Elizabeth North was born in Hampshire  naval officer. She married an ing a writer. She now lives in residence at Bretton Hall *Worldly Goods* is her eighth *The Least and Vilest Things*, *Everything in the Garden*, *Flore Enemies*.

ELIZABETH NORTH

Worldly Goods

PALADIN
GRAFTON BOOKS
A Division of the Collins Publishing Group

LONDON GLASGOW
TORONTO SYDNEY AUCKLAND

Paladin
Grafton Books
A Division of the Collins Publishing Group
8 Grafton Street, London W1X 3LA

Published in Paladin Books 1988

First published in Great Britain by
Methuen London Ltd 1987

ISBN 0-586-08697-8

Printed and bound in Great Britain by
Collins, Glasgow

Set in Times

For Jenny and Gareth

Part I

1

The River Swale, which has a course of nearly seventy-two miles through a tract of remarkably diverse country, rises amidst wild, almost mountainous scenery in the extreme north-west of Yorkshire and flows, with the Ure, into the Ouse at Myton-on-Swale in the heart of the great plain of York.

At this confluence in 1319 took place a battle: on one side forces mustered by the Archbishop of York and on the other marauding Scots. It is commonly known as the White Battle because of the number of clerics actively engaged in it.

The course of the Swale is always deeply interesting. From Muker, the first of the larger centres of population, along its banks to Catterick Bridge, where Swaledale proper may rightly be said to end, the scenery is full of charm and beauty and at times sublimity.

No one among the Forestiers could understand what kept Polly up there in these wilds. Like most southerners they suspected it was about as welcoming as Iceland. Of course it was terribly picturesque, Julia would say, and could appeal to Polly's artistic nature, but she had only gone there because of marrying a major in the Royal Artillery who, along with other members of his regiment, drove tanks over rough, high country.

It was thought that Polly was hard up. 'She'll have a widow's pension,' Julia once said, 'but I rather think she works, part-time, perhaps teaching.'

Christmas cards were exchanged yearly, but Polly's cards said very little, having no family of whom to give news. She usually promised to visit her Sussex cousins, but had not done so for a very long time. When the letter arrived announcing Nina's engagement, Polly had some difficulty remembering who this was. Their youngest? The child in gumboots she had met when visiting the family some ten years back?

'Perhaps you know the family of the young man,' Julia wrote. 'They live in Leeds.' Julia's writing was something of a scrawl and Polly couldn't quite make out the name. Crossley? Crosby? 'No,' she wrote in reply, and thought of adding: 'Leeds is about as far from Swaledale as London is from Chichester,' but reckoned the irony of this exaggeration would be lost on Julia.

There was a flat bottom to the valley outside Polly's window. After the rains, this reflected patches of still water where the Swale had overflowed its banks. Snow on the hill opposite, and Polly could see the weather coming from the west and going on eastwards. Otherwise the view was mostly of fields dotted with sheep. This from the front, while from her back window, it was of a long slope of fields and more sheep up to where the tree line ended.

She lived alone but did not see herself as lonely. She had friends from the village and in Richmond. None of these were really Yorkshire people, but incomers like herself. She also had a lover who was, like herself, a teacher, but this affair seemed on the wane. This dark winter there was less zest in the making of assignations. A wedding? Yes, she would go to it, maybe make an extended visit of it. That way she would show the man that she had a family like he did, even if in her case they were no more than cousins. She wrote back to Julia. 'Yes, let me know when it is going to happen. I'll hope to have time off for it. Not sure if my old car will make it, but . . .'

The Forestiers themselves had hardly ever travelled north. They had been to Scotland just before the war, twenty odd years before this time (we are in the late 1950s) but never to Yorkshire.

'They have no summer to speak of up there, I believe,' Julia was often heard to say, although since getting to know Campbell, Nina had visited the place several times and reported back that it was okay, not really that much different, and anyhow who was this cousin that her mother talked about?

'She is a Masterson,' said Julia. The Mastersons were her side of the family. 'Related to Great-Uncle Arthur,' she went on, 'and by the way I rather think that we could use his house again for the reception . . . when the time comes of course.'

'Dear Polly, Harold and I are both delighted that you'll come. There's no date fixed as yet. Nina is still working. She's in London now,' and added a comment about girls, careers and that this was a good thing really, wasn't it?

Julia wrote at her bureau in the drawing room. This is a dark house, built to face east and west with sun falling only in the garden. A window beside Julia revealed a terrace and beyond a lawn, a cedar tree, some snowdrops. Later she would stride along the village street towards the post office, a large, breezy and familiar figure much given in a spontaneous and unself-conscious way to organizing things.

A quiet house now with all three children away from home, but Julia – in winter and in summer – filled it with fresh air, opening windows to hear calls of rooks from elms or sounds of tractors from the farm across the road or the occasional aeroplane overhead.

These days she would banish the silence with phone calls to friends and relatives, her voice echoing towards the study where Harold sat, as he sat every day, working on his transla-tion of Marcus Aurelius.

It could be said that these anticipated events occurred at a good time for Julia. A wedding creates a focus in your life, something she felt lacking these days, perhaps because she had just come through the menopause. Or rather not come through it, since it is not something which leaves you as it found you.

Her afternoon was for the garden, meetings or more calls on people. In between times she would cook for Harold. 'Her cooking efforts' he would call them. Domestic skills pass down through the female line and Julia was the first Masterson to manage without servants. Thus all she would pass on to Nina was the sense that to present a meal entirely on one's own, whatever the quality, was something of an achievement.

Harold kept a diary noting her activities and moods. 'J brisk. J quiet.' She was at her best when keeping up with friends and relatives. This was her forte. The whole wide world must know by now the details of the young romance – at any rate Julia seemed to think it most romantic – that Nina had been working for a magazine, researching the price of property; that Campbell, being in that business . . . and so on . . .

'He is an estate agent,' Julia was telling someone on the telephone. An estate agency for Julia was a concern which advertised in *Country Life* where you saw page after page of houses for sale, photographs of extensive grounds or parkland – quite often houses you had known or visited when young for weekend parties, mansions with moorlands or streams by which you had picnicked. In regard to property, Julia had never actually been a vendor or a buyer, Glebe House having been left to Harold in the will of a childless uncle.

As for the engagement, thought Harold, the writing had been on the wall for months. Earlier entries in his diary read: 'N at home with Viking, spooning mostly.' The Viking was a nickname he had coined for Campbell.

Harold also logged the seasons and the weather. He would open his study window, tap the maximum/minimum thermometer which hung outside, then close the window, hunch his narrow shoulders and make a note in his diary as to temperature and weather situation. 'Low cloud. Snow imminent.' That sort of thing. Glebe House was on a coastal plain, a long, low house, the sea but half a mile away. Between house and sea – a garden, then a church and then the cemetery.

The Viking element in Campbell was the reddish hair and rugby-playing muscularity. 'I think he is an entertaining person,' Julia said, soon after Nina brought him for his first visit. 'I wouldn't go as far as to say that,' said Harold. His other favourite word for Campbell was 'ebullient'. The young man always spoke at length, with fervour and with optimism on the benefits of enterprise and of achievement in the modern world.

All well and good, Harold would think, retiring to his study, wearing his eyeshade and shawl as always, and forced unwillingly to reflect upon his own achievements.

The only good sign, which suggested some delay in the proceedings, was that the girl herself seemed in no hurry. Being courted by the Viking had wrought no observable change in her. The whole project seemed in any case a questionable exercise. New divorce figures had been published recently and the chances of a lasting match seemed limited.

But he would see it through as he had done five years before for Nina's elder sister. We must see Harold as an honourable man, only dishonest when it came to putting money on horses. This he did nearly every day (via telegram to a London turf accountant), but allowed it only to be known about on Saturdays.

We are into January. A dull afternoon. Julia was on the telephone again. Being of a generation not raised from child-hood to the habitual use of this, she raised her voice, telling yet another friend or relative how pleased she and Harold were. 'Oh yes,' she finished, 'we like him very much indeed. He has such varied interests.'

One of these interests was an in-depth study of battles fought on Yorkshire soil. 'This battle,' Harold once asked him of the conflict mentioned earlier, the one which took place where the Swale, the Ure and the Ouse have confluence: 'All those vicars fighting Scotsmen. By the way, who won?' 'I think the Scots, I am afraid to say,' said Campbell.

'Afraid to say?' Harold chuckled, enjoying the image of the church in disarray. For that establishment he had little sym-pathy, and of his wife's devotion to it he would simply note: 'J at matins. J at evensong.' More frequently J went to both. But he was not ungrateful; nor did he disparage the fact that these acts of worship calmed her. He would watch her drifting back from church across the garden, note the dreamy look which suggested sacred music was still echoing inside her head.

For himself, all that he wanted was the tolerable. For Harold, to be disappointed was the norm. Those who expected other-wise were those missing the main point in life. As to success and failure, by which Campbell judged the world around him, what of them?

Harold's own life achievements? A degree in classics. No career. What could one say? He was a gentleman and had been born with expectations that his unearned income would be adequate to see him through. His enterprise? He had travelled to the Himalayas once. A noteworthy expedition this, in the 1930s, to conquer Everest. Although as far as Everest was concerned, he hadn't been included in the final party to attempt the peak.

His study: low-ceilinged. The outlines of stone flags could be seen and felt through the once-expensive faded carpet. Southern midwinter: dark, muddy, damp and miserable. Northern midwinter: likewise dark, muddy, damp and miserable. Although statistics speak of an average difference of up to five degrees Fahrenheit, mild spells last longer in the south, and that is about as much as one can say with certainty.

More often Campbell spoke of battles of the Wars of the Roses. Towton Moor, 1461, was included in his area of special expertise. One day he would write a book on it. Across the dinner table at Glebe House, he would elaborate on how the Yorkists fell on the Lancastrians and how the little river called the Cockbeck flowed with blood.

Of Yorkshire itself, Campbell spoke less. He had been educated in the south and was not anxious to extol his place of birth, presenting himself rather as a man of England than a Yorkshire man with typical pride of place. In fact the Forestiers learned more from others. Their present vicar had spent time in Yorkshire as a chaplain to the RAF. More bombing missions had been flown from there, he explained to them, than from any other English county. It was a fine place, a grand place, through which many rivers flowed into the North Sea and where skies were higher and vistas quite incredible.

'I'm sure it's very beautiful,' Julia would say to Campbell, although she'd heard of less salubrious parts of it from Nanny who had left the family to go and work in Halifax.

Yorkshire is a chunk of land stretching almost all the way across the north of England. From a high point in the Pennines on a clear day you can stand in Yorkshire and see the coast of Lancashire near Morecambe. A few other facts: it is by far the largest of the English counties, covering 3,897,940 acres. The population, at the time of which I write, was 4,845,320, which was larger than that of Denmark by a few thousand and a million more than that of Norway. These figures date back to the time before the counties were redivided in the early 1970s.

Polly's exaggeration of the distance between Swaledale and Leeds was more than slight. Especially in regard to time taken travelling. By the late 1950s much of the A1 was dual carriageway, and by using this you could approach Leeds from the north-east in not more than two hours.

Most of the Crosbys lived on this side, well away from smoky areas. Having contributed to the building up of cities, Leeds in particular, the moment they could afford to move away from that which they had created, they did so, first into suburbs and then into commuter villages. The head of the family, Richard, now lived in a manor house as far out as Northallerton, but in regard to Campbell's parents, they had less elevated aspirations.

Pound Close: up a private road, the trees surrounding it, planted at the time of building, now matured, the stone of this and other houses nearby, weathered. This is undulating country, west of the plain of York, east of the Pennines. Pound Close, built in the 1930s, with a solid feel to it and high sash windows. Phyllis stood in Campbell's room, about to tidy it. In her hand – a photograph of Nina; this she'd found on Campbell's dressing table. A good enough likeness, emphasizing all about the girl that worried Phyllis. Nina is standing in the porch of Glebe House. Her fringe almost conceals her eyes. She leans as if hoping to fade into obscurity. Nor did the porch look quite as porches should, but dilapidated and unsound.

Phyllis looked out of the window – across the gravel drive – square lawn beyond: no snowdrops yet. Phyllis would feel no resentment about this. Like most Yorkshire people, she expected winter to last. Winter is a time for getting on with things.

Somewhere in the house, the daily woman hoovered. Once Phyllis had finished in here, Mrs Everard would come in and clean. If you were Phyllis, you left no room entirely in the hands of someone other than yourself.

Another look at Nina: it was hard to put your finger on what was wrong with her. Bernard said shy, but in Phyllis's opinion that word hid a multitude of sins.

Yes, good looks and an impression of aristocratic cool, but in Phyllis's experience, these upper-class girls thought they could get away with murder. Well, not murder, but with not being especially polite or painstaking.

Perhaps, however, Nina was a slight improvement on the girl

before. Campbell had been visiting a girl who lived in Scott Hall Road, Leeds, a typist he had met through work. Such girls could cause trouble, get a hold on a young man.

Phyllis replaced the photograph and closed the door on Campbell's room. An uncharacteristic move, this. She always practised what she preached and one of the few disciplines she had instilled in Campbell was that any task begun should at all costs be finished.

Phyllis Crosby, mother of two, grandmother of three, broad-shouldered and grey-haired. A woman who moved carefully and by dint of constant vigilance remained on top of most of the materials of life. She pondered few imponderables, but accepted, sensibly, that human beings were less easily controlled. She was a woman who believed, however, that by planning in advance as much as possible, one could forestall catastrophes or at the very least foresee them. (This is no suggestion that the north is full of thoroughgoing and efficient women of this kind and the south peopled with the impulsive and less provident kind we find in Julia.)

'I think we ought to meet them,' Julia said. 'Meet whom?' said Harold. 'The Crosbys.' 'Must we?'

Between the two women communication had already been established, letters early on exchanged expressing pleasure that 'the young', as they both called them, had finally made up their minds. Julia's tone – enthusiastic, saying she and Harold had become so fond of Campbell and so on. Phyllis, less effusively, had said that she and Bernard had become 'attached' to Nina, adding that they would do their best to make her feel at home.

Of course they would, thought Julia, it hardly needed saying, did it? Now she wrote back to arrange a meeting, London possibly. A trip there would mean staying with her elder daughter, Laura, who lived in Sevenoaks. She could have spent a night with Nina but, since Nina was home most weekends, there was less point. And Nina's flat was not the most comfortable of places.

It would be an encounter of more or less social equals. Neither of the Crosbys spoke with a Yorkshire accent, although it could be said that Bernard had a more decided way of speaking than do many southerners. Some Yorkshire people end their sentences in a tone of voice which suggests there is nothing to be said on any matter. They say things like: 'He did right then.' A pause follows.

But it would not be a meeting of financial equals. The fortunes of the Forestiers had long been waning, while over the last hundred years or so, the Crosbys had prospered increasingly. Before the meeting Bernard contemplated this, although by now he was resigned to the fact that the Forestiers had nothing whatsoever to contribute to the match other than the person of the bride herself.

The girl – since one must not call her shy – was perhaps remote, but not unappetizing. Bernard often looked over the young shape of Nina and wondered how much of it the boy had had his hands on. Not that these thoughts were ever expressed, nor hardly allowed to surface in his consciousness.

His office faced the General Infirmary. He would look out there and think of death sometimes. It might be convenient perhaps. His final illness might be sudden. Phyllis often forecast this.

Bernard in winter, less than at his best. Golf courses freeze. There was the club house, but less excuse for spending time there after work. Long evenings at home.

His first-floor office: large arched windows, Bernard's desk sideways on to these. His little empire, carved from his share of Crosby money, fought for, stablized, established, ticking over nicely thank you, in spite of Campbell's pushy presence urging changes and extensions.

While Harold would have opted for as late a wedding date as possible, Bernard couldn't help but hope it would be over with as soon as possible. At least home life would be easier.

Nina's visits and her silent noncommittal presence bore down on the household. And when she was not there, Phyllis pointed out interminably that southern girls did not always settle easily, quoting from examples in the family of wives who had become homesick and kept rushing south or had their mothers to stay on long extended visits.

As if there were some chance of stopping Campbell in his

tracks, thought Bernard, looking forward to his lunch. He always took this at the Conservative Club some streets away. Bernard, walking along Great George Street, approaching the bulk of the town hall from behind, cutting down beside the Headrow. Bernard with his walking stick, navy blue greatcoat, grey felt hat, crossing the Headrow, going through Park Square where there are eighteenth-century buildings, where solicitors have their offices, where brass plates are polished daily and pigeons flutter among lime trees.

Julia strode at speed across the foyer of Brown's Hotel with hand outstretched. She was enlivened. She loved forging links, learning about children, houses, dogs, ponies, vicarages and villages. Phyllis and Bernard were to be family and she could never have enough of family. Her two brothers had been killed in the First World War and her only sister had died recently.

She is not at all like Nina, Phyllis thought. 'It was most surprising,' Phyllis would say afterwards to those two people who received her closest confidences, her sister and her daughter. 'Nothing like her in the slightest, perhaps the nose, but otherwise . . .'

While Julia's report on Phyllis – to Laura later that evening – was: 'Rather gaunt in a strange way, but awfully nice of course,' because to Julia everyone was awfully nice unless they were on the tiresome side, which was about the worst she would ever say of anyone.

Bernard's verdict would be: 'Not really what I expected either.' Privately he decided Julia may have been enormously pretty once. She had a lightness in style and yet a measure of earthiness. He had seen her type in films. She could for instance have done just as well as Celia Johnson in *Brief Encounter*, the only film really to have moved him in his cinema-going days.

Tea was served. Bernard had been looking forward to this. It was not a meal that Phyllis ever made a great deal of, having decided in recent years that a man of Bernard's age should be kept as low on carbohydrates in his diet as possible. She had ordered brown bread and butter, but couldn't help but notice how Julia spooned dollops of Brown's Hotel strawberry jam rather liberally on to her plate. Bernard had to order another silver jam dish of it.

As far as conversation was concerned, no problems here, since Julia chattered on, speaking of Yorkshire, mentioning all the good points she knew of. 'You grow such lovely and successful roses up there, don't you?' 'Yes,' said Bernard, roses being the only part of the garden in which he took an interest. 'It's the soot from the mines,' said Julia. They nodded. Soot is not from mines, it is from industry, but like the Crosbys we must let that pass.

'I do love tea,' said Julia, reaching for the plate of cakes which had just arrived, taking the very éclair that Bernard had had his eye on. 'Tuck in. Feel free,' said Bernard, not looking at Phyllis, who was to say afterwards that of course women who threw themselves around a great deal and had a surfeit of nervous energy, would naturally have a craving for foodstuffs high in sugar content, not to mention fat content. She and Bernard would only need a light meal tonight.

The two women established the exact age of each other's grandchildren, which was as follows: Phyllis, via her daughter Nicola, had three granddaughters, while Julia, via Laura, had Edmund, four, and Venessa, one and a half. They compared notes as to the characters of these same children. 'You're one up on me,' said Julia. 'Poor Laura's dying to have another, but Jim's digging his toes in.'

This, decided Phyllis, was rather more than she needed to know about Nina's family, but she went on smiling and it was Bernard who said that Nicola, he reckoned, would go on having babies until the cows came home. 'You were saying that only the other day.' He turned to Phyllis. 'Was I?' Phyllis's expression changed not one bit. Bernard was glad that he was meeting members of the steering committee of the Federation of Estate Agents shortly to discuss tomorrow's annual general meeting.

Around the three of them, the heavily carpeted foyer with its swing doors, waiters standing discreetly by pillars. Outside, the Piccadilly traffic. 'We're much looking forward to meeting Harold,' Phyllis said. 'Oh, he hardly ever leaves home.' Julia sat back, full, wiping her mouth with a linen napkin. She has sad eyes from time to time, thought Bernard. Perhaps there had been something of a brief encounter in her life.

How odd, thought Julia at about the same time, that here we are and no one's even mentioned why we're here. 'It's nice that there's no hurry for the wedding,' she began, then realizing the implications of this remark, she continued: 'I mean that Nina is devoted to her work of course . . .'

Phyllis nodded as if doubtful as to the accuracy of this statement, remembering that Nina had often said about her work that it was fairly boring, low-grade sort of journalism – just making phone calls, lists and things.

'Campbell is such fun,' said Julia, undefeated. Phyllis smiled. She had this habit of smiling with her lips and not her eyes, which could be quite forbidding. But Bernard laughed. Campbell fun? Good heavens! Campbell the thorn in his mother's side, the cause of so many murmurings at night and sleepless nights? Bernard couldn't help but feel extremely tickled. 'Nice woman,' he said afterwards. 'Yes,' said Phyllis, but it should be realized that 'nice' when used by Phyllis carried far less weight than, for instance, 'sensible'. 'I'm not sure what the purpose of it was,' she said. 'The meeting? Did there have to be a purpose?' Bernard asked. 'One would have thought so.' Phyllis looked puzzled. This was most unusual. It might be several days before she was herself again.

As for Julia, she never questioned that the meeting was a good thing to have organized. Connections must be made. All the same, she dashed to call a taxi, somehow not feeling like bothering with a bus or tube at rush hour. A taxi to Charing Cross, leaning back not sure what she felt, but homesick suddenly, which was silly because she was going to Laura's. Edmund would be waiting for her to read aloud to him, while Laura bathed Vanessa. With Phyllis she had felt – what was it? As if her voice had been pouring out into nothingness, as if a muffled but invisible hand were raised to catch remarks and absorb them. She bolted out of the taxi and ran for the train, not wishing to reflect on this further.

A brief encounter or a sad encounter in her life? Not relevant, although it might explain the difference between this mother and her youngest child. What is relevant is that Julia prayed at night, slept well. Sometimes woke up in the morning weeping, but was usually all right by breakfast time.

'I don't quite know exactly what I thought of them,' she said to Harold two days later. He took her suitcase to carry it upstairs. 'It hardly matters, does it, what you thought of them? Was there any evidence of congenital deformity or disease?' She followed him. 'Of course there wasn't!' 'Then that's all right. You didn't have to like them. You only had to see that they were sound. We're mixing blood with them, you know.' He went downstairs. Julia stood in the bedroom looking out as the sun went down behind the cedar tree. We leave her there.

What was it, Phyllis asked herself, as she returned to normal programmed days of winter. Nina? Was it a perverseness in her that had made her set her style in opposition to her mother's? Phyllis never would be sure which would be preferable: that Nina should become more like her mother in the course of time or less.

What was it? At dusk she would fold heavy wooden shutters over windows. Thus sealed, Pound Close had a fortress feel to it. Remember the marauding Scots. Reflect that most of England has been uninvaded since 1066.

Up here night falls earlier. This is the difference. Lower sun and darkness sooner. More living to be done in lit-up rooms, more money spent on rooms to brighten the interiors and dispel the gloom. As well as this a search for more activity to sustain the spirits.

Up in Swaledale Polly found work helped. Love helped as well, but as we have seen was less reliable. But in the case of women kept by husbands, women whose lives were structured by the need to stay at home and keep their households going, solutions differed. Muriel, the wife of Richard Crosby, spent winter afternoons playing bridge and hardly noticed when the sun went down at half past three around Northallerton.

Another office, this in London. The view out of the window is irrelevant. A man speaks to a girl who stands across the desk from him: 'I hear you are engaged, Miss Forestier.' 'Yes, actually I am.'

Then he reminded her that, upon employment, she had said she wanted a career in journalism. 'Oh that!' said Nina: 'Yes, I know I did. The fact that I'm engaged does not mean that I shall get married soon.'

He scratched his head. 'I see. Am I to take it, then, that in your case the word engagement has no future connotations?' 'Possibly.' She turned her profile to him. The window here is relevant. She gazed out of it. 'I suppose you read it in the papers.'

'After all I am a journalist. I do glance at the social pages in *The Times*, the *Telegraph*. Even the *Yorkshire Post* from time to time does not escape my notice.' 'Under forthcoming marriages, I suppose.' Her head moved slowly. She was face to face with him again. Impassive and with eyes lowered. A glint of tears perhaps.

Oh no, I can't have this, he thought, hastily congratulating her and suggesting that at least employment here had brought about a happy fate for her. 'I believe the young man met you here? I understand the meeting took place here between these walls?' 'I'd like to give my notice in.' Was it impassiveness or what was it? 'I'd like to say that you have been entirely satisfactory in the work.' She nodded: 'Well, it wasn't difficult, was it?'

'All the same . . .' He scratched his head again. He'd meant to say that she had cheated and shown cowardice in not announcing that she'd changed her mind on something fundamental in her life. And further he'd meant to say that, had she stayed, he would have considered offering her some work in feature writing. Instead he found himself explaining that, as long as she informed him when the wedding was, he would look for a replacement for her at a time to coincide with this. 'Weddings go rather well in June, don't they?'

What held him back? What was it in her that had stopped him in his tracks from sacking her immediately. She remained across the desk from him. What was she waiting for? 'Well . . . ah . . . you wear no ring. Where is the ring I ask myself?'

She reached into the pocket of her skirt. The ring was sapphire and diamond, an antique. It would keep its value until lost one day when hanging nappies on a washing line.

2

Another burst of telephoning had begun. 'Max 45. Min. 40,'
noted Harold. 'Big show will be in June. Countdown begun.'
From a drawer in his desk he took an envelope. This contained
a schedule of valuables held in the bank in Chichester. The
only two remaining items which would be worth realizing: two
Georgian sauceboats.

For Julia – a pause for letter writing: 'Dear Phyllis, As I
think I may have mentioned when we met, we have this cousin,
Polly Grant, who lives in Yorkshire. She'll be coming to the
wedding and she'd be most grateful for a lift. This may be on
the early side to make arrangements, but now it seems that
June's the time . . .'

'Is it known why?' asked Harold. They had just had lunch.
'Because she's given in her notice.' Julia piled the plates. 'And
oh, by the way, I've earmarked Dorothy to do the flowers. I'll
have to go and tell her.' A windy day. Doors banged and
windows rattled as Julia went out. Dorothy was her best friend,
a widow, living in a pretty cottage just along the village street.
Silence resumed.

A few mornings later on a Monday, Phyllis was in Campbell's
room, completing the task begun a month before. In her mail
this morning there had come the letter which had almost put
her off this task again. How typical of Campbell! She had just
rung Bernard at the office, an unusual step, to find out whether
Campbell had returned from London.

Meanwhile she soothed herself by sorting out his belongings,
boxes filled with mementoes of his childhood. He had wanted
to be an admiral, then a general, then a numismatist. Model

ships, toy soliders, coins filling cardboard boxes stacked in corners. Men needed hobbies, women had to sort out the remains of these.

With her was her eldest granddaughter, Louisa aged six, a biddable child in a Viyella frock and polished sandals. 'I say, Grandma, will we soon be trying on our bridesmaids' dresses then?' Louisa had been overhearing things. 'We'll see, dear,' Phyllis said, but smiled. This was her favourite granddaughter.

Outside rain fell. Louisa was saying she had only been a bridesmaid once and that her best friend Susan had been a bridesmaid twice. Phyllis nodded: 'I see, dear,' and looked around the walls of Campbell's room. These maps of battle-fields were dust traps. But perhaps he would complete his book. Men must be allowed to try. Men had to experiment. There were Crosbys like him, often one in every generation. Better of course that such offspring should be male, not female. Girls, if they were reckless, rash and over-ambitious, could spread such damage.

Was the role of mother to fit a son for marriage? Some would say so. She had done her best with him, to shape him and smooth him and direct his energies, but then whoever could say with certainty that they had done their best with anyone?

The rain stopped. Sun gleamed through the poplars. The lawn was now edged with snowdrops. In a way Campbell's absences at weekends had created peace. As she would say to Nina in the years to come, the male presence was a disruptive force, but one which one accepted, didn't one? Task more or less completed now, followed by Louisa, Phyllis went down-stairs to make the daily woman's mid-morning coffee.

Mrs Everard sat in the kitchen. What a weekend, she was saying: 'By, didn't it sile down!' This means it had been raining hard. And Mr Everard was a right misery, was Mr Everard. Yorkshire people have a way of emphasizing by repeating. Phyllis always spent at least twenty minutes listening to Mrs Everard. Listening to a daily woman is almost as important as paying her.

The passages of Pound Close, thickly carpeted; the doors of walnut, closing silently. Louisa ran into the kitchen. 'I say,

Grandma. Can I play out, Grandma? Please say yes, Grandma. I'll put on my duffel coat, shall I?'

The first stretch of the M1 would be open in a year or so. It would range through forests, roll over hills, slope into river valleys. These would be clearly labelled so that drivers of coaches, trucks and cars would know when they were crossing the rivers Soare, Trent, Don and Calder.

Meanwhile Campbell used the A1. In spite of improvements, this was a longish drive. He was trying as usual to break his previous record for the London to Leeds trip. He had climbed out of Nina's bed before she set off to work and was now framing in his mind the words he would use to justify the earlier wedding date, both to his mother and his father, although the former would be the more inclined to question him on finer points.

The journey gave him time for thought and forward planning, sometimes for dreams as well. This road had once been Ermine Street. It reminded him of Roman legions marching. Perhaps he was at heart a soldier. He had often wished he'd stayed on in the army after doing national service. Nevertheless, I am a fighter in life and will win through, he told himself. Soon he would have Nina. By sheer persistence he'd achieved what had at first seemed inaccessible. He'd overcome what many people thought to be a disadvantage – his place of origin. Not that Nina seemed to think this was important. She would never have penalized a person for a geographical accident of birth. Nina believed all men were equal. Nina, he would often say to people, had ideals. Not many, but the ones she'd mentioned were pretty admirable.

Some people say the north starts at Grantham, some claim it is earlier than this – at the mythical line which links the Wash to Bristol. To Campbell, any such dividing line was increasingly irrelevant. Ease of travel, innovations such as the M1, would bring the two ends of the country close together. Social mobility would grow as people sped from north to south and vice versa.

He'd seen pictures of the new motorway. Sketches had been published recently of families walking hand in hand over bridges, shielded by shining glass from rain and gales, while underneath swept streamlined, highly-idealized futuristic traffic.

Bernard decided not to wait. It was getting on for lunch time anyway, so he asked Miss Hosier, his long-time secretary, to give the message to Campbell that he must ring his mother on arrival and then left.

He was halfway along Great George Street when he saw Campbell's car sweep round the corner. Bernard stepped into the doorway of the medical bookshop, outside which he would often pause to consider titles on display in the window.

Today there was *Stimson on the Inner Ear*, which puzzled him less than *Diabetic Feet* or *Gut Hormones*. He only paused here if feeling especially fit. Odd world that of the medicos, whose offices and consulting rooms spread up the hill beyond the Infirmary. There, where one of his ancestors had set up home in a street of brand-new residences, rooms which had once been living rooms or bedrooms were now rooms where highly trained men leaned over patients exploring gut or bladder, pancreas or inner ear, probing under flesh or through such orifices as men and women were provided with – as if these orifices were for the convenience of consultants' hands or instruments.

Mid-afternoon and Phyllis drove out with Louisa, first calling at the local shop for groceries. Those who live in villages should feel it incumbent on them to support small shopkeepers. Then on along the winding street, past stone houses and terraced cottages. All buildings here had bright woodwork and were kept in spanking shape by commuters – either owners of businesses, as were the Crosbys, or high-ranking salaried executives. This village was for three years running the winner of the trophy for the best-kept village in the West Riding.

Outside the village – a stretch of woodland. Here Phyllis stopped the car again and went with Louisa in among the trees, carrying the binoculars she used for bird-watching, showing the child how to adjust them in order to focus on a robin or a sparrow. Girls need hobbies. They grow up into wives who ought to have an interest of their own, albeit one which will not distract them overmuch.

Then back into the car, a small Austin, and on through glistening countryside, liking this time of year because of the tidiness of it. The roads were at their emptiest at this time of day, although we are in a time when roads in general were emptier.

With Louisa chattering in the back, Phyllis headed west to reach rising, bolder land, taking a steep road, then winding into a private drive. Helen came to the door. Her hair was down. She was wearing narrow black woollen trousers and her feet were bare. Such girlishness in someone nearing forty! 'Have you come to tea? How lovely!'

'No, dear, thank you, just to see you.' By this time Helen had taken Louisa by the hand and led her through the house and the conservatory and let her into the garden to play with Lena, the golden labrador. Helen's excited voice still echoed. Yes, she was going through a bad patch almost certainly, thought Phyllis, following.

Helen Garside, formerly Crosby, Bernard's younger sister, born late in life to elderly parents. Such a mistake in Phyllis's opinion: such children always tended to be spoiled and self-indulgent.

An evergreen hedge surrounded Helen's garden, but at the end of this, a gap with a view down to the valley, the river and a railway viaduct. From the picture window in the long lounge, Phyllis watched Louisa romping on the lawn with Lena. Beside her, Helen put her hand behind her head to lift her hair and let it fall again. All the usual signs were there. Phyllis never could decide if children would have helped or not. The answer was almost always no – for their sake less than Helen's. Although her delight in Louisa's presence made one think. 'And how is Charlie?' Phyllis asked. She was relieved to see no signs of bottles or of glasses. It was known that Helen drank alone sometimes. And the house was reasonably cared for. Charlie was fine, said Helen. He'd be home this evening, but away on business for the rest of the week. Oh dear, thought Phyllis. What it was to be wrapped up exclusively in oneself and just one other person!

* * *

27

In the Crosby family it was a tradition that wealth should be apportioned equally between male and female, so Helen had inherited as much as her two brothers and her sister when their parents died. And Charlie had a salary of sorts. There is no completely satisfactory way with money, Phyllis thought. If the woman has the larger share of it, the man will feel inadequate. This was almost certainly part of Charlie's trouble. Perhaps the best way was the way she, Phyllis lived – with something of her own, but less than Bernard.

But whereas Phyllis's money (from the Ramsey side) had gone towards the building up of Bernard's business, Helen's had gone into this – all that surrounded her. They had built this house: extravagance was not the word for it.

The room in which they now sat was huge – white carpet (most impractical), golden velvet curtains, creamy leather three-piece suite – even a white grand piano, redundant now since Helen, who had had some training, hardly ever played these days. There was also the latest kind of record player, piles of records, piles of magazines, a television with the largest screen available. As if one could buy happiness! For Phyllis, in spite of the wide window and excessive light, the place had a claustrophobic feel to it.

'I have some news about the wedding.' She hadn't intended to tell anyone outside the immediate family as yet, but Helen needed some preoccupation even if it were only buying clothes. And after all she was Campbell's godmother. 'June almost certainly,' said Phyllis.

'Oh lovely!' Helen made one of her extravagant gestures. 'I am so looking forward to having Nina living up here.' She had taken to Nina in an unexpected way and Nina likewise seemed enthusiastic, always insisting on visiting the Garsides whenever possible. What was it? It could of course be Charlie who, with all his faults, was so attractive that girls went for him.

Helen was talking about a holiday they were planning in the south of France. The Garsides went in for that sort of thing. 'We might go on there from the wedding, I suppose.' She stretched herself along the floor, head propped on elbow. One of her poses! Blonde Helen, who as a child had been told much too often that she was beautiful. Perhaps she still was. Many people spoke of her as if she was, but Phyllis always said: oh no! To *think* that one is beautiful is often to *behave* as if one is.

Louisa came in from the garden, pink-cheeked, carefully shutting the door behind her. She sat on a small chair which Helen kept for visiting children, eating crisps and drinking lemonade. Most unsuitable and it would spoil her tea, but Helen needed to feel that she sometimes did the right thing, so Phyllis had not objected.

'And are you really all right, dear?' she repeated before leaving. 'Yes, of course.' Helen jumped up and began to tidy some scattered records. There had been music, loud music playing when they first arrived. Phyllis suspected Helen of dancing on her own sometimes.

How sad for Helen that her only sister had died recently. The responsibility had thus come to Phyllis to keep an eye, as she would call it. There was very little she could do, but a display of concern was always necessary. To love a man was all very well. Would that everyone could love as strongly as was possible; but to be held by it, controlled by it, led nowhere.

At least I have had visitors, said Helen to herself, something I can talk about when he comes home. And the wedding to tell him about. This would prevent her from searching in his eyes in the way he recognized as questioning.

One good reason for having Louisa for the day, for Phyllis, was that it took some of the burden off the shoulders of her daughter. Perhaps an even better reason was the pleasure of seeing this same daughter at the day's end. Lovely Nicola, thought Phyllis as the family came in out of the cold twilight. First, the middle girl running and then Nicola, large, stout and smiling, carrying the baby. Best moment of the day so far. Good looks were quite irrelevant when considering young women of the kind that Nicola was. What one considered was bloom, bright eyes and energy.

Louisa was jumping up and down and telling her mother that the wedding was to be in June and wouldn't she please get on with the making of the bridesmaids' dresses? The baby crawled across the carpet, reached Phyllis and was held by her.

'So they can't wait?' said Nicola. 'I don't know, dear, but we shall see, no doubt. But reading in between the lines . . .' 'She can't be pregnant can she? Surely not! She wouldn't leave it as long as June. I say, she didn't get the sack, did she? Poor Nina, I do hope not.'

We must see Nicola as sound and staunch and like her mother in all sorts of ways, but a hundred times less judgemental. Whatever Nina was to say about the Crosbys in the years to come, she would never hear a whisper against Nicola. Who was also flawless in her parents' eyes. They had so loved her that they could not bring themselves to send her, as they had sent Campbell, south for education. Love given had been thus rewarded with as whole a person as we'll meet within these pages.

Louisa and her sister ran along the passage to the television room. 'Hey, Mo!' Louisa said. 'We'll have our dresses soon. Won't that be exciting!' Mo sat and watched TV, ignoring her. Then yawned deliberately to show how boring talk of weddings was. She was a different case. Melanie, three. She would be four just before the wedding. She was nicknamed Little Mo after the tennis player Maureen Connolly, who was the youngest ever to win at Wimbledon.

'What's wrong with June?' asked Nicola, recognizing in her mother signs of being on the warpath in this matter. 'There is nothing *wrong*, dear,' Phyllis said. 'Only that it would have been nice to know about it earlier. The Forestiers have evidently known about it for some time.'

'Oh well,' said Nicola. 'I'll get in touch with Nina and find out what she's got in mind for bridesmaids' dresses.'

It was all too much, thought Phyllis, who would offer time and time again to pay to have these made for Nicola. Young married women these days! Especially Nicola with her warmth of heart and bursting love towards these three children and a husband whose intention was first and foremost to enjoy himself.

'I want to be a page,' said Mo, returning, having had enough of Louisa's chatter, and went on saying this and saying this and spoiling any chance that Phyllis might have had of a rewarding talk with Nicola.

'Do shut up, Mo,' said Nicola. 'We'd better dash, Mum. We're going to a dinner party and I've got to iron my dress and Peter's got to fetch the baby-sitter.'

Phyllis restrained herself from the usual word of warning to her daughter in regard to her alarmingly over-active social life. It was all to do with being so popular, outgoing and generous.

'I want to be a page,' said Mo again. 'I said – shut up!' said Nicola: 'Girls can't be pages.' 'Why?' 'Oh, I'll explain sometime.' And so she would. This patience, this minute attention to the whims of children! Nicola was of a generation who believed that mothers should at all costs listen and explain at length. She ought to have more help of course, but she was also of the generation who believed that to hand responsibility to someone else was to betray the child and fall short in the conscientious role of motherhood.

''Bye, Mum,' said Nicola. Phyllis kissed them all and let them go and, because of Mo's continual moaning, a little less reluctantly than usual.

If Nicola had any fault, it was with Mo. When Mo was born, she went over to the Dr Spock method of rearing children. Mo was fed on demand and had been demanding ever since. She was red-haired and reminded Phyllis of Campbell at the same age. Say no more. She had a square head, dead straight hair and had once put the family kitten in the spin-dryer.

'It's June,' said Helen, handing Charlie a gin and tonic fat with ice. He fixed a cigarette in his holder. She registered his every gesture, but tried not to show that she was doing this. Together on the long settee, they stretched their feet towards the coal-effect electric fire, his arm around her.

'I will miss you,' Helen said. 'Not coming, then?' 'What do you mean?' 'Not coming to the wedding, then?' 'Of course I am. I mean I'll miss you this week.' 'Oh,' said Charlie, shifting slightly.

She dug her fingernails into the palm of the hand furthest away from him. If she dug her fingernails into the palm of the hand nearest him, he would guess she was deliberately displaying tension and distress. 'I'll miss you too,' said Charlie.

'You don't have to say that.' Any minute now one of them

31

would have to leave the room, but if he left, he would know that she would stay sitting there with a stricken look on her face that would haunt him all week long. If she left, it would be to go upstairs and be heard weeping or, if not to be heard weeping, to be known to be stifling sobs.

Stillness outside. Frost had settled earlier. She would be alone all week. She would hear every creak of woodwork, every scratch of leaf against windowpane. She would become one with the sounds.

Cooking was a pain to Phyllis. She followed recipe books exactly. If it were roast meat, it was roasted to perfection. If it were pastry, it was of the required consistency. Meals arrived on time and were well balanced, but there was no pleasure in the preparation, only the sense of having done it right and with the benefit of long experience. Tonight there was a casserole. Bernard had already eaten. Campbell came in late and was about to eat.

'Cam, dear!' She kissed him as he came in, fresh-faced, large, his best suit rucked because his restless movements ruined all his clothes, however much she made him spend on them. 'That suit needs cleaning.'

He had stayed late at work to make up for the morning. In fact he had been out most of the afternoon assessing property. He had rung, yes, but given very little information. Now he sat there, eating, and between mouthfuls was telling her about the properties he'd seen, mainly in order to delay her onslaught.

'Er . . . did Nina get the sack, did you say, dear?' Campbell looked up. His mother was all-seeing, wasn't she? 'I didn't say that, no,' he said, bending over his plate and eating much too quickly. So like his father, Phyllis thought regretfully. She had tried correcting this. 'I rather thought,' she went on calmly 'that would be why she had decided go get married sooner rather than later.'

Here we go, thought Campbell, trying to contain his temper. He could be calm, controlled and rational with nearly everyone, but when his mother cornered him like this, stood over him as if he were a child again . . . 'It might be, mightn't it, because she *wants* to . . . marry me I mean. I *told* you: she has given in her notice.' 'You are talking with your mouth full, dear.'

One of the most frustrating moments in Campbell's life had taken place a few years earlier, when he was in the army. He had been in Cyprus waiting to be taken in a plane and dropped over Egypt for the Suez action. Two days he had waited.

But this was almost worse, worse than that moment when the orders came – dispersal rather than attack. Lay down your arms. Remove your parachute. Putting down his knife and fork, he pushed his plate from him. In Campbell's case, the United Nations might be said to have a lot to answer for. His mother simply didn't know, did she? His mother wanted blood, it seemed. He left the room.

Upstairs he threw himself on his bed. His mother always had deflated him and here she was once more pricking balloons which floated in the sky with words like love, hope, yearnings, dreams, printed on them. And now she was attacking Nina, suggesting there were flaws in Nina's love for him. She *wants* to marry me, he muttered to himself, and felt like standing up, opening the window and shouting over this and other gardens, telling all and sundry and the world at large. He even thought of going to see Margaret, the girl who lived in Scott Hall Road. She no longer worked at Crosbys' but she had made it clear that he could visit her.

Phyllis replaced the casserole in the oven, leaving the heat on low. He would be bound to come back down and finish it. She did not regret at all the anger she'd aroused in him. Only by scenes of heightened emotion could one force young people into serious consideration of the steps they were about to take in life.

Nicola slipped out of her party dress, letting it fall on to the floor. Peter clung to her. 'Speaking of weddings, you should go in what you're wearing.' 'ie practically nothing at all?' 'ie nothing at all,' he said, removing her bra and knickers. 'The best texture that I know is skin,' he said, 'your skin.'

'You big jelly,' she said, once they were both in bed, although he was neither large nor jelly-like. Peter was tall, slim, blond and athletic. Without any particular skill at sport, he enjoyed them all. He also enjoyed buying showy cars in which to drive not only to sporting occasions, but to take Nicola to dinner parties all over the Ridings, West, North and East – even as far as that place which is now, to the regret of those living there, known as North Humberside.

'And so our Nina is to join us sooner than expected?' he said later. The use of 'our' in Yorkshire indicates that someone is kin to the speaker or a neighbour or a close friend. The use of it sardonically suggests the speaker is several removes in generation from those who would have used it habitually. Nicola snuggled up to him. He was everything she wanted. Our Peter and our Nicola were snuggled up together. 'I love you just as much as ever,' said our Nicola, and our Peter said more or less the same. Don't mock them. There is more of this. Nice, isn't it?

How she would come to envy them, their closeness and their nicknames. Happiness attracts, but it can also overwhelm. Nina would sigh, despairing at its unattainability.

It could be said that the most truly Yorkshire person in the family was Charlie Garside. As a child Charlie spoke with a Yorkshire accent, although this had by now been largely eradicated, first by service in the navy, in which he had become an officer, and then by association with officer-like types in his job in advertising. These were the years before it was trendy to hold on to an accent of regional origin.

Charlie's mother retained her accent. Nina was to meet her one day, sitting in Helen and Charlie's kitchen. Mrs Garside, in spite of generous hand-outs and presents from Charlie and Helen, always bought her clothes at jumble sales. And always wore a hat, and was the first person to call Nina 'our Nina'.

Charlie stayed downstairs this evening. He was considering a dilemma, which was whether or not he should hurry on upstairs and make it up with Helen by making love to her. This was tricky, very tricky. For, if I do, thought Charlie, she will think I am doing so in order to reassure her that I will be missing sex while absent. But if I don't, she'll think I'm saving myself for week-long indulgence.

3

From Harold's diary (a Saturday in mid-March): 'Max. 40. Min. 35,' although the north-east wind which kept blowing made it feel much colder. Harold had begun to think of this as Viking weather sent by Campbell to discomfort him. It made the log fire in his study smoke. 'N home hogging drawing room fire. Julia off on wild-goose chase to do with Sacred Broodies.' The term Sacred Broodies indicated the Mothers' Union. They, together with the Broodies (which indicated the Women's Institute) made up one of the many activities which kept Julia out of the house for hours at a time. 'Viking expected,' Harold added. Then he remembered another person who might be arriving. 'John – tomorrow possibly.'

Nina was trying to draw up her wedding present list. Campbell's mother had suggested this. As soon as people received their invitations, they would ask for it. Nina sucked the end of her biro. All she could think of that she really wanted was a record player. But this probably wasn't the sort of thing you could put on a wedding present list. She lay parallel to the fire on the long sofa which she'd lounged upon ever since she could remember. She pushed the fringe out of her eyes, put down the list and picked up a copy of a fashion magazine, partly to take her mind off John who had been away from home on national service since before she got engaged to Campbell.

In many ways John was the most important member of the family to her, but the questions he would ask would be discomforting. What was more, he would expect objective, logical replies.

It was quite possible that, were it not for John, she would have accepted one of Campbell's earlier proposals and by now be in Yorkshire married and it would all be over.

It was easier talking to Laura these days. At least with Laura you could stick to trivia like bridesmaids' dresses and trousseaus. Laura's habit of mind and conversation were easy to cope with, even if finally not something which one looked up to.

She looked at her watch, rolled off the sofa and lay on the floor for several minutes looking at the ceiling, then went into the kitchen to make her father's tea.

Harold was doing calculations: cost of wedding versus saving on the cost of keeping Nina at weekends, including extra firewood, food and general wear and tear. And, if no wedding, how long would she hang around? From this his thoughts ran to the general economics of a family. At what age could you say to a child: that's all – get out? And did this vary between sons and daughters? Then take education, investment in this on a daughter plus outlay on her marriage. Let us suppose this education to have been advantageous. What, then, were the ethics of the idea that the man she married benefited from this rather than the investing parents?

Not many people had asked Nina why, in the end, she had said yes to Campbell. Most people had seemed quite unsurprised, probably because of all the time she'd known him and been going around with him. In any case, explanations in regard to relationships, she'd learned from John, were simply abstract concepts having little relevance to life. According to John, most human conversation was philosophically meaningless, the only exceptions being (a) statements deriving from sense experience such as 'Because of the Aga cooker, this kitchen is the only really warm room in the house,' or (b) tautologies, an example of which would be, 'A triangle is a three-sided figure.'

She assembled cups and saucers. Most of these were of fine porcelain, the remains of several inherited services. None of them matched. Whenever Campbell was visiting Glebe House, he would turn over whatever piece was to hand and read the maker's mark off the bottom. Likewise he'd handled the silver teapot which she'd just placed on the Aga to warm. Campbell had once seized on it, inspected it and declared it might be worth five hundred pounds.

Arguably those who have grown up with such things accept

them with a churlish equanimity, but Nina disapproved of inherited wealth full stop. John had explained to her that it was shameful, as were all divisive elements. A new world was coming; things would change. We must all vote Tory, John would say, since the more the right wing governed, the sooner the forces of the left would muster and overthrow the establishment. Possibly there would be a revolution, possibly blood on the streets. All of which might have been a good reason for not marrying Campbell. He stood for capitalism, did he not? And she as his wife could be a sitting duck for hoards of revolutionaries as they poured out of the cities. She would explain that she was on their side of course, but would this save her?

She huddled by the Aga waiting for the kettle to boil. Add electric kettle to list, she reminded herself, then, looking around the room – add whole new kitchen with Formica work surfaces.

Before dark, she decided that instead of listening for Campbell's car she would go down to the beach, possibly one of the best places that she knew to be alone. She was better at being alone than she was at being with other people, which may have been yet another reason for marrying Campbell. She'd been out with several young men and they, like Campbell, talked a lot about themselves and their experiences. Nina would sit there listening, but would not in fact be listening. Eventually they would realize this and not ask her out again. Campbell was different: he didn't notice when she wasn't listening.

The English Channel, calm and smooth; the beach, flat and sandy stretching out in front of her at low tide, beach going on forever, gulls and sand dunes. Perhaps if John tomorrow asked her why she was marrying, she would tell him how she had come here often while making up her mind, pacing up and down in the manner people were supposed to do when coming to decisions. But John would know as well as her that it was the place and the kind of day it was that filled your mind wherever you were. Decisions were not made that way. Decisions happened and you didn't usually know which way you'd choose until you'd chosen it.

Wrapped in a heavy old fur coat of her mother's which came down to her ankles, Nina decided that life was almost certainly to do with more than having vaguely cosmic thoughts, which was a pity because she did like having them. Life was to do with doing. 'What do you want to do?' someone asked her when she left school. 'I might be a journalist,' said Nina and found a job on the local paper, but this only reported on weddings, funerals, council meetings, whist drives and so on. And only for five pounds a week, whereas in London she earned twice as much.

To walk home she went through the cemetery. She would hang on to the job till June and that was something, wasn't it? The humiliation of that interview had faded quite remarkably. She paused by a grave. Time probably was everything.

The wind dropped as she passed the church again and entered the alleyway which led to the old vegetable garden. This was no longer cultivated, but there remained a few fronds of asparagus which brushed against her as she passed.

At night she had begun to dream of walking here, a dream that she was passing through the garden and that beside her was an unseen, unidentifiable presence wearing strong boots, clumping determinedly on beside her. Whoever it was, it wasn't Campbell.

Sometimes in the same dream she would be climbing shallow steps ascending in a wide and easy curve to reach an eminence, while the person who accompanied her was doing it the hard way, up the craggy precipice and still struggling long after she had reached the top. Here she stood, knowing she was so high up that she could see out across flat misty countryside as far or further than anyone had ever seen.

The eccentricity of Glebe House arrangements appealed to Campbell; in particular, Harold's frequent absence from both meals and general conversation. This smacked to Campbell of Mr Bennet in *Pride and Prejudice* which he'd read in O-Level English Literature at public school.

The study also fascinated him. He'd only been in there once when Harold had unrolled the scroll which was the family tree. There displayed were Forestiers, Mastersons, Giradoux and many others. Campbell sat awe-inspired, noting the noble occupations of Nina's ancestors: the baronets, colonial administrators, the odd bishop and attorney general.

And when the father actually appeared at meals, as he did this evening, Campbell felt extremely flattered and assumed it was his presence that had caused this rare event. Having taken note of Harold's interest in the classical, he would introduce such topics as the Roman occupation of York, calling it Eboracum to impress the old man that he was, like him, a man of learning, even erudition.

So what with that and with her mother's chattering, there was little need for Nina to contribute. So she sat and thought of John and wondered if he would turn up tomorrow and if Campbell would still be around and how the meeting of the two would go.

Then Campbell began to talk about the new branch of Crosbys' which would soon open at Wakefield. His father had at last agreed to it. And after this her mother talked about the meeting of the Mothers' Union and the vicar who had attended, saying how nice he was. He was comparatively new. 'I never thought I'd get to care for him,' she said, adding that she felt extremely sorry for him since he had a crippled wife who couldn't help him in the parish, a great disadvantage naturally.

This is the same vicar who had been to Yorkshire and had eulogized the place. Nina didn't mind him. He seemed rational and probably didn't believe in God at all but, because of his position, had to make it look as if he did. Even John said that he seemed intelligent.

'Definitely an improvement on old Fire and Brimstone,' said her father, referring to the previous incumbent. Nina thought there might be an argument. Blind belief was more in her mother's line, the man before had been a particular favourite.

Her mother looked into the distance sadly. This was the usual outcome these days of a disagreement which was so completely basic that it made you wonder how they had survived together all these years. She often saw them as two combatants who had boxed a draw, flaked out, punch-drunk.

The dining room – not often used, except when visitors were present. A single-bar electric fire barely took the chill off it.

The subject changed to property, introduced by Campbell,

naturally. Prices, he was saying, had broken records in their rise over the last few months. He went on to elaborate with various examples. Harold sipped the red wine which had been brought by Campbell. At least the Viking never arrived empty-handed. It was not one of Harold's favourite clarets but you couldn't have everything, he told himself, listening as Campbell moved from property to other items of especial value. A pity that I didn't hang on to the sauceboats for a little longer, he reflected. Then a further thought occurred to him. 'I wonder . . . couldn't it be said – it's surely not that things have become more valuable, but that money has become worth less. In which case,' Harold went on in his questioning and professorial tone, 'in regard to objects, in relation to each other they have stayed the same.'

'Indeed one could say that,' said Campbell, leaning forward eagerly.

'Staying the same but at the same time moving fast?' Harold brightened in the eye department as if he were on the track of something. 'This, for instance.' He picked up a pudding spoon and held it vertically in his fist. 'How much has this gone up in the last ten minutes – or let's say since it was laid here? Could we say one half-penny? One farthing possibly?'

Campbell threw his head back, laughing. At this point Harold rose to leave the table. Campbell sprang to open the door and closed it, sat down again, his mouth still open as if he was planning a further peroration on the subject of the worth of things, amazing leap in prices and so on; but did not do so. There was a passing silence.

Julia sighed. There were moments – albeit rare – when she truly believed that the pecularities of her household and her failure to make it ordinary were unique and tragic. She began to clear the table, putting china and cutlery on the serving hatch, as if there were still someone on the kitchen side to take them off and deal with them. Pretensions oh pretensions, Nina thought.

'What are you thinking about?' Campbell asked a few minutes later when he was alone with her. 'Oh value and so on,' she said, 'objective truth.' She was thinking about John again in fact. He didn't have that many views on worth and value, but he did go on about objective truth a lot.

'Objective truth is hardly the same as worth and value,' Campbell said. 'You are confusing things.' Perhaps she was. He sometimes criticized her mind these days, although more often he disparaged her in the more practical areas of life. Sometimes it seemed as if, in having chosen her, he'd taken on a job of reformation.

Enough has happened in my life, thought Harold in his study without learning of further changes. He wished he'd brought his unfinished glass of wine with him. He made up the fire and stood in front of it. Yes, I have made adjustments in my life, he thought. The world has swivelled on its axis and it could be said to be a world I don't belong to any more. I have experienced two major wars, several minor ones, the dissipation of the British Empire more or less, the atomic bomb, a general strike and several devaluations of the pound. I've made adjustments in my mental attitude towards the world and, bugger me, I can't but hope there aren't that many more to make.

He waited. The other three were in the kitchen. Then they were in the drawing room, at which point Harold went to find the half-empty bottle of red wine and carry it back to the study.

A man is of his time, he told himself, and can be of no other time. Had he lived longer, how would he have faced such things as men who walk upon the surface of the moon, heart transplants and the micro-chip? Although he would have welcomed, as should be quite clear by now, the sixties and the permissive society which would have made it perfectly acceptable for Nina to have gone to live with Campbell with no marquee, bridesmaids, champagne and the rest of it.

Eventually he heard them going up. Then silence, but for creaking floorboards which he took to be the Viking creeping into Nina's room. Weddings were intended to precede this sort of thing, not follow it. Harold shrugged his shoulders, finished up the wine and wandered through the house to make sure everything was locked.

* * *

'At last!' said Campbell. 'Mmmmm,' said Nina. It always quite surprised her, this. He was so well brought up, so deferential to her parents, so incredibly correct and then, regardless of their presence in the house, he would come and fling himself on top of her.

You saw a person and you thought: I can't imagine doing it with him. Then here you were and had been doing it for months with him. Time did change everything. Sex was at first a great adventure. Now it was urgent, not to say essential, really. She would lie there afterwards and think about it all. This was the nubbins of it all, the central issue and the focus. This was the reason for everything that would happen between now and June, when upwards of two hundred people would arrive to witness an event which would not have occurred if Campbell hadn't wanted her. 'Sex is quite momentous, isn't it?' she whispered. 'It certainly is,' said Campbell ardently. He began to whisper at some length about the future and his plans for both of them. Sex seemed to make him especially optimistic. Strange that a bodily function could affect the mind like that.

Yes, sex must be crucial, mustn't it? It tortured people. At the same time it made them full of energy and spirituality, made them dreamy, airy and romantic. People also killed for it. But it was commonplace, since everyone you ever saw would not be there had it not occurred between their parents. It was both extraordinary and ordinary. People did it all the time, but hardly ever said they had been doing it. You saw them and you would know they had been doing it, but they would look the same afterwards as before.

She said, 'You know, I can't imagine other people doing it.' 'Of course they do,' said Campbell. 'I know, but all the same, I can't imagine it.' 'I'm glad we're getting married soon,' said Campbell, who had much the worst of it in many ways because of having to get out of bed and go along the passage soon. It was much easier in London where he could spend the whole night with her. And it was so cosy afterwards – rather like being in bed with your parents when you were a child, in which case having a sexual partner was no more than a replay of an earlier experience.

'Time's funny isn't it?' she whispered. Once Campbell told

her that two hundred years ago, to get to London or the south of England he would have had to travel by boat down the Ouse to Hull and then along the coast to Tilbury. 'What do you mean?' 'Just that if we'd been born two hundred years ago we wouldn't have met.' 'We wouldn't have been us in any case,' he said. 'I *know* we wouldn't.' Then she began to wonder how far north she would have gone to marry him. Was there a sliding scale to do with passion and geography? I love you so much I will go to Edinburgh to be with you. I love you even more, so I will go to Inverness to be with you. And what degree of passion would take someone as far as Shetland, say, or Iceland, or as far as Greenland?

And what of love itself, words of which they spoke as he lowered himself out of the bed, made for the door on tiptoe and headed out towards the drafty passage. How true was it? And if true, what exactly did it mean? To love is probably to need, decided Nina, at any rate I hope it is. Need is the word I'll use to John tomorrow.

This brother four years older than her, who came and went according to his own whim or will, never assuming people would expect him at any particular time. There was so much that was unknown about John. If asked what he was going to do after national service, he would say: 'I suppose breathe, live and walk around and earn enough money to make it possible to go on doing these things,' and if it was then pointed out to him that most people by his age had decided on a path in life, he would reply: 'Oh, is there a stipulated age by which one is supposed to have decided on a path in life? Is there a law? How interesting! I never heard of it.'

He may even have chosen to avoid Campbell on this day. At any rate they missed each other by half an hour. A narrow squeak, thought Nina, although the meeting between the two of them would be inevitable, but maybe not until the wedding when there wouldn't be a lot of time for the surfacing of fundamental differences.

'So where is everyone?' He put his motorcycle helmet on the kitchen table, likewise his gloves, and began to unzip the complex fastening of his leather suit. 'Well, Mummy's at the vicarage or seeing someone. Daddy's in there.' She jerked her head towards the study. 'And . . . er, Campbell's just left.' She lowered her voice somewhat. 'And I've got to go soon to . . . to catch my train.'

But John wasn't someone with whom you discussed arrangements. He was someone with whom you discussed ideas or listened as he gave you ideas. He eschewed small talk and could appear comfortable standing alone on social occasions. To look at – more like father than mother: with horn-rimmed spectacles and, at this time, because of RAF service, short hair.

Perhaps he would talk, as he often did, about his work, which was as a medical orderly in a psychiatric unit; about the terrible cases of men damaged mentally and in some cases irretrievably by war. Most of the family soon had enough of John's accounts of all this pain and anguish, but Nina lapped it up and listened endlessly.

'So you're still working?' said John. 'Yes, for the moment.' 'Then getting married?' 'Yes,' said Nina, turning to the sink to deal, quite willingly for once, with cups and saucers left from tea.

He sat down, lit a cigarette and drummed his fingers on the table. 'So one must assume you love him then?' Nina gulped and ran the tap into the sink. 'Well sort of, yes.' 'That makes sense.' 'Oh, does it?' Something like relief was spreading. 'Love? Lust? Desire?' said John: 'I dare say chemistry would be the nearest word to use.'

'Oh absolutely!' Relief was not the word for it. To think that only half an hour ago she had considered leaving on an earlier train to avoid this confrontation. 'How are your patients?'

He rubbed his nose. 'I never thought I'd wish for the death of someone.' He started on a story of a man who screamed all day and night and how this man, who'd been a bomber pilot, had crashed his Lancaster and seen the body of his bomb-aimer spread across the runway. 'Yes, I almost wish he'd die,' said John, and Nina said, 'Do you? How terrible for you.' Perhaps she was irrelevant, possibly it didn't matter what she did and maybe it wouldn't matter what he thought of Campbell either. Even the fact that Campbell had so wanted to be part of an invasion force and to be parachuted into Egypt might after all now go unquestioned.

'He's rich I gather?' 'Campbell? Well, you could say so, but he is not a partner in the business yet.' She went on to explain that Campbell's parents were quite democratic in a way, believing that young people should work hard for what they earned, which meant that Campbell didn't have that much of a salary. 'You call that democratic?' 'Well, I thought it was.' John began zipping up his suit again. 'I'll take you to the station if you like.'

Mild weather had been streaming in since yesterday when on the beach she'd thought about these things or tried to think about these things. No east wind now, flat roads ahead, the roar of motorcycle engine drowned all else. She clutched John's back and put her feet on the pillion stirrups as he accelerated. She wished he could have driven her like this for ever.

At the station yard he left her, circled and shot off again, John going in a puff of exhaust. Of his own love life – or rather lusts, desires and chemistries – nothing was known.

On the platform at twilight – figures standing, waiting like herself. Opinions shouldn't matter. They were abstract. They changed nothing. Real things were to do with catching trains and having sex and clothes and getting organized.

4

In the south, daffodils by now, but in Harrogate clumps of crocuses still clustered around the trees along the Stray. This common land consists of many acres of mown grass. It spreads and slopes, a green and open space. The town's grey buildings are relieved by it. Overlooking this, a teashop. Here sat Phyllis and her sister, exchanging news and catching up with plans.

Easter would be early. 'And Nina will be with you?' Cicely Cornelius sipped lemon tea. 'You will get used to her, I promise you.' Cicely already had a daughter-in-law. 'I was rigid with nerves when Caroline first appeared, but now I'm really rather fond of her. One of the main things in life, I often think, is simply getting used to people.'

Here they had sat at weekly intervals during all their married lives, comparing notes on family and children; also husbands, although inadequacies in respect of these had long been accepted by the two of them. And, having dealt with next of kin, they would move on to extended family. For instance Helen, whose name was often mentioned as they drank their tea or coffee and listened to a trio playing. 'She is going through a bad patch I'm afraid,' said Phyllis. 'Oh not again!' said Cicely.

Phyllis held her cup, looked out on the windy day and thought of all the things she had to do before the holiday.

'And will you see that loony aunt?' asked Laura. She and Nina were walking along Oxford Street. 'I mean the one who tried to kill her husband.' Laura took a great interest in the ins and outs of other people's families.

'I don't know.' Nina explained that over Easter they would be staying at the Crosbys' seaside house: 'I don't think she is loony really. It might have been an accident.' '*What* might have been an accident?'

Nina walked on. They were shopping in her lunch hour. 'Well, there was an accident. In a car or something.' Campbell was always vague when speaking of the Garsides, lowering his voice as if there were some further mystery about which he had been sworn to secrecy. 'I'm sure they love each other. They are always touching. They're fairly old, but I am sure that they have – you know – sex a lot.' 'Why? How are you sure?' Laura was insistent. 'Did she tell you that they did?'

'Of course not. I don't know her all that well.' Except that Nina did feel that she knew Helen well. Perhaps because the older woman was so extra friendly, chatting about nothing special, making Nina feel quite talkative herself. At Helen's house it never mattered what you said.

'You did say she was said to be deranged.' 'Oh did I? What I like about her is that she is silly.' 'Silly?' Laura's voice rose in incredulity: 'That's ridiculous.' Laura seemed to think that no one grown-up could be silly. They had stopped by Selfridges. There were summer clothes on show by now and it was sunny, spring-like in a way, but windy. 'I don't feel like buying anything,' Nina said.

They walked on. People turned their heads in their direction. Nina hoped it was at her they turned to look, but it could as easily have been at Laura, who was blonde and had a sexy walk and always wore high heels.

'Anyway,' said Nina, 'maybe she did try to kill him. I don't know. People who love each other often hate each other. At any rate they do in books.' 'In *books*, yes,' Laura said. '*And* in real life. What about Ruth Ellis?' 'But she was a prostitute or something.'

Ruth Ellis was the last woman to be hanged in England. Nina had read somewhere that, when a woman was hanged, they put a belt around her skirts so that her knickers didn't show as she swung, which was extraordinary when you came to think about it. Once you were dead, what would it matter what showed? And if it did, you should insist on wearing trousers.

'What's he like?' 'What's who like?' 'Her husband.' 'Charlie? Well he is attractive . . .' 'Sexy?' 'Sort of.' Nina couldn't explain. All she could think of was that Charlie was the kind of man you could stand close to and feel comfortable about. Sometimes walking on her own in London, she would imagine meeting him. She knew he spent time here on business. She often dreamed of having older men make love to her, but Charlie was the only one she had ever met who might come up to expectations. There was a softness to him. He had pale eyes and pale hair which he combed back. 'He cooks,' she said to Laura.

'Cooks?' Laura was again incredulous. 'Yes . . . foreign dishes, adds cream and wine, that sort of thing.'

'It all sounds most peculiar,' said Laura, as they stopped for lunch. She had left the children with a friend and come up for the day from Sevenoaks to help with shopping. She might well have grumbled that they hadn't bought a thing so far, but her mind was probably more on the problem of her husband, Jim. 'Why doesn't he want another baby?' Nina asked. 'He can be very obstinate,' said Laura, which didn't seem a proper answer somehow.

Jim was a doctor with a serious outlook on life. He kept the Forestiers informed on recent advances in medical science. He was a fairly boring person who always meant what he said but would spend a long time saying it.

Helen was doing her accounts, calculating how she could afford both wedding clothes and holidays, checking in particular the joint account. On the day they married she put all her money into both their names.

The task was comforting. The evidence was that, in regard to other women, Charlie couldn't be spending that much on them. All the same, the usual signs were present. He was so full of life these days, excitable, frenetic. Sometimes he would come home saying: 'Are you happy? Say you're happy,' and she would say yes, she was happy.

Once Helen wrote to a woman's magazine agony columnist. 'I have this problem . . .' The agony columnist wrote back: 'You can never know what someone is up to all the time unless you never leave his side, even when he goes to the lavatory.' This surprised Helen since in those days, columnists in women's magazines were more inclined to suggest that someone with her problem was not coming up to scratch either sexually or domestically. Or they might, for instance, have suggested that Helen stage a romantic evening with a candlelight dinner or even that she wore lacy and alluring clothes. 'Either follow him to the lavatory whenever he goes or leave him,' wrote the columnist. 'A third alternative is to accustom yourself to live in permanent and excruciating anxiety. Your fourth alternative is to find an occupation which will distract you when you are assailed with doubts.'

Most of the time now Helen tried to keep to the fourth alternative. She shopped, she walked the dog up the hill behind the house. She also cleaned the house a good deal, having dispensed with her cleaning lady. Within the family she had been criticized for this, especially by Phyllis who believed that Helen needed company and someone to keep an eye on her. But then the cleaning lady had been nosy, always commenting when Charlie was away, saying things like: 'So, he's off again,' or: 'You'll be worried. I said – you'll be worried,' and going on about her own husband's infidelities.

Even so, there were so many things Helen couldn't do when anxious. She would play records, yes – the healing powers of music, but she couldn't face the piano which she could play quite well. Even shopping sometimes was impossible. Going out meant facing people, meant not being close to tears. There was the fear of meeting someone who knew what haunted her or, worse still, someone who might have seen Charlie with another woman, imagining whispers . . .

There had been a time when Helen didn't worry when he was in London, because at that time he had had a girl in Skipton. Although there was always the possibility that the girl from Skipton had gone to London with him, from which it followed that she was the sort of girl who could get off work easily or even did not have a job at all. In which case she could have been a married woman, but a married woman who could spend a night in London could have been a woman uncommitted to her marriage and thus more of a threat.

One of the worst days in Helen's life had been the day she had found out about the Skipton girl. An unnamed Skipton phone number scribbled on his business card: this wouldn't have been troubling, but when he saw her looking at it, he said, 'Oh, for heaven's sake, what is it now?' in the tone of voice he always used when he suspected she suspected him. Helen, almost choking, suppressed the panic in her voice. 'Just thought I recognized the number,' she said quick as a flash but then couldn't think fast enough of anyone she knew in Skipton whose number she might have confused with this one.

Is one supposed not to mind, she was asking herself just before Easter: a wildish day, but the wind was less biting; you could lift your chin to it. She opened the window and heard the blackbird singing in the laburnum tree in the centre of the lawn. Children were home from school. From nearby gardens their voices echoed. At least it could be called spring now, although the changes in the seasons mean less to those living on a knife edge.

'The pains of hoping to be close,' said Cicely: 'That's Helen's trouble, isn't it?' Although she was the older of the two sisters, she could have been mistaken for the younger, having always spent a great deal of time and money on her appearance. Her role as Phyllis's main confidante was paramount. Her brand of wisdom lightened problems and distanced them. 'Harry's given up all that,' she said: 'He's put on an atrocious amount of weight and been struck down by lethargy.' 'Has given up all what?' said Phyllis. Then realized and began to laugh.

'You look tired, dear,' said Cicely. She considered Phyllis to be reckless in expense of self and spirit in continual vigilance in regard to family. She, herself, conserved her energy and took a rest each afternoon, regardless of the demands of her social calendar.

The phone rang. It was Charlie's secretary. Could Helen give him a message when he returned tonight? Helen put down the receiver with shaking hand. At least the secretary was not with him. I can go shopping after all, thought Helen, and her mind, as if released from bondage, shot forward to imagine details of the shopping trip.

Halfway down the hill she stopped the car. Where had the

phone call come from? Could the secretary have been in London after all and called from there? I have been fooled again, thought Helen. She could picture Charlie in the room beside the girl who made the call. A hotel room and Charlie saying: 'Call my wife and tell her – think of anything to convince her you are not with me.'

My life is a minefield. Helen sat in the car, intending to turn and head for home. There she would ring the office in Leeds to check whether or not the secretary was there.

A women stood outside her house. She stared at Helen. A woman she knew slightly, a near neighbour. Helen pretended to be searching in her handbag as if, on the way to town, she had forgotten something. Then she drove on down the hill, along the valley, left again and up the hill. She got out of the car, went into the house and stood by the telephone, touching it but unable to lift it.

The two sisters kissed and parted, Cicely to shop for a length of silk to cover a cushion and then to have her hair shampooed, set and silvered at the best salon in Harrogate. Later she would drive home to her fine house in the plain of York and rest before she gave a dinner party at which a uniformed maid would wait at table.

Phyllis stood outside the teashop. The wind blew hard as it usually does here. Old women have been lifted, carried past the cenotaph on ballooning skirts and landed outside the Midland Bank opposite. In Harrogate old people dwell, not to say proliferate. Most are in homes, but there are still some who live in the manner to which they have become accustomed in large grey houses on the edge of town. As did Aunt Winifred.

Poor frail Aunt Winifred. Phyllis kissed the dry old cheek, then set about the weekly check through medicines. Aunt Winifred's paid companion could not be completely trusted to administer these correctly. Aunt Winifred was childless now, her only son having been killed in the First World War. She was not completely bedridden, but was in bed today, propped up on pillows. From her high-ceilinged bedroom you could see out across the town towards the North York Moors.

Cicely is right – I am quite tired, thought Phyllis as she went downstairs again. She also had to check up on belongings: Aunt Winifred's book collection, silver and portraits. The young doctor in weekly attendance admired such things and was sometimes given them. These were Crosby possessions.

To marry is to take upon oneself another family, thought Phyllis as she made her way back up the massive staircase. The only other Crosby who occasionally came to see Aunt Winifred was Muriel. Phyllis sat by the bed and raised her voice to keep Aunt Winifred abreast of family news. The old lady smiled and nodded. One more winter and she will be gone, if not before, thought Phyllis. Since she had now run out of news, she picked up the *Yorkshire Post* and read aloud from this.

'I don't think we are hearing much today.' The paid companion, Rose, looked in. She was a short dumpy woman with straight grey hair hooked back in a plastic slide. She chattered on.

Not to marry, decided Phyllis, could be to end up like Rose with no one but a married sister living in Canada. She folded the newspaper and put it down. Aunt Winifred's eyes were closed. Perhaps I try too hard, thought Phyllis. She often suspected that Muriel on her visits read bridge articles aloud.

On the way home she called on Nicola. 'You look pale, dear. What a pity you can't come to Sandsend with us.' This was the way of it; families were created, then diffused.

'I'm fine. Don't worry, Mum.' Nicola went off to fetch Louisa. School holidays began today. I'm sure there's something very wrong, thought Phyllis, putting the baby in the pushchair and taking Mo's hand firmly.

'I'm staying with my other grandma over Easter,' Mo said. 'Either hold on to my hand or to the pushchair handle, dear.' Phyllis had to raise her voice because of gusting wind and passing traffic. 'I'm staying with my other grandma over Easter. I'm staying with my other grandma over Easter.'

'And did you do your shopping?' Charlie asked. 'My shopping?' 'For the wedding.' 'No, I didn't after all.' Helen hastened on to say what she had done today, though none of it was strictly true, except the checking of the joint account.

They ate. They went to bed. They made love. Nina was right

here. They did it often and were extremely good at it. It never failed them. They indulged themselves at length and ended up after twenty minutes on the far side of their king-size bed.

Afterwards Helen leaned on one elbow looking at the shadows under his closed eyes, wondering how he could give so much of himself to her and yet almost certainly have given just as much the night before to someone else.

He was awake looking at her. 'Can't you sleep my darling? Don't be anxious, Helen. Please, please don't be anxious' He pulled her down towards him, then turned her, clasping her. 'Oh, my darling, there is no one quite like you.'

No one quite like me? Careful, Helen. No one quite like me, for heaven's sake? But she couldn't ask him what he meant by that or he would leap out of bed and go and sleep in his dressing room. Not only that, but the whole of Easter might be spoiled.

At least he had a dressing room. Otherwise he might go out into the night and drive away. She counted twenty and in half a minute he was asleep again. If he had a conscience, it would appear it never troubled him at night. For all she knew, there might be enough on his conscience to ruin her life for ever if she knew the details.

Then he was awake again. He must have felt her tension. 'Listen, Helen, if you really loved me, you would sleep.' Conditional: his love for me is always conditional on my being as he wants me. I must lie here breathing as if fast asleep and counting suspects from the past and present, women passing through my head along with dates and times and opportunities as well as alibis . . .

5

If you are a southerner in Yorkshire, you never quite forget it. In the background of your consciousness is this steady beat reminding you that you have travelled from your roots and may be only perching here. You are not uncomfortable but perhaps exposed. You sense you are existing somewhat on the edge of things. Down there (down south as you may come to call it), beyond you spatially, is the main sweep of the country and arguably the heart of it. You are also aware that, in the minds of people living in those busier and boskier parts, the north is usually irrelevant.

But to admit to a dregree of geographical insecurity is by no means to admit regret. Quite the reverse in Polly's case. She remained in Swaledale not because of its beauty, but because of the challenge of it all. In Polly's opinion the place where you belong may not be the place where you function at your best. Which is not to say that she was always crisp and confident. Far from it, especially this spring.

The floods shrank in the flat of the valley and the fishermen were out again. Love was not worth it, Polly thought, stamping down across the fields to stand on the bridge over the Swale and to lose herself in watching the swirls and eddies and being stared at by fishermen under green umbrellas.

It was worse in the school holidays. Those were the times he used to come and see her unexpectedly. Those were the times she would look out of the window and see his car, the times when at first she'd been surprised to see his car.

These holidays she would sit and read in order to prevent herself from looking out expectantly. Too many bloody windows, Polly told herself back inside the cottage where she now sat and read in order to keep herself from looking out.

Love is anticipation, peak and aftermath. Things happen when you least expect it, when you have begun the process of recovery, when at last the memories of the first euphoria have begun to fade. His car again.

People don't say what they've come for. In the past she used to help him out. This time she wouldn't. She made him coffee, stifling the sexual need his presence had aroused in her within five minutes of arrival.

If men want encouragement, they should ask for it, thought Polly sitting there, not making conversation, not taking the lead as she had always done. Most of all it hurt to remember that there was a time when this man, once given the signal, used not to be able to wait before tearing his own clothes off as well as hers.

She watched his car go, knowing there would be no need to look out hopefully again. An expense of spirit in a waste of what? Of anger at the gross ephemerality of it all? She took an envelope from the mantelpiece. The invitation was accompanied by a letter from Julia which said that someone from the Crosbys would be getting in touch with her about a lift.

She examined the card. The inscription of her name on it insisted on the presence of a bond which, even though so seldom called upon, held permanence. She licked the envelope of her reply, put on her coat again and trudged towards the post office.

Pause for the view: sky, colourless above the flat-topped hill. Same east, same west. This vista was one of suspended animation.

How do I know this is north not south, thought Nina, looking out of the window of the tiny bedroom she'd been given. The sea was pale and calm beyond the beach. The sand was gritty, but there was sand like that on southern coasts. Was it the misty light or what was it? Families played, children wearing duffel coats and woolly hats were running on the beach in wellingtons.

The Crosby seaside house was like a miniature of Pound Close: as if someone had lifted up Pound Close, shrunk it and set it down with all its contents, which were, as were all Crosby possessions, of lasting quality.

If I was dropped by helicopter, Nina thought, with blindfold and having been given no clue whatsoever as to where I was landing, would I guess? I'd sniff the air. But sea air is much the same all over, isn't it?

'Let's go for a walk,' called Phyllis, directing Nina to a cupboard underneath the stairs where there were sweaters, coats and macintoshes to be borrowed. Bernard was out playing golf and Campbell was in the little sitting room, papers spread everywhere, working on a chapter of his book. 'It's nice for men to have occupations on a holiday,' said Phyllis.

They set out, Phyllis carrying her binoculars, taking the cliff path where brown earth and chunks of grass were always falling into the sea so that the path continually had to be remade further inland. The sun might have been behind the mist somewhere.

Phyllis, in between raising her binoculars to look at birds, was in a reminiscent mood, mostly about her early married life, a time of comparative hardship when they had been building up the business, the stringencies she had been forced to observe, the savings made by such activities as boiling up bones for soup and gravy. But, as she pointed out, there were far fewer temptations in those days in the form of expensive tinned foods which might be useful for emergencies but were in no way nourishing.

'Frozen foods are supposed to be all right,' said Nina. 'Oh, do you think so, dear?' said Phyllis, going on to speak of women in the family – how they managed or did not manage domestically. There was her brother's wife, Joan Ramsey, for instance, who was always buying new, so-called labour-saving gadgets. 'And Helen of course is far from careful.' 'I thought her money was her own,' said Nina. 'It never is, dear, really, is it?'

Sandsend is up there to the north of Whitby, the lights of which could be seen at night. But Whitby was spoiled, the Crosbys said, full of amusement arcades which encouraged people to waste money.

It wasn't a holiday in the sense that you could stay in bed for as long as you wanted. What the Crosbys called a nice lie-in meant that breakfast was at nine instead of eight o'clock. Then came the walks, which couldn't go on that long because of having to get back to get lunch ready, although, as Phyllis often pointed out, one could be less meticulous on holiday. Cold meat and salad, fruit and cheese instead of a cooked main course and pudding could be served at midday.

During meals everyone said in detail what they had been doing: Bernard's game of golf, how he'd played and what people at the club had said. One morning he'd been discussing business with his partner who dealt in household goods. People now, he said, were buying more and more of these and, because of hire purchase facilities, which meant easy-come and easy-go, were buying rubbish and poor workmanship. Nina said, wasn't that just normal greed like everyone had? Then realized that, by claiming greed for all human beings, she was claiming it for herself, which would make them think she was marrying Campbell for his money. So she said she might look for a job in Leeds after she was married. 'We'll see,' said Campbell, and no one else said anything.

The next day Phyllis led her inland up a chine between two woods where a great variety of birds could been seen, and told her what a pity it was that, for instance, Joan Ramsey didn't have any interest to speak of outside the house, which was probably the cause of her buying so much equipment. On the other hand, Muriel Crosby went much too far the other way, being very preoccupied with playing bridge, which was all right in small doses but could lead to sad neglect of other responsibilities.

The trees they walked between were hawthorns, stunted and with branches always pointing inland. No sign of leaves or buds as yet. 'Caroline Cornelius,' Phyllis said, 'is most artistic. She has taken up lampshade making, something she can do at home of course.' Soon Nina wished she hadn't said anything about working after marriage.

When they came back from this walk, Campbell had fallen asleep over his table of papers. Phyllis removed the fountain pen from his hand, put the top on it and said they would have tea without him. After this she reminded Nina of the wedding present list and Nina went upstairs to write this out.

She also read. There had been a list in *The Sunday Times* recently of the best fifty novels ever written in the English language and she was working her way through these. She was trying to improve herself. She was always trying to improve herself. She wondered if all those women that Phyllis talked about also tried to improve themselves and whether trying to improve yourself counted for anything or not.

That evening Campbell went out with his father to the golf club for a drink. She was permanently apart from him it seemed. She sat with Phyllis, looking through the wedding present list.

'Well done, dear,' Phyllis said, 'but I should leave out ovenware if I were you. Nicola has got tons of it. People are always giving ovenware. Plates, cups and saucers?' This was a little vague, said Phyllis. It was better if you specified a dinner service, mentioned both design and make and wrote down where it could be bought. Let people make their minds up as to which parts of it they bought. 'I think it's rather greedy asking anyway,' said Nina.

'Oh, do you, dear? But since they're going to buy you something anyway, it should be made as easy as can be for them, shouldn't it? Now for the linen. You've forgotten tea-cloths. Nick is always saying what a bore it is to buy them.' Essential to a wedding present list, it seemed, were cheapish items to cater for those with little cash to spare. 'Of course,' said Nina.

'Towels . . . navy blue?' Phyllis drew in her breath. 'I thought you had to put a colour,' Nina said. Phyllis hummed. 'It *is* unusual, but if that's your choice . . .'

In respect of larger items, Nina had already cancelled record player, but she had left in refrigerator. 'Oh,' said Phyllis. 'Now I come to think of it, Joan Ramsey has just the thing . . . in very good condition . . .' I might have known it, Nina thought, crossing out refrigerator.

Outside the window, darkness now, but in the bay a single light. It bobbed a little, possibly a boat.

So many people made mistakes with wedding present lists,

Phyllis was saying, quoting as a prime example Jane Crosby, the unhappy wife of Simon Crosby, son of Muriel and Richard, who had gone as far as asking for certain shades of carpeting and even for a washing machine which, as was obvious, was something one did not need for the early years of marriage. 'Did she get one?' Nina asked. 'You look tired, dear,' said Phyllis. 'Yes, I am,' said Nina, and went to her room. Outside the light remained, still bobbing. Then it began to dwindle. Boat going out to sea, light dwindling, dimming, disappearing. Nina didn't feel like reading, so the only thing to do was to sleep.

If people disapprove of you, you have two options. You can either say to them: you've got me – so put up with me; or you can try and drag yourself up to meet their standards. In the morning Nina, determined to spend some time with Campbell, went into the little sitting room and sat beside him. 'Am I so awful?' 'What do you mean?' 'I just wondered . . .' 'I am marrying you, aren't I?' True, what more could one person do for another than marry them? 'Okay now?' he asked her. 'Sort of, yes.' 'Oh, by the way, we ought to be thinking about a house.'

It was really tricky getting married. You got one thing out of the way and then another problem came along. 'Well, you're up here all the time. If you can't find a property, who can?' 'There's a lot of work before the Wakefield office opens,' Campbell said.

But then he put his arm round her and read her a sentence from his chapter on Towton Moor. 'A dreadful ardour inspired all ranks. Men thirsted to be at their enemies' throats . . .'

'Do you really think it was as bad as that?' Most of the time here she'd wanted to be with him and now they were together, it was disappointing. This might have been to do with not having sex. The house was so small and Phyllis, as if warning them, had several times complained of sleeping lightly.

'I'll see you later,' said Nina, and went off for a walk on her own, avoiding Phyllis, and found a dell on the gorsey, brackeny slope of a cliff and a boulder to sit on, and thought about all the things the Crosbys disapproved of, starting with greed. But then they didn't need to be greedy, having everything they wanted. Surely, in some cases, greed was excusable? She thought about this for a time and then found she was thinking about falling cliffs, and if they were always falling, the land would be forever getting smaller. So the sea was greedy. Some greed *was* excusable. Then she wondered about jumping up and down near the edge of the cliff to see if she could dislodge a piece of land so that it would fall off earlier than it otherwise would. That would be a way of making her mark on the world, but she would not be famous for it, only dead.

'I was wondering where you were, dear,' Phyllis said, back at the house. 'Oh, I found this sheltered spot. It was okay there.' 'I think it's nice to get away now and then on your own and have a think about things,' said Phyllis. Poor Nina, she was thinking, what a lonely child she is. I'll cheer her up by giving her the lettuce to wash.

Poor Nina, she went on thinking later, as the sun came out and she stood in the garden looking at the sea which had been grey all weekend, but now was blue. Here was the space she, Phyllis, wanted. *And* she wanted solitude sometimes. *And* she didn't really enjoy telling people how to live their lives and warning them of other people's mistakes. But if one knew how life could best be lived, then one had to tell them, didn't one, dear? Even if all the time you knew that it would make little difference in the end and that, as sure as the land would fall away, those who strove would keep on striving until they could no longer strive. Then the striving would be handed on and those who followed, having also learned from their own mistakes, would repeat the process and repeat the process, because the passing on of wisdom is what people do as they get older.

The colours brightened. A colony of gulls swooped and arched. Her sharp ears caught the sound above her head of a skylark. From down on the shore came the sound of fine shingle being pulled out and dropped back, pulled out and dropped back.

Helen went into the conservatory. The passion-flower plant needed pinning back. It sprawled and climbed up and along the sides and roof, knotting itself, new growth sending out tendrils which clung fiercely to older, stronger stalks. She should have dealt with this last autumn, but had not felt like it.

Then she went outside and found the earth was soft. She plunged her fork into the soil. But she must also cut down overgrown border plants also left since autumn. So much she'd neglected in the autumn! What had been the crisis then? How funny – I've forgotten now. This made her want to giggle.

On the first day of the holiday she had decided he was overwhelming her with love as if to build up a credit he could draw upon if darker days returned. On the second day she decided that he could be soothing her or lulling her into non-suspicion. But, no, it was all quite genuine, she decided on Easter Monday. Proof almost positive, so almost positive that later she would go inside and touch the piano keys.

On Bank Holiday Nina called in on her way back to London. There was the dog, the piano and the piles of magazines. This was what she liked about it all. The sun came out. They sat on the lawn and Helen put a record on indoors. The voice of Frank Sinatra poured out of the windows. Lena ran to catch a stick thrown by Nina.

Beyond the garden, the steps, the valley and the train crossing the viaduct. Charlie came and put his arm around Helen. You wouldn't believe that they could hate each other. He had been gardening and had rolled up his sleeves. Lena brought back the stick. Nina crouched to throw it again, pushed her fringe out of her eyes, turned her face and smiled up at both of them. My God, thought Charlie, when this girl really looks at you . . .

It's all to do with different kinds of loving, Polly decided as the milder weather from the south reached Swaledale and the skies cleared. Men love and women love, but the two loves are completely different. They travel, but in parallel, and there is no true confluence. If occasionally there seems to be a meeting place, that is pure coincidence.

She opened her window. The patches of snow on the hill to the south had dwindled into tiny white markings in the dimples in the ground. A fast RAF plane skimmed between two clouds. A tank from Catterick crossed the skyline with its gun raised.

The bracken was still ginger-brown with the new season's growth well hidden under it. Only little ponds in the flat valley now. Soon the ground down there would dry and let it all seep away. You never knew whom you might meet at weddings.

Part II

6

The big event in Harold's life: was it climbing Everest or not climbing Everest? Had he got halfway up or had he got only halfway up? Depends how you describe it. Some would say it was an achievement to have been included in the expedition. And he did get to the top of a lesser neighbouring peak. There is a picture of him standing there. Would that be the only evidence of his existence or would there one day be a book with his name on the spine of it?

Most of the family didn't think so. Their attitude to Harold's work was on the whole one of indifference. For instance John said that it was a useless and redundant occupation. Latin was a discipline which would no longer be needed in the modern world, and in any case the stoicism of such as Marcus Aurelius was unreformist. Nina more or less agreed with this. Laura reckoned it would never be finished, which made it, for her, a non-event. As far as Julia was concerned, all she did was to make polite enquiries from time to time and fail to listen to replies.

Once he used to quote to her from it, but did this no longer, even though it would have been increasingly appropriate. 'Occupy yourself with few things if you would be tranquil' was a case in point. Instead, he found himself snapping at her, raising his voice to ask her why she couldn't leave a few things for the silly girl to do herself, to which Julia would answer that the silly girl was still at work.

'D-Day minus 30,' Harold wrote. 'Max 50. Min 45. Coldest late May day since records (meaning mine) began. Estimated number of guests attending Great Disaster: 250.' He stood outside for a time, looking towards the church spire beyond the early summer foliage. Were there no church, he speculated, there might be no wedding. Then he thought of Julia and her frenetic efforts to preserve the place, to ensure the flowers were done, to make sure people knew exactly what was going on parochially and considered further that, if it were not for people like her, there might be no churches anyway. By now their fabric would be heading for decay. Spires and towers would be condemned and pulled down for sake of the community. How would it look, the English landscape, thus denuded of these identifying features?

But there was a church and there would be a wedding, also wedding business to be done, on which he allowed himself half an hour before settling down to work each morning. This summer he would not go to Goodwood. His last visit had been late last August, a good meeting, a golden day – perhaps never to be repeated in his case. He watched the early meetings of the flat on TV, reading the runners in the papers and cabling his bookies by phone at moments when Julia was out in the village arranging beds for visitors and extra helpers or rushing at the herbaceous borders with hoe in hand. Carter, the man who used to come once a week to tidy up the small acreage around Glebe House, had suddenly given in his notice, offering no reason. Carter: the only person to be able to work the old Atco mower – that is apart from John who hardly counted since he was at home so seldom. 'Grass longer than ever recorded,' Harold added to his diary.

One thing to be grateful for – no marquee here, no buggering about with guy ropes tripping people up for days on end. The reception as expected was to be held at the home of Uncle Arthur Masterson. This, like a hundred other items in connection with D-Day or Disaster Day, had been arranged by Julia. Harold was now sitting indoors trying to capture the word which could most aptly be applied to Julia at this time. Satisfied, he completed his entry for the day. 'J approaching critical mass.'

She was, however, soothed at night by her Bible reading, texts as recommended by the Bible reading fellowship. Last night it had been the feast at Cana. Harold looked over her shoulder. 'Turning water into wine, eh? Why didn't we send an invitation to J.H. Christ?' Then turned his back, chuckling to himself. But some nights she would be restless, wondering why she hadn't heard from so and so, a friend or far-removed relation who had not replied to their invitation. Some nights he noticed her body as she slipped her nightdress over it: her skin still fine and pearly in contrast to the muscled, reddened hands and weather-beaten neck.

Harold shuddered to imagine what her mood would be when all this was over. Even now she had started going quiet at times, looking into the distance, occasionally expressing doubts about arrangements, most recently that Dorothy didn't seem to be taking such an interest in the choice of flowers as might have been expected. 'She seemed so keen to do it at the start, you see.'

Usually when Julia came in from errands, there would be a bang of the door and a call of: 'Harold, I am back. Hullo!' but this morning, having heard her approaching footsteps, there was a silence, so he went outside and saw her there on the lawn staring up at the cedar tree as if it were the cross at Calvary and she nailed up on it. Heavy-laden was not the word for Julia standing there sniffing. 'I went to Dorothy's. There was no one there. She's gone, completely gone, and in the shop they told me that she's gone with Carter. I mean I've seen her nearly every day for weeks and weeks and never had an inkling . . .'

Well, that's best friends for you, thought Harold, but did not dare say it and anyway it needed no saying. He had always found Dorothy a wildish and enticing widow, whose anxiety to please Julia mistook for friendliness. 'There is,' she sobbed, and could hardly get the words out, 'a notice up outside the cottage. It is for sale!' Harold offered her a large white handkerchief. 'Have a good blow. That's right.' 'I'm sorry. I am being silly.' 'Tell you what – let's have a sherry.' 'Terribly terribly silly. I know she needed someone. Well, she must have.'

There is good in this woman, Harold thought, pouring sherry. Too many churches and no such thing as saints, but if the world was peopled with women like this, it would be a fine and most forgiving place, even if more of a bloody bugger's muddle everywhere.

* * *

Helen's outfit was complete at last. It had taken her three shopping trips. On the first of these she chose a white silk spotted shirtwaister dress with a permanently pleated skirt. Just the thing – a touch of the *grande dame* look. To go with it, she would need a wide romantic hat, also of course shoes and a handbag in a yet-to-be-decided colour, but possibly navy to echo the spots on the dress. Or red?

She had tried the dress on again at home. 'Yes, very nice,' said Charlie, but didn't sound whole-hearted and when she went to shop for shoes, hat and bag, she saw another dress, something that she absolutely had to get, one of those impulse buys – a two-piece, extravagant in both price and style, longwaisted, cream and with a full skirt in the current bouffant fashion. Deciding that impromptu buys were often in the long run most successful, she wrote a cheque and walked on air back to the car. The pleated spotted dress would do for other occasions, like Phyllis's St John's Ambulance Garden Party later in the summer.

Then there was the trip to buy shoes, hat and bag to go with the cream two-piece, which was going to be very demanding in regard to accessories. In between times she considered the current joint account and became a little worried. There was the holiday to come. The holiday was all-important.

The third trip drained her of energy. Charlie came home unexpectedly that lunch time and found her lying on the bed. He always became upset when she was tired, believing he was somehow the cause of it and that she was accusing him by lying down and admitting tiredness. 'It's my own fault,' she said, leaping up to display what she had bought, at which he was suitably amazed and impressed, agreeing that it was worth every penny. 'Do you really think so?' 'It's your money, darling.' This was unusual. It had always been 'our' money. Was he distancing himself from what they shared? Don't panic Helen.

'Oh, and I've booked the car across the Channel,' she said, which was not the case at all. 'I thought that we were flying.' 'No, driving, darling, you remember?' 'All right.' Nothing more was said. He left. His voice had that resigned tone. She rang a travel agent and booked the car across the Channel.

Look at yourself in the mirror, Helen. Have confidence. Think forward to the wedding. Think forward to the holiday. Then you will be alone with him, no threats from others, no chance of him running out on you, time to say: Charlie, I know I'm not the only one, and if you could be honest . . . It has always been not knowing that has hurt. Say it to him in the car as you did before, which is why he would prefer to fly.

Now he was away again. She was assessing the effect of the whole ensemble. From the bedroom window, a clear view of the rising hills, fields intensely green today and dry-stone walls intensely grey. She stood in front of the long mirror. I can put my hair up, backcomb it for height, which will be appropriate for the silk turban. I shall be all in cream and gold and wear a single red carnation. But I must not hope for too much from the occasion. I must remember that I often get things wrong. What will I get wrong this time? Could it be that I shall look too glorious, as if I have been trying to outshine the bride? Could it be that navy and white poker dots with a picture hat might have been better after all? But what shall I do with this ensemble if I revert to first thoughts, which, as they say, are often best?

No, I have chosen. I shall stand this way, leaning back very slightly to emphasize my small waist and with my head tilted back a little and the champagne glass held delicately by the stem. And all those Forestiers will see that there is someone in the Crosby clan to stun them. And who knows that I may not make some new friends, may be asked to visit these new relations by marriage at some future date? I feel I have a special relationship with Nina, something in common which she feels as well. They will say of me: is she really Campbell's aunt? She doesn't look old enough. And I will look them in the eye, full face, since my profile is a tiny bit disappointing in comparison, and they will see someone of honesty, integrity, liveliness and sensitivity. Charlie approves: that is the main thing. And I won't say what I have to say to him until we are across the Channel, so that, whatever happens afterwards, it won't spoil the wedding.

* * *

A house had turned up on the books of Crosbys'. It was on the outskirts of the city in a long road called Firs Avenue. 'I think it's pretty nice,' said Campbell. He was in bed with Nina in her flat. 'Come up next weekend: see what you think.' 'I've just been up.' 'That was a month ago.' 'Six weeks, actually,' said Nina, 'and I'm supposed to be going home.' 'But this is where we're going to live.' 'I'm having the first fitting of my wedding dress.' This was being made by a woman who had once been a London dressmaker, but who now lived in Chichester.

Campbell sighed. 'Then the weekend after.' His mother had seen the house, approved it and had offered to lend him the deposit. 'You buy it,' Nina said. 'I'm sure that it will be all right.' 'It's not as easy as that. *You* have to like it.' 'Does it face south?' She was very tired, getting more and more tired all the time. She was beginning to think that she could be like the vicar's wife who had a wasting disease. She was also hungry. He hadn't bought her dinner tonight and they'd only had scrambled eggs. 'As long as the house is sunny,' she said. 'But otherwise I shan't know whether it is where I'd like to live until I've lived in it.'

Campbell buried his face in the pillow. Then he got out of bed and stood with arms folded. Naked and standing up, the sight of Campbell was not one to fill Nina with overwhelming love. His dangling sexual organs embarrassed her. While she said over and over again while making love that she loved him, the actual part of him intended to cause her pleasure, while she needed to feel penetrated by it, was the least appealing part of him. 'I'm sure the house will be okay,' she said.

'But don't you see? It matters what you think.' 'I don't mind, honestly.'

There were so many things she didn't mind about, it sometimes drove him wild. At times he wondered if she was really there at all. He kept on having to come down here almost as if to confirm to himself her existence, her presence, the presence of the person for whom his whole life was in a state of flux. As if he hadn't enough to do with the new office, supervising alterations, choosing decor. No one did it right if you didn't do it yourself. All his life he was going to be weak in delegation, which lack stemmed from his inability to choose people of the right calibre for his staff. He already half realized this about himself, but couldn't quite admit it, especially in Nina's case. After all he had chosen her.

And she was very much there, lying in bed, her bedroom drawers overflowing with discarded clothes, some of them new ones which she claimed were trousseau, but kept wearing. 'You never seem to mind about anything,' he said. 'Well, that should make me a very accommodating person.'

He began to dress. Someone who truly loved him would spring out of bed, put her arms around him, coax him back, but she just lay there, not looking at him, lit by the yellow street lights through the thin curtains.

She has let me down, thought Campbell, walking round the block of streets. She *can* be marvellous, but isn't trying. And Nina, huddled in bed, wondering how she would cope with losing him for good and whether it would be too late to keep the job and could they buy back the sauceboats, cancel the caterers, marquee, etc., and what about the money she'd been given to pay for clothes and which she'd spent? And where in the world were the words she'd used to break the news to everyone? It all came down to words in the end in almost everything. I don't suppose he'd let me down, thought Nina. Well he couldn't really.

All I have to accept, decided Campbell, is that life, as my mother has been saying ever since I can remember, is far from perfect. I shall go back and tell Nina that life is far from perfect and she'll realize she has disappointed me and mend her ways. Doubts tear at me, thought Campbell, striding up and down outside the flat in the small hours of a London night when even the buses had stopped running.

No one, absolutely no one, knew how he aspired. If it weren't for him, they would be there for ever, stuck there never doing more than consolidating, blind to all he was doing in the way of forging ahead and carrying with him the little one-horse world that was Crosby and Crosby of Great George Street, Leeds.

Nothing, thought Nina, nearly dreaming, nothing but sleep and feeling the shape of the bed as it fits your body contours. Sleep and food until there were other things to worry about.

I'm sure the house will be okay and anyway it's not exactly mine because it will be bought by Campbell and his mother and the life I live in it will be another life and nothing to do with life as it is now, full of anxiety since I do not know whether he will return or not.

Were it not for streetlights, I would be in total darkness, but were it not for streetlights, I would be living in another age or perhaps have died in childhood or have married at sixteen and died by now in childbirth. I am glad I am leaving this flat, this room, because it has become such a mess, although it doesn't look so bad when only lit by streetlights. But if he doesn't come back, where will I be? Oh, I suppose I'll feel I have been jilted, but I would pretend that I had realized just in time it wouldn't work and say to people: 'Yes, I nearly married,' and seem to be a person of considerable experience. I'm sure the pain, if I could face it, wouldn't last for ever. Except that I am someone who cannot face pain or put myself at risk from it. And anyway, now I come to think of it, his suitcase and his other clothes and possibly his wallet are still in this room somewhere, so he'll have to come back for those, which will make it difficult for him to leave again. Except that if he did, I could end up a nicer person on account of suffering and learn to think of others more. My mouth might also become more generous.

She was still here, asleep or pretending to be. He came in quietly and lay beside her with his hands behind his head, feeling protective and mature, ready to assert to the whole world if necessary that he understood the responsibilities of having given his word. No man would say of Campbell Crosby that he had left undone those things he ought to have done. Honour equals honourable behaviour.

'I think I love you,' said Charlie's secretary in bed in a hotel room. Charlie's heart sank. This was said to him more frequently than he welcomed. 'Sssh . . . you mustn't.' He held her close to comfort her. 'I keep thinking of you all the time, you see,' she said into his shoulder. Oh here we go again, thought Charlie, holding her even closer and telling her he wasn't worth the love she offered him. She was young, unmarried.

'You've spoiled me for others.' She began to cry. Charlie wanted to leap out of bed this minute. 'I don't mean,' sobbed the girl, 'that I am shop-soiled. I only mean that there is no one like you. No one will ever make me feel like you have made me feel.'

Such was often Charlie's trouble in regard to women that he'd had. This hurting people hurt him terribly. This night had been intended as a treat for her, the first time he had brought her with him on a conference, their first whole night together. Now it seemed it would be the last. Most of his liaisons lasted longer than this.

The place was Scarborough. Squawks of seagulls echoed in the courtyard well as they dived at dustbins. At dawn Charlie left the girl asleep, walked up to the cliff, sat against the castle wall and gradually felt the sun warming him. You win some, you lose some. Swings and roundabouts. Charlie felt like crying too.

7

Phyllis wrote: 'Dear Mrs Grant, I hear you are in need of transport south to my son's wedding. Julia Forestier wrote to me of this. I'm afraid that we ourselves are planning a leisurely trip down, so might not fit the bill. However, my sister-in-law, Joan Ramsey, has expressed her willingness . . .'

Joan Ramsey wrote: 'Dear Mrs Grant, My sister-in-law, Phyllis Crosby, has asked me to get in touch with you in regard to offering you a lift south for my nephew's wedding.'

Polly wrote thanks and yes she'd be in touch again, and Joan wrote that they'd have to set off very early on the Friday, so would Polly like to stay the night with them in Leeds? The final corespondence read: 'Dear Mrs Ramsey, Thanks so much. I'll arrive, should God be smiling on the West Riding Road Car Company, around seven P.M. on the Thursday. Please don't bother about feeding me. I usually travel with my nosebag.'

All sorts of spurious and probably finally unrewarding events will keep a person going, thought Polly, walking across the sloping cobbled market square of Richmond one fine morning. And, after all, she told herself, I have been between lovers before and really need no one but myself. Although even to say I am *between* lovers suggests that I assume another will turn up. She always felt on top of the world in Richmond. It wasn't warm on this last day of May, but so light that it seemed it would stay light for ever. Oh why go elsewhere, Polly asked herself.

The same bright light shone on Nina in the front room of the house in Firs Avenue, and the hall was pretty because the sun lit up the stained glass semicircle over the front door making blue and red patterns on the bare wooden floor. Normally she didn't like stained glass because it reminded her of the church at home and the silly illustration of St Paul being suddenly converted. Sudden conversions were in any case impossible, since everything was gradual, except maybe for accidents.

The only thing apart from Nina in the house was the old fridge which had belonged to Joan Ramsey, but she went into the larder – or walk-in-pantry as it is called in Yorkshire – and found a six-month-old copy of the *Yorkshire Post* and did the crossword. She was supposed to be choosing the decoration for the house. Campbell had dropped her off on the way to work. Having finished the crossword, which was quite easy, she went upstairs with a notebook and pencil to write down what colours she would like on the walls up there. A little man Phyllis knew was going to do the work for them. Having decided white walls everywhere, she sat down again and read the *Yorkshire Post* and wondered what had happened to the people mentioned in it. How many people who had got engaged that day were still engaged, how many married now, and what had happened to the family whose house had been burned down and had the man who set off on a bicycle to India got there yet? Then, feeling uneasy, Nina tried to think of something else to do and came to the conclusion that most of life was to do with trying to find new things to do. It was uneasiness that led people into taking vitally important steps.

Then Helen turned up with a flask of coffee, some cups and chocolate cake. She had heard where Nina was and thought how lonely it might be. She also brought some copies of magazines such as *Homes and Gardens* to give Nina new ideas about the house. They turned the pages and agreed that best of all the rooms illustrated was one with a pale floor the colour of sand and furnished with sofas and chairs with wide blue and white stripes. 'It looks like a beach in summer,' Nina said. 'Doesn't it just!' said Helen.

Then Helen went home. Soon Nicola would arrive with Louisa and Mo. She would be taking Nina out to tea with Jane Crosby, the mother of another bridesmaid. Being with someone as easy-going as Nicola could be fun, but sometimes it could make you feel inadequate, since, however hard you tried, you could never be as nice as her; so you might as well give up trying. Attempts at self-improvement were fraught with obstacles.

Nicola drove fast in her white Morris Traveller. Mo stood behind Nina and played with her hair. 'Leave off, Mo!' said Nicola. 'It's okay,' said Nina, 'I like it.' Mo's hands gave her a tingly feeling down her spine. Nicola said Jane would be very anxious to impress them both. 'Usually I believe in taking people as they come,' she said, 'but in Jane's case I lose patience rather.'

It was odd to be going to see Jane on wedding business when, according to all that had been said about her, her own marriage was on the point of finishing. She lived in a place called Cottingley which is famous for the fairies in the photograph which, as was discovered more recently, was faked. In Jane's front room on her upright piano was a picture of Jane as a little girl wearing a fairy costume.

To get there they had driven west through stony villages which were not like villages, being joined or nearly joined together – more like one long town without a proper centre. There would be a stony field or two and then another village. The sky was darker and the hills were sharper. It was more like what Nina had imagined all Yorkshire would be like, with factories in river valleys.

The house felt as if it had been hermetically sealed. The central heating was on and humming, although it was by no means cold outside and Nina had been sitting at Firs Avenue without a cardigan. Perhaps Yorkshire people expected cold or in some cases didn't go outside enough to test the temperature and warm themselves up. Jane's mother was present at the tea party, carrying in tiered tables loaded with plates of tiny sandwiches, slices of fruit cake and home-made biscuits. She was wearing a tight-fitting dress, pearls, and had obviously just been to the hairdresser's. This was Mrs Bosomworth. Nina wondered if she would have become engaged to Campbell if his name had been Bosomworth.

Jane herself wore fashionable clothes, a full skirt with a wide belt, which made you realize that there were worse things than being unfashionable. She looked not so much unhappy as discontented. We should feel sorry for her. 'What a lovely wedding dress you had!' said Nina, looking at yet another photograph on Jane's piano. Everything was polished in this room, especially the piano. The photos rested on a lace tablecloth which hung over the lid. The Firs Avenue house was the same kind of small house as this, but it would be important not to let it look like this.

The three little girls tried on their bridesmaids' dresses. Emma, Jane's daughter, and Louisa looked good in theirs, but Mo looked odd in hers and said she hated it. 'Well hate it then,' said Nicola.

On the way home Nicola said one of Jane's problems was wanting everything to be perfect, which it never could be, although you could get nearer it with one child than with three. 'Why didn't she have any more?' asked Nina, but Nicola said it was tricky talking with this lot in the car.

'Should I have asked Mrs Bosomworth to the wedding?' 'Definitely not. You have to draw the line somewhere.' Just then Mo was sick down the back of Nina's cardigan. They stopped by a dry-stone wall and Nina shivered while Nicola cleaned up the mess. Then Nicola went behind the wall and was sick as well. 'Perhaps you both have gastric flu,' said Nina. The grass around the wall was very dark, and beyond all this grey clouds were piling over the hills further west. 'No,' said Nicola. 'Mo is often carsick, but in my case it is something else. You can guess what, but whatever you do, please don't tell Mum.' Nina guessed. 'I'll tell her after the wedding,' Nicola said. 'I'll be past the three-month stage then.'

When Helen got home from seeing Nina she felt confident enough to go through some of Charlie's suits to pick some out for cleaning. Confidence was necessary to perform this task in case she came across incriminating evidence. Waste bits of paper she could throw away, but bills, receipts or notes she stacked together on his mantelpiece. To sort them out she had to look at them. Within ten minutes she had found the bill for the double room in a hotel in Scarborough. Charlie, usually so careful, you slipped badly here. Was it the girl's tears on the pillow while the seagulls screamed outside at dawn?

It was now five thirty in the afternoon and Helen began to

shake. Once there were glaciers which gouged their way into the Pennines, pushing the land to one side and another, spreading themselves as they fingered and forged their way west, groaning as they gashed and twisted, exerting the force of tonnage more massive than any ocean-going ships the earth has seen, but sharp-edged like ships' bows, breaking, sculpting and creating, forming peaks and rivers.

Summer had withdrawn again. She wished for sun as there had been at Firs Avenue, not because she yearned for the sun itself, but because this morning she hadn't known what she knew now. In the conservatory she began to put ties on the most recent shoots of passion-flower, but her hands shook too much, so she put on her coat and went outside to diffuse the tremors, hoping to be calm before he returned, telling herself that perhaps he couldn't get a single room, but knowing that she couldn't ask him if that was the case. Then she remembered that she had left all the suits lying around the dressing room and not packed them to take to the cleaners. She'd found the evidence, but he must not know she'd found it. She went upstairs again, put all the slips of paper back into pockets and the suits back in the cupboard.

'Sins of the fathers,' said Phyllis in the evening, 'or rather of the mothers.' She was speaking about Jane. 'You mean the sins of Mrs Bosomworth?' said Nina. 'I wouldn't know about that,' said Phyllis. No, she meant the sins of Muriel. Simon Crosby was in many ways a neglected child. No wonder he had married early and unwisely. 'Didn't his mother love him?' 'Of course she *loved* him, but there are different ways of loving, aren't there, dear?'

Nina and Campbell said they hadn't yet decided on all the decoration for the house, so went off again to Firs Avenue. Campbell took with them a second-hand carpet, a fine example he had bought in a Wakefield furniture sale. On this carpet, they made love. It was nine thirty and still light, though cold. Birds sang in the cherry trees which lined the avenue. Pink fluffy blossom waved in the breeze. It was fun having your own house and making love on a new, if second-hand, carpet. Campbell reminded her that she was going to have a Dutch cap fitted before the wedding. He was fed up with using French letters all the time.

This is perhaps our last glimpse of Nina as a girl who thought she was unconventional. Not that it was all that unusual as the 1950s approached the 1960s to have had sex before marriage, but by doing so, you could feel that you were a little bit avant-garde maybe. Soon, Nina thought, I will be living here and won't be even the slightest bit unconventional.

'I'm worried about you drinking on your own, darling,' Charlie said soon after he got back and found her with glass in hand. So she told him how she'd enjoyed her day so much that she'd come home, done masses of gardening and now needed a pick-me-up. The longer she could conceal the agitation, the more she could build up control. I may be wrong, she kept on thinking. There may have been no single rooms that night.

They watched TV until ten, when she announced an incipient hangover and went to bed. He followed her, sat on the edge of the bed, held her hand, stroked her hair, declared his devotion and went back to watch more TV.

Let me lie here forever feeling triumphant that I haven't spoken. Let me be the woman who sails over it all. Let me be up there in the sky looking down on all this. Make it distant for me, please.

Nina was reading in bed a book by a young Yorkshire social realist writer in which working-class people had huge high teas and made love a lot. Then she slept and dreamed of those heavy boots again, tramping alongside her through the vegetable garden. Campbell lay awake worrying about the new office. He had taken on a new assistant who did Goon Show impressions, making the girls in the front office laugh hilariously. It was possible that the boy did impressions of him as well, of Campbell, behind his back.

Bernard had a pain down the left side of his face. Sometimes it spread down his neck into his arm. He was almost certainly about to have a stroke. If he survived the night, he would call in at the medical bookshop tomorrow to check on the symptoms. Many of the books in the shop were so technical as to be beyond his understanding, but he could surely purchase a simple medical dictionary. But then Phyllis would comment. Perhaps he could keep it in the office. Miss Hosier would notice, but at least she wouldn't comment.

Aunt Winifred was weakening. Phyllis had her on her mind. One should not hope for people to die for the sake of convenience, but it would be better, Phyllis decided, if Aunt Winifred went within the next week or so, thus enabling the funeral to take place with a decent interval before the wedding. Best of all would be for the dear old heart to go on beating, let us say, till mid-July, by which time everyone would have returned and settled down again. But, in Phyllis's experience, death always struck at the most awkward times. For instance, her own mother had died one Christmas Day in enormous pain, which meant that for ever afterwards Phyllis could not wake up on Christmas Day without the visual memory of her mother's twisted mouth and terrible last hours.

Peter never woke when any of the children cried, so it was Nicola who went into the room next to theirs. Sally, better known as Toots, the bellowing red-faced baby, had to be lifted out of the cot. The sliding side of the cot had been tied firmly ever since the occasion when Mo let Toots out to roam the house in the middle of the night. Now Nicola, putting her hands under Toot's arms, lifted her – 'Bother you, Toots!' – and carried her downstairs. Dawn chorus, bottle for Toots warmed, Toots settled. Then a visit to the toilet, then sitting outside in the passage, mind reeling. What to do? Wake Peter and tell him now? Get the doctor? No, it might be nothing serious. Go in the morning to the surgery. Peter would have to take Louisa to school or ring one of the mothers on the rota. Almost certainly the doctor would say: take it easy; but she'd have to tell her mother. Then the decision would come as to whether she should go to the wedding and, if not, whether the children should or should not be bridesmaids.

Friends who'd had miscarriages said they'd felt 'something

go' inside. Nothing had 'gone' inside Nicola. At least she hadn't felt it had. Having put Toots back to bed, she went downstairs again and found the book which said: 'Any sign of bleeding is to be taken seriously.' Later in the chapter it said that a miscarriaged embryo, especially in the case of a mother who had already borne healthy children, suggested a fault in the embryo and not in the mother and that, although it might constitute an emotional blow, parents thus afflicted should, in a sense, be grateful that nature had taken its course and a faulty being had been spared a faulty life.

Shakily Nicola crept back into Toots' room, listening for regular breathing, resisting an impulse to lean right over into the cot and kiss the baby. If you were about to lose a child, those existing became all the more precious. She would never say 'Bother you, Toots' again.

8

We are all but a phone call away from heartbreak, thought Phyllis as she drove to Nicola's. We should never uncross our fingers. By virtue of our motherhood, we are vulnerable, our children likewise. What was she to wish for Nicola? Another child or not another child?

Mo was in the garden filling the paddling pool with the hosepipe. Not at all a warm day and Mo was only in a tee shirt and shorts. Her shoes and socks were soaked. Phyllis turned the hose off, took Mo by the hand, led her upstairs to find clean dry clothes. Nicola called out from her bedroom anxiously to find out what was happening. 'It's perfectly all right, dear. I'm collecting clothes for Mo and will take her home with me. You rest. Completely.'

'I'll only go if I can take my tricycle,' said Mo. Phyllis corrected her. '*Please*, Grandma, *may* I bring my tricycle!' Mo sighed and repeated the words parrot-fashion. That would have to do for now. Phyllis managed to fit the tricycle on the back seat of her small saloon. There was just room for Mo beside it. 'Mummy lets me go in the front or I am sick,' said Mo. So Phyllis went into the house again to fetch a bowl and a towel and Mo travelled in the back, but wasn't sick. Thank goodness Nina left this morning, Phyllis thought. One child in the house will be quite enough.

A threatened miscarriage to someone who already has three children and is only just over two months pregnant is not an occasion for informing more than a few close members of the family. While Mo was taking a reluctant early afternoon rest, Phyllis made some phone calls. Nicola, having so many friends around the country and being far from reticent about such things, would certainly be ringing nearly everyone she knew.

So it would be as well to ensure that no one closely concerned became offended by hearing the news from other sources. She ended each call with the words: 'It's very early days of course and we must all keep our fingers crossed.' So everyone who knew about Nicola crossed their fingers and Mo, who was listening over the banisters, in spite of not completely understanding all the implications of what Grandma said, crossed her fingers and went back to look out of the window of her bedroom and feel homesick.

Nicola had not protested. Because of this she felt some guilt. She really shouldn't have let Mo be dragged off like that. She was less anxious about Louisa who was staying, happily, with a school friend round the corner. Nicola lay there putting finishing touches to the bridesmaids' dresses. Toots was being cared for by Mrs Arnold, Nicola's cleaning lady who, in the afternoons, would take the baby home with her where there were several little Arnolds.

I should really have taken Toots as well, thought Phyllis, because I have been to Mrs Arnold's house and it is not one of the cleanest. The other grandmother, Peter's mother, could have helped perhaps, but she had recently opened a fashion boutique in Manchester. This made her disgracefully unavailable at times of family crisis.

Mo tricycled over and over again down the slope from the terrace at Pound Close, along the border at the bottom and then, by getting up speed, found that one burst of hard pedalling would take her up the slope again. She was strengthening her legs with the intention of one day soon tricycling out of the drive and home to Harrogate. She thought she knew the way all right.

Phyllis watched her when she had time to watch. Otherwise it was too risky to leave Mo tricycling for long on her own and Mo had to come inside and sit while Grandma was on the telephone arranging things or in the kitchen cooking. If Mo did not do exactly what Grandma said, Mo would not be able to be a bridesmaid.

In the early morning she had to be very quiet because Grandma needed all the sleep she could possibly get, so Mo would stand at the window and wonder about climbing down on to the porch roof, then sliding down a drainpipe, but feeling rather ashamed that she was not brave enough to do it.

Crying for Mummy was another thing she must not do, especially at night. Not because Grandma told her not to cry for Mummy, but because, if she was heard crying, Grandma would come in and see her lying there and, if there were tears on her face, Grandma would say, 'Oh, you've been crying!' and Mo would have to say, 'No I haven't' because being comforted by Grandma reminded her too much of being comforted by Mummy which would make her cry even more. Learning to cry silently was hard but she managed.

She also got better and better at opening the bedroom door in the evening so that no one heard. Then she would sit by the banisters out of sight and hear Grandma ringing Mummy to tell her how good Mo was being and that it was really much better for Mo to stay here because coming over to see Mummy would upset things. Mummy wasn't ill, Grandma said, but having to be very careful. The wedding was getting nearer. Then they said she would be going home on the Monday. Then they said, no, Mummy had to go on being careful for another week.

'I don't much mind if I'm not a bridesmaid, you know,' Mo said one night when Gramndma was kissing her good night. 'We'll see,' said Grandma.

On a Sunday Daddy came with Toots and Louisa. Mo showed them her speed test down the slope, across the lawn, along the border and up again. Then she sat on Daddy's knee and Daddy said how quiet she was. 'What is it, chuck?' he asked and Mo said, 'Nothing.' Only just sat there because he smelled right and felt right. But then he had to go indoors and talk to Grandma on his own. Louisa said, 'Mummy isn't going to the wedding.' 'Why?' said Mo and Louisa said, 'I know what's wrong with her but I'm not telling you,' and jumped on to the tricycle, pedalling it fast down the lawn. Mo had to run to catch up. She was holding this stick and managed to shove it in between the spokes of one of the back wheels, which made the tricycle stop suddenly, fall on one side, throwing Louisa into the rose bed, scratching her face. After this, Louisa behaved in a very babyish fashion, screaming and yelling that she wouldn't look pretty as a bridesmaid with scratches on her face. Mo was smacked by Grandma and Louisa taken home by Daddy.

That night on the telephone Mo heard Grandma telling Mummy that maybe it would be best if she and Grandpa took only Louisa to the wedding. So next morning Mo said. 'I don't want to be a bridesmaid, Grandma. Please, Grandma, do I have to be a bridesmaid?'

Each evening Peter would come home, lie on the bed beside Nicola, gin and tonic in one hand, kicking off his shoes and staying there until Toots was brought back by Mrs Arnold to be put to bed. 'Having you all to myself, chuck,' he would say, 'is heaven, absolute heaven!' They had the television in the bedroom and sometimes friends called. Then at night he would snuggle up to her and say, 'If only this could last for ever,' and Nicola would say, 'You big softie!'

Not able to make love of course, but lovely, even though most of the time Nicola was thinking about Mo and whether she should have been firm with her mother and kept Mo at home. Another week passed. 'Peter, love,' she said, as he lay with his head between her breasts, 'I think Mo should come home now. Mum and Dad can take Louisa to the wedding. They can't manage both of them.'

'But you've made the dresses. All that trouble! Of course they'll manage.' And when she told him that she knew Mo really didn't want to be a bridesmaid, he pointed out that Mo was benefiting hugely from her stay at Pound Close, was much improved and considerably less spoiled. 'We should definitely let her go,' he said: 'There is *something* to be said for your mother's kind of discipline.'

This one remark of Peter's shattered an illusion: the belief that they, that he and she agreed – no, more than that – were in total harmony as to how their children should be reared. I must keep calm, Nicola thought. The main thing is that I love him and he loves me, even if there is, as I have long known in my heart of hearts, another side to him which makes him almost devious. He's like a child himself. She stroked his hair and his long thin back. It was as if she had to choose whom to please, the father or the child? Men did not love children as children needed to be loved. She cried silently just as Mo was crying silently ten miles away.

'D-Day minus 8,' wrote Harold. 'News arrives that Carter and Merry Widow have set up love nest in Brighton. Sandown Park going soft. Rain intermittent. Min 50. Max 63. But let us rejoice. J has found replacement flower-arranger. N and Viking due here tonight. Final briefing at vicarage. More rain forecast.'

But it was dry and almost warm as the two of them went through the garden, holding hands, under the rose pergola and out along the alleyway, hearing the cuckoo in the height of song somewhere beyond the elms. Nina wore her new tight pink cotton trousers. In regard to the coming interview, she said to Campbell, 'I don't think it will be embarrassing or anything.'

Because the vicar was a well-heeled vicar with a private income, he had made quite a few improvements at the vicarage, which was Victorian and much too big for most vicars these days. But here you could see what could be done with this kind of house, given good taste. Many vicarages these days were sold off, and new, more easily maintainable ones built in their grounds. A vicarage near Tadcaster, which had been on the main-office books recently, had sold for fourteen thousand pounds and several really rather pleasant modern houses built in the grounds – an estate known as Church Close. All this Campbell related at length to the vicar, who offered them sherry (sweet, medium or dry) as well as gin or Scotch.

Nina need not have worried that the interview would be embarrassing or anything. Our vicar is suave and sociable and saw the whole thing as a formality, albeit a formality designed to emphasize the part the church was to play in their union. And perhaps, he considered, the very act of approaching the vicarage together could be in itself enough to give them pause for thought.

'I must say this is a very fine room,' said Campbell on being shown into the study. He then continued his peroration concerning the fate of vicarages in general and added that it was a pleasant change to find one kept in the manner for which it had been purpose-built.

Then they would have started on the business in hand, had not Campbell spotted some maps of wartime airfields which the vicar, out of some quirky nostalgia for his chaplain days, kept on the wall above his desk. At these, Campbell rushed with great enthusiasm, pointing out that he had in fact visited many of these airfields and there was one now which, the vicar might be interested to know, had been turned into a place known as a trading estate – ie a place of small factories, light industry and wholesale warehouses, to which the vicar said he had heard of such things.

Nina sat down on the sofa, found a recent copy of *Punch*, cocked one leg over the other and turned the pages, laughing every now and then. While the vicar nodded and Campbell extended his review of wartime airfields by explaining that in fact one or two of them had, funnily enough, been sites of earlier battles.

The vicar kept a set and charming smile on his face, glancing occasionally towards Nina – or rather towards the spread copy of *Punch* which only just concealed the tightness of her trousers in the crotch area. She was in turn rather hoping that the vicar *was* interested in what Campbell was going on endlessly about, because otherwise he would be thinking what a bore this man was and wondering why she was marrying and might just possibly call her back or send for her at some stage and tell her she should think carefully about what she was doing, which she didn't want to have to do because she never had and probably never would and it was much too late to change her mind in any case.

Anyway what they had really come for was to discuss hymn tunes and details of the service order. And talking about that would be pretty straightforward and much easier for everyone than talking about the meaning of weddings, which she guessed would be uncomfortable for the vicar himself, because everyone knew he had a terrible time maritally with a wife who was crippled and couldn't help him in the parish, let alone, you know, in bed and everything.

You hardly ever saw this wife, who had a nurse and a bedroom downstairs at the back of the house, which she never left except on very fine days when the nurse would push her around the village in a wheelchair or through the cemetery to the beach, which was the way that Nanny used to push Nina in the pram, Nanny being fond of reading tombstones. Nina recrossed her legs.

The ordained purposes of marriage, said the vicar, when he finally managed to get a word in edgeways, were threefold. 'Oh yes?' said Nina, closing *Punch*.

He handed them a prayer book each, open at 'The Solemnization of Matrimony', explaining that of course he absolutely realized that they of all people would know the ordained purposes already, but he had to treat them in this matter very much as he would any Tom, Dick or Harry – at which they all three laughed and Campbell sat back throwing one leg over the other in an expansive gesture, feeling himself to be approved of by the vicar.

The order of service which they planned to use would be the one which has now been replaced. Nina, looking through it, hoped they wouldn't have to read it out just now, especially the passage about men's carnal lusts and appetites and how marriage was a remedy for sin. But luckily the vicar skipped those bits: he seemed to want to concentrate more on the area of mutual society, help and comfort, which he said was something many young couples didn't realize was the true reward of being married. And so on.

Nina swopped legs again, looking over at the vicar, it having suddenly occurred to her that he was really rather a desirable man, reminding her of Charlie, about whom she still had sexual fantasies. Perhaps she should have gone all out to marry an older man who would die and leave her well off as well as wiser and ready to be courted by much younger men again.

'One doesn't,' said the vicar, 'have to say obey these days, but of course it is entirely up to . . .' Campbell squeezed her hand. 'It's up to Nina, I think.' Both men were smiling at her, Campbell widely and the vicar, it seemed, warmly. Decision time once more, when she should really speak out, shouldn't she? Or was it just a moment during which she could look reflective? 'Um,' she said, wondering which would sound the most effective both now and on the day itself. 'Oh yes, I'll say obey, I think, I might as well.'

Campbell laughed somewhat uproariously. Was she not delightfully ironic at this moment as well as charming and seductive? He touched her pink cotton-covered thigh in a gesture of intimacy, he rather hoped the vicar noticed. 'Let me fill your glasses,' said the vicar, moving towards his decanters, remembering how he had once believed this girl to have something worthwhile in her. He sat down, smiling, leaning forwards.

This girl: in fact he wanted to take her by the shoulders and, raising his voice to emphasize and re-emphasize the three main purposes, which were, since he had skipped them earlier for gentlemanly reasons and for brevity, as follows: (a) for the procreation of children, (b) as a remedy against sin and to avoid fornication and (c) – the one he'd touched upon, for mutual society, help and comfort which one should get from the other, both in prosperity and adversity. This last above all, since the girl sitting opposite him, flaunting her health and revealing the outlines of her sexuality, could know nothing, absolutely nothing. He wanted to run into the back room, carry out his wife, unwrap her wasted lower limbs and say to Nina: see here, girl! Here is the burden some people have to carry with them for as long as they both shall live, let alone the other burden which was that he, the healthy party, found himself some nights praying for an easeful death for this woman to whom he had made his promises some fifteen years before.

He stood outside to say good night to them in the dusk, hearing their voices fading as they went into the alleyway. Then he moved towards the little gateway leading from his back drive into the churchyard. Some nights relief came in the form of reading, some nights in the church in the dark where, whether there was a God or not, the empty building and the shape of it could be said to speak of the transcendent.

We leave him feeling his way past the pews to kneel under the chancel arch where in due course he would perform the rite of which we have just spoken, which was his job after all and not unjustifiable when two parties have requested it. We will learn very little more of him, except that as he prayed, the girl in pink trousers featured hardly in his thoughts at all. And if he did consider marriage, it was the nature of the bond in general and its waning strength these days: people now lived in expectation of health; only in cases such as his own was sickness the norm.

The other two, tracing the steps Nina would take with her father in eight days' time and feeling the brush of asparagus in the failing light, stopped to kiss. 'I can't help envying him in a way,' said Campbell. 'Why on earth?' 'Well, I always do rather envy people whose jobs tie in so completely with what they believe.' 'He may not.' 'May not what?' 'May not believe.' 'But he couldn't do what he does unless he did believe.' 'Perhaps,' said Nina, 'he can't think of anything else to do. I mean what else is he trained for?' But Campbell was talking about himself and his own occasional doubts about what he did because, although one did try awfully hard to be absolutely honest in all dealings and there were of course professional bodies to protect the customers or clients as he preferred to call them . . .

Into the main garden of Glebe House, where she paused to pick a stalk of grass from the edge of the unmown lawn, putting the stalk in her mouth to chew the juicy end of it, pondering the nature of being a vicar while Campbell talked. It could be rotten actually, couldn't it, being part of something which meant nothing any more – at any rate nothing to do with what it had started out being to do with – namely Jesus, loving kindness and humility. Although humility, when you came to think about it, got you nowhere. Campbell didn't have it and, in spite of having so many things wrong with him, managed very well. Perhaps there was only loving kindness in the end.

Soft rain was falling. It rained harder as they sat at dinner. 'Good news!' said Julia. 'I've found someone else to do the flowers.' 'Oh good!' said Nina: 'Not that I'd have minded much if we'd had to do without. I can't see the point of them.' Upon this, her mother left the table and the room in tears and her father shouted, which he hadn't done for years, mentioning how in ancient Greece they dealt with baby girls at birth by exposing them on mountainsides. Then he left as well. The study door slammed. 'Typical!' said Nina: 'Absolutely typical!'

Campbell looked down at his plate, at the mess of stew in front of him. He put down his knife and fork. 'It's just a row,' she said: 'You've heard of rows?' 'It has made me most uncomfortable,' he said, and later, on the drawing room sofa where a year ago they'd cuddled and there'd been excitement in the air, Nina yawned.

Such a low ceiling this room had, the shelves seemed ready to fall in on him. The whole seemed tawdry, unappealing. 'I rather think it was your fault,' he said. 'People can't help what they're like,' she said. 'Of course they can. You *know* they can.'

'In fact I don't know that.' Perhaps she'd prove it to him in the end, she thought, wondering if people married people to prove to people they were wrong. Then thought about how she had said goodbye to the boss today. He had shaken her hand, wished her luck, then picked up the telephone to make a call. Mind you, she had made quite a few mistakes at work these last few weeks, but that was all to do with leaving anyway. When you are coming to the end of things, they matter less. You don't take trouble any more. It seemed as if boats were burning everywhere and it was all her fault.

One day just after breakfast, Aunt Helen came to ask if she could help and Grandma said, 'No thank you, dear.' But Aunt Helen said she had this idea of asking Mo over to her house, which would have been especially nice because of Lena the dog and all the ice cream that Aunt Helen kept in the ice compartment of her fridge. Grandma was going to say 'No' but Mo danced around saying, 'Yes, Grandma, please say yes,' several times at the top of her voice, so in the end Grandma said, 'Yes.' It was only a few days before they were leaving for the wedding and she did have an awful lot to do, she said. But Mo must sit in the back of the car and, if she felt sick, have the window open, but not too wide.

As it happened, Aunt Helen's car had a sunshine roof, so Mo was able to be driven along with her head sticking out. They went to Aunt Helen's house, made a picnic, collected Lena and took her to a place where you could walk by the river and throw stones into it, or better still, sticks for Lena to fetch. Lena swam in the river with her nose making waves like the bow of a boat. Mo slipped once when throwing a stick and all but fell in. Luckily, however, she only got her shoes and socks wet.

By that time the sun had come out, so Mo went barefoot while her socks dried out hanging on a bush – or nearly dried out. Then the sun went behind some clouds and they went to a café not far from the river for some tea. When they got back Grandma was standing in the drive looking as if they were late. She said she'd tried ringing Helen.

Nor was Grandma pleased about the shoes which were still wet. It meant that Mo would have to put on her best shoes which were supposed to be for the journey to the wedding. 'I wish I could go there with Aunt Helen and Uncle Charlie,' said Mo. 'Certainly not,' said Grandma. Later Mo heard Grandma saying to Grandpa that she didn't know what had come over her, letting Helen take the child off like that. It had been a bad few hours waiting.

Charlie was seldom at home alone. He stood outside the conservatory, drink in hand, looking out over the valley, hearing sounds echoing up, cows lowing as they were driven back to the fields from milking, dogs barking. The train came slowly over the viaduct. After it had passed he noticed how the mass of buttercups in the field had reflected yellow on the underside of the stone arches.

How many more times would he stand here? He felt over-whelmed by failure. He had dug this garden for her, cut the hedges all for her, dreamed up and oversaw the building of the conservatory, but might as well have done nothing.

She came through the house to stand before him, kissing him. 'I've had such fun with Mo!' He put his arms around her waist, feeling the bones of her ribs where she had lost weight. She'd had to have the cream two-piece taken in. 'Keep your arm there,' she said. He hadn't wanted sex for weeks. It must be over with whoever it had been this time. Whenever he was sexually involved with someone else, he wanted more of Helen, whether on account of titillation or of guilt, who knew?

9

By Tuesday there was only drizzle in the south, but flurries of snow on hills in the north, which would make people think of setting off in winter coats. Sales of summer clothes were everywhere effected, but in Leeds, the fashionwear manageress of Schofields – a large and classy department store – said that they were making up for loss of trade by selling quantities of cardigans and light woollen skirts. On Tuesday in the south it was dry with a still, calm feel to the air, a sense of promise that, although the temperature was still sub-average for the time of year, the sun could break through any moment now.

Nina was laying out the presents in Uncle Arthur's dining room. The table was huge, designed to seat at least twenty people. The room reminded her of the room in the film of *Great Expectations* where Miss Havisham had her cobweb-festooned wedding cake.

The green-edged dinner service occupied the main part of this end of the table near the door. Plates piled, cups and saucers piled or balanced. When you considered that there were more parcels waiting back at Pound Close, there would be at least twelve of everything. 'We'll never have twelve people eating,' said Nina to Laura who was helping her. 'And anyway I hate dining rooms. We'll always eat in the kitchen.'

'Honestly,' said Laura, 'you keep saying what you will do or won't do, but you'll change. Anyway things break.' Nina went on to the ovenware, of which, as Phyllis had warned, there was a vast amount. At first she arranged it in kind, a section for expensive items like Le Creuset, which was then made only in the orange glaze, a section for Denbyware and a third for Pyrex, placing these more everyday items at the front to show those who had given them how pleased she was to have them.

Then she changed her mind and decided on a less categorized arrangement, mixing them all up. Each time she moved a piece, however, she had to make sure that she had also moved its accompanying card. But in the end it may have turned out to that the name of someone who had given her, let's say, one Pyrex mixing bowl, would be credited with the gift of a whole set of Le Creuset including an especially nice round vegetable dish with a hollow handle which made it both lighter and cooler to the hand.

Laura did her share of the table quicker in spite of giggling about some of the more awful presents like the crocheted purple and yellow tea cosy sent by Mrs Carter, the deserted wife of Carter. Likewise the set of six forks which were not proper forks, having one fat prong and two thin ones. These were, Nina said, cake forks. 'People eat a lot of cake in Yorkshire,' she said, telling Laura about all the cake shops where she'd seen crowds of people of all incomes queueing up for éclairs and cream-filled doughnuts. 'How disgusting!' Laura said: 'It must be the climate. Is that crazy aunt of Campbell's coming?' 'You mean Helen? Yes of course she is.' Helen had given Nina navy blue sheets, towels and pillow cases, all with a thin white stripe. They were about her favourite present. Helen had said leave them at the Firs Avenue and not to worry about putting them on show, but Nina wanted everyone to see how nice they were.

'She'd have been better if she'd had children, maybe,' Laura said. Nina said she didn't see why. People were always going on about how having children changed you. She was sorting out cards which went with presents, nearly all of them inscribed with the names of couples, with the name of a man and the name of a woman and a common surname. And yet in every case the woman would have bought the present, wrapped it up and written the card. And all these couples had at some stage been on the receiving end of presents. You got married, you got presents and later gave presents. Marriage after marriage after marriage, all signified by handing over goods. She held up a card. 'Best wishes from Mr and Mrs Simon Crosby' – who might not be Mr and Mrs much longer, but had to go on looking as if they were until they weren't.

Outside: greyness. Beyond the dining room windows the marquee was going up. It would not shield these windows, but those of the huge saloon along the wide corridor. Uncle Arthur himself was not in the house that day. He was on the way home from the South of France where he spent most springs. His housekeeper had brought a tray of coffee and sandwiches in for Laura and Nina at lunch time.

In fact the mansion at this time was to be sold and was under offer to some Americans, Uncle Arthur having decided to submit himself to the care of an old people's home in Bournemouth. Uncle Arthur, by far the richest relation of the Forestiers, had run through the remains of a considerable fortune: he had continued to live in the manner to which he'd been born and, having sold all the contents of value, was now forced to sell the house itself.

Campbell spent the morning at the main office on account of his father having already set off south. At lunch time he went to fetch his hired suit from Moss Bros. Being rushed, he ran from the office all the way along Great George Street, turning by the town hall, crossing the Headrow and jogging breathlessly down crowded, narrow shopping streets. He'd tried to deal with the morning suit earlier, but there'd been some trouble about his size and he had to make this return trip. Coming out of Moss Bros carrying the cardboard box which contained the suit, he bumped into Margaret. Margaret said, 'Look who it isn't!' and, 'Long time no see!' Campbell stood there, panting and smiling.

And there was so much to do that day, so many jobs, one of which was to visit Firs Avenue and hand the keys to the next-door neighbours in case of trouble in his absence. His mother had said this was of prime importance since so many people knew from the *Yorkshire Post* where he and Nina were going to live and when the wedding was. And, after all, there were quite a few things in the house now – his carpet and a more recent purchase – a Georgian chest of drawers.

Then there was the report he had to write on a house he'd looked over yesterday, a lovely place, two farm cottages joined into one, out near Wetherby in one of the best of all commuter districts, the kind of place which would suit himself and Nina one day. 'Oh, Margaret!'

'Go on! Give us a glimpse! Let's see what you've got in there. Not that I can't guess. The big day, isn't it?' Campbell also had on his list to buy several new shirts, some socks and underpants. Luckily when they were married, Nina would probably buy all those things for him, not that he could quite imagine her doing so, but his mother was always telling him how Nicola bought clothes for Peter.

Margaret walked beside him so he had to slow down. He hoped he wouldn't meet anyone else he knew. 'Going anywhere special?' she asked. 'Back to work.' But he was hungry and in the end it seemed the best thing to do was to take her into a coffee bar where they could get a quick sandwich. She sat down opposite him, let her shoes slip off and gripped his ankle between her stockinged feet, saying that she had the afternoon off because she had been to the dentist that lunch time. 'Was it painful?' 'Worth the afternoon off, if I can think of anything to do to pass the time.'

I mustn't, I mustn't, said Campbell to himself, but did. Which meant that he would now have to fetch his car, drive Margaret to her place in Scott Hall Road, then back down into town to shop for the socks, etc, then back to the office where so many small items required his attention that he might not start on the house report until six at the earliest.

He would always try to cram the doings of two days into one, would Campbell. He would always rush. Thus he would frequently fail to please those who waited for him. But that afternoon he was very gentle with Margaret, whose face was swollen after her visit to the dentist and who could not do for him quite as much as she had in the past. It would be the last time, anyway. She said she would never forget him and wished him happiness. 'I mean it like – and if ever . . .' She had creamy skin and her hair was red like his. 'We're two of a kind, you and me,' she said, leaning over him, stroking his broad hairless chest, a girl who appreciated men's bodies and handled them with genuine enjoyment.

* * *

As every item was laid out, Nina pictured the person who had bought it, going round the shops, wondering if they could afford this or that, spending money that they'd counted on using for their own purposes, suddenly having to fork out for someone who had decided, for whatever reasons, to get married. Presents were so terrifically personal: they said something about the feeling of the giver for the receiver. The table was now hidden under assorted brand-new household wares, and all for her. She felt crushed by it all and with a small ache somewhere.

As Campbell zipped his trousers, put on his shoes, looked at Margaret lying there, Nina was writing a list of cheques received. Not that she could remember all of them. Then she had to make a list of the presents sent to Pound Close. She chewed the ballpoint pen and thought how weddings were as much as anything to do with lists on paper. One of the requirements for marriage could be the ability to spell and to remember things. Laura was talking about this friend of hers and Jim's who was having an affair with someone, in spite of having three small children, and how difficult this was because Laura liked both this woman and her husband who was beginning to suspect. She told the story as if it were a film she had seen.

Nina went into the marquee. The smell was of canvas and of still-damp growing grass captured and enclosed. One of the men working on the tent whistled at her, not realizing she was the bride, perhaps. There they were, six or so of them, working on this huge construction all because of something she had said and something she had done. Later she followed her mother – who had just arrived – from the front door of the mansion through the main hall and towards the door which would lead out into the marquee. 'We'll stand here, receiving guests,' her mother's voice echoed, 'shaking hands. It has to be, let me see, me and Daddy, then you and Campbell, then Campbell's parents. Yes, I think that's right. Are you all right, darling?'

Like a circus tent it was, ready for a performance to begin, but it might be all right somehow since nothing had turned out really badly so far. Once they were on the plane and away it might be all right as well. Her first flight on an aeroplane and the place looked hot and sunny in the travel brochure. The hotel was white with a garden in front of it, then there was a narrow road and then the beach. She would wear the pink shorts and suntop which went with the pink trousers and then there was the new bikini.

'Yes, I'm fine,' she said. In spite of the unreality of the situation, sometimes she felt she was the only person in the world who was all right and that she would live for ever.

Cost of marquee hire, cost of tips to be given at the taking down of the marquee, cost of catering plus cost of tips for catering staff, cost of cars, cost of tips to Uncle Arthur's staff., The cost of anything can never be assessed without the cost of tips to those employed, reflected Harold. The list and the additions he made passed the time in his study when the house was too full for concentrated work. Even his study was less of a haven. It contained the camp bed on which John was to sleep. Harold kept tripping over this.

He had lunch with Nanny and the grandchildren who behaved much better than they ever did with Laura or their grandmother. Harold commented on this. 'That's the way of it,' said Nanny. She was coaxing Vanessa to eat spinach. 'Down the red lane, darling.'

Nannies are people who are so devoted to a family that they come back from wherever they are currently employed to help on grand and important occasions. Nanny had been in France recently with a Roman Catholic family. She was telling Harold about young Xavier who was something of a scallywag and would stop on a walk whenever he saw a statue of the Virgin Mary and kneel down on the damp grass to pray. 'That's the way of it,' said Harold.

After lunch Nanny dressed Vanessa in an angora cardigan she had knitted, then lifted her into the old pram and pushed her through the cemetery towards the beach just as she had pushed Laura, John and Nina. Many new tombstones had been raised there since she'd last pushed anyone through the cemetery towards the beach.

Vanessa was really too big for the old pram. But she was also too small to be a bridesmaid . . . in Nanny's opinion, that was. If the weather didn't warm up, those little dimpled arms would be cold in those short sleeves.

After the wedding Nanny would go and stay with her sister in Wolverhampton before looking for another temporary job. There is a limit to how many families a Nanny can get really fond of. Mind you, Xavier's Mummy (in fact a duchess but to be called *madame* because the French didn't have the same idea about titles as the English) said there was always a place for Nanny in Avenue Victor Hugo, Paris. But it is very tiring as you get older, being in a foreign country and worrying about small change and the value of the franc and not being able to buy Marks & Spencer's undies. Which you couldn't then, but can now, but which makes no difference to Nanny who has been dead and buried in a Wolverhampton cemetery these fifteen years.

Edmund held the handle of the pram, only letting go to stand still while Nanny stopped to read a new tombstone. He was very bright and although not yet five had begun to learn to read. 'What's rip mean, Nanny?' 'Rest in peace, darling,' said Nanny. Rest in peace, darling Nanny, Wolverhampton 1970, aged 72, after long and faithful service to the families of . . .

George Ramsey was possibly the most reluctant wedding guest of all. He minded especially about missing the Yorkshire versus Middlesex match which opened at Headingley this very day and, had it not been for the fact that his granddaughter, Joanne Walker, was going to be bridesmaid, Joan didn't think she'd have got him to go at all, even though it was his nephew and not hers who was getting married.

That morning Joan said, 'I think she is a history teacher.' 'You think who is a history teacher?' 'This cousin of Nina's who is coming with us. She arrives tonight.' 'I hope she hasn't too much luggage,' said George, setting off for Headingley. The only disappointing thing about the match was that, since England were playing the West Indies at Lords, neither young

Trueman not Johnny Wardle would be appearing for the home side.

Polly's luggage included a large square cardboard box which contained Nina's wedding present: a mahogany cabinet with brass handles bought in a local junk shop and believed to be a Victorian medicine chest. Since the young couple would have absolutely everything they needed she had bought them something they couldn't possibly need but which had interest value. Perhaps even nuisance value. Let them learn that life was not all matching tableware and pillow-cases. Let them reflect on this.

Coming down from Swaledale, Polly felt like a hill person coming down into the plains to test the safety of these lowlands and to scout for enemies. Her suitcase was old and heavy, not yet full, but would be fuller once she had stopped in Harrogate to change buses and to shop for clothes. She left both suitcase and cardboard box at the coach station and went to several shops, reminding herself that she had recently noticed that navy blue suited her. But came out of a department store with a steel-blue silk shirtwaister dress that had made her feel relaxed in the fitting room. Easy to wear is what matters for me, she told herself, then remembered that, whereas navy blue would have just about gone with her white shoes, steel blue required a different shade of footwear.

For most of her life, Polly wore sandals or wellingtons or fur-lined boots. Today the shops were full of shoes with pointed toes, so she had to buy a pair half a size too long in order to accommodate her widish feet. Really to choose clothes well, you had to be in the habit of it. People like her who lived in corduroy trousers and flannel shirts should stay in their own environment and ignore invitations. The only dress she had was for occasional functions at the college of further education where she taught. And for her weekly classes she had two skirts only. One of the reasons Polly so seldom went south was that she had not got the clothes for it.

Then it was time to go to the hairdresser's where her short hair was trimmed and set into a helmet shape. Would it last until Saturday? All this trouble and expense and she would still look dowdy and peculiar in comparison to other wedding guests. But, sod it, she thought, cheering up on the bus to Leeds, for a time telling herself that once she had begun drinking champagne, she would forget about not looking right. The thing was to *feel* right, feel in tune with herself. It never really mattered what you looked like to others. But it did all the same.

For Joan, this evening was the culmination of a week of non-stop planning to do with journey, clothes (both hers and George's), leaving the house in order as well as trying to keep at all costs calm because of migraine. George had been warning her all week against mounting panic leading to migraine: as if she needed warnings!

She had two pairs of spectacles, one for distance which she wore all the time and one for reading. On her way south she would have to keep changing these in order to read the map for George. Today she had tidied the guest room, made the bed and made early preparations for the picnic they would have en route, knowing that George would be reluctant to waste time and money stopping at a restaurant, especially with an extra passenger. And I must remember, she said to herself, putting a casserole in the oven for tonight's meal, that this woman is a widow, very lonely possibly and without children I believe, so perhaps I ought to put away the many photographs of children and grandchildren.

The house spoke of extreme devotion, of time spent, as if all the rules of housekeeping had been strictly observed, although there was a lack of frills. Even the valances round the divan bases of the twin beds in the guest room were straight rather than gathered and matched the brown carpet, which would presumably save time and money on the laundering of them. A single ornament on the narrow windowsill and on the wall, a water-colour of Whitby Abbey. Polly looking for an ashtray, opened a drawer of the bedside table and found a case containing needles and several colours of sewing thread. There was also a tin of biscuits. Joan Ramsey came from a line of women who knew how to do the best for houseguests, even though she found intrusions of this kind a strain.

Her reason for not providing an ashtray for her guests: George, in addition to being a solicitor, was an insurance agent and, knowing the cause of so many calamitous house fires, forbade smoking upstairs. So Polly had to stub out her cigarette in the washbasin.

'Ah Nina!' she said to Joan downstairs. 'I hardly know her, but as far as I remember, she was an insouciant child.' Joan was not sure of the exact meaning of insouciant, but it sounded right for Nina, although she had only met her once or twice at Pound Close. 'You don't have children, do you, Mrs Er, er . . .' 'Polly, please, for heaven's sake. And no, I don't have children and I'm sure I missed out on a highly important experience, but since I can't know what that highly important experience is like, I'm hardly likely to mind too much. So I'm happy, well not happy, but, you know . . .'

Joan blinked, but felt a little easier. Much easier. This woman wasn't nearly as formidable as she had expected. Small and could be pretty if not oddly dressed. But drinking a good deal quicker than most women Joan knew. She poured more sherry and began to feel less at risk from migraine as Polly elaborated on her views of life and marriage and said how, basically, all weddings were mistakes but that people had this impulse and the church was there. 'A lottery,' said Polly: 'No, no more sherry, thanks, I mean, what else is there?' 'I think there is some whisky,' Joan said, getting up. 'No, when I said what else is there, I meant what else apart from marriage could there be?' 'I've never really thought,' said Joan. And Polly said: 'But yes, a Scotch would be delicious, if I may.'

Joan rushed to pour some before George came in, so it would be a *fait accompli*. She'd just heard him parking his car in the drive.

He looked like the solicitor he was, though what it was that made people look like solicitors, Polly couldn't at the moment analyse. George had a round face, thinnish grey hair and a stocky physique: also an air of suppressed energy which fitted uncomfortably into the neatness of his home.

'Ah, so you are drinking Scotch!' he said, after shaking

hands. 'Well, what about another?' He held the bottle up invitingly – at least it looked invitingly to Polly, though Joan could read clues in both the gesture and the tone of voice which conveyed to her his displeasure. This guest after all was her complete responsibility: she had agreed to everything with Phyllis without consulting him.

'Yes please,' said Polly. The polarization of the male/female axis in this house did not occur to her until the meal was being served – so carefully, so nervously, with starched table napkins, spotless mats on polished table. Joan looked towards George every now and then as if to search his every look, word, gesture for either approval or disapproval. What a life of panic and containment there was here. People should not live like this. I could have gone by train. I've added to the strain by coming here. It hurts to feel one is impinging on the lives of others.

Joan undressed slowly, still remembering what Polly had said about all weddings being mistakes finally. From this it followed, didn't it, that all the worries she'd had over all the years of being wrong for George were wasted worries and all the guilt about seeming unable to make him happy, wasted guilt. At the same time she was worrying about whether he, like she, could smell cigarette smoke from the guest room next door.

'Are you going to be all night?' George muttered from the bed. She was putting rollers in her hair. Then she must check through her suitcase, in which everything was packed except for the dress for Saturday hanging in the wardrobe. 'Shan't be long. You go to sleep.' But he wouldn't until he was sure she was there. Not because of any real need for her presence, but because he liked to know that every single light was out and the day properly over.

'I thought you had been to the hairdresser's.' 'Yes, but my perm isn't very strong and the rollers will keep the set in.' Then he sniffed. 'I'm sure I can smell smoke.' Joan dropped a roller which fell under the curtain which ran around the dressing table. Rather than bend to pick it up, she took another from the box in front of her. She had just heard the spare room window open.

Polly stood by the open window, smoking. The road was deserted, most lights were out in other houses, a glow from the city in the sky beyond the trees. The solstice in suburbia where every inch of ground was cared for, had been cultivated or built upon, where continued efforts from people such as Joan were required to defend this land against the encroachment of the wilds where Polly came from. Men married so that they could go out and earn and leave their patch in the hands of capable women who, like Joan, went grey-haired before their time.

Joan crept into bed. George's arm came round her. Only a habit. 'You haven't opened the window, Joan.' 'Nor I have!' But she delayed moving and he took his arm away with a sigh as if to get out of bed himself. 'No, George, I'll do it.' 'No, Joan, I'll do it.'

She must lie there, apparently unconcerned, her head uncomfortable in the rollers, knowing he was by the window in his pyjamas with his hand on the catch.

Some things in life are well-timed. Just as George opened their bedroom window, Polly stepped back from hers to put the cigarette out in the basin, having decided that the garden below was too neat to receive a cigarette butt. And George got back into bed with no further comment on either smoke or windows. What a relief, thought Joan.

On reaching home, Campbell rang Glebe House to say that he would be leaving at first light and would arrive in good time for the 3 P.M. rehearsal. He didn't speak to Nina because she was already in bed, said Laura, with a sore throat. But he was not to worry. Jim had arrived and given Nina some penicillin and it was really nothing. Then Campbell remembered he had failed to call in at Firs Avenue to see the neighbours, so drove back there and they asked him in for coffee, which he couldn't really refuse. Not only had they said they would look in every day, but they would get some groceries for Nina in a fortnight's time. They also made some rather lewd honeymoon jokes. They weren't at all the sort of neighbours he had hoped for. The wife said, 'We'll be thinking of you,' nudging him with her elbow.

Back at Pound Close he found a note from his mother reminding him of all the things he ought to be taking with him, also instructions about locking up and where to leave the key for Mrs Everard. Much more interestingly there was a letter from a man with whom he'd corresponded now for several years. It concerned Towton Moor and invited Campbell to serve on a committee which was being formed to organize the upcoming fifth centenary celebrations, ending with the words: 'We must all join forces to commemorate what was undeniably the bloodiest battle ever to be fought on British soil.' This was a triumph. What a pity there was no one with whom to share the news! But of course in future there'd be Nina.

Meanwhile there was the speech he would have to make at the wedding reception. He picked up notes made so far, lay back on his bed to think what more to say, but slept and dreamed that he was in a building like a market hall, marshalling bands of people. Nina was there somewhere. So were the new neighbours. Everyone got into line except Nina and the neighbours. Then his mother appeared and told him that he'd been relieved of his command. Next he was parachuting out over the coast near Glebe House, seeing Beachy Head, but knowing that his target area was down there beside the church – to the east of the elms but not of course among them. Nina, in a white dress, was bending over a child, a bridesmaid who was not a child but looked like Margaret. Next thing, Nina was taller than he was and he was the child, running from person to person along the village street telling people all the interesting things they ought to know about a battle he had witnessed. Then he woke, set his alarm for four o'clock and slept thereafter dreamlessly.

Mo got out of bed in her blue pyjamas and padded barefoot across the shiny boards towards the window and parted the curtains. Her head just reached over the windowsill. She could see over the rooftops that the sky had one star left in it. It was getting light. The hotel room was huge with huge high beds in it, one for Mo and one for Louisa. Grandpa and Grandma slept next door. The hotel was in the middle of the town with a narrow street below the window. For supper last night a maid brought them boiled eggs and cornflakes and Grandma had told them all the things they could choose for breakfast. Then, after breakfast, they would go to the seaside with Joanne and

Emma and in the afternoon see the wedding place where there would be a rehearsal as there had once been for the Sunday School nativity play at home when Louisa played the Virgin Mary and Mo was a donkey.

Most people going south that day took the A1, then the North Circular to reach the A3 Portsmouth route, thereafter turning left at Guildford; but Campbell knew a route by which you could avoid the worst part of the journey. He would branch off the A1 near Biggleswade and take minor but much more scenic roads.

The sky, clear as he set off, translucent blue like the sapphires in Nina's ring, although the one star Mo saw down in Chichester had faded by this time. Campbell saw the orb of the sun rise over bypassed Doncaster, but by the time he reached his minor road, there were clouds. Not that he noticed these, driving in shirt sleeves, his jacket thrown across the pile of suitcases in the back seat.

However agitated, however late, he was incapable of not studying the lie of the land through which he drove, assessing its potential for development, admiring or deploring property as he passed, houses with windows too small or asymmetrically positioned, noting properties which had had the misfortune of having their values lowered by road widening, although no doubt their owners would have received adequate compensation. Life on the whole for Campbell, in spite of everything his mother said, must be seen finally as fair and well arranged. He would expect it to be so. He would blame others if it were not so.

Unexplored England, thought Campbell, passing through unheard-of villages and small towns which, because they had been missed by railways or main roads, had been left behind in the progress of the centuries. Like old men, Campbell thought, like people who dodge progress. Such was the way he passed the journey. One day he would have a larger, faster car with perhaps a radio. One day he would buy Nina a car in one of the bright colours that she liked – for her birthday. He would park it outside the house so that she would wake up, see it and give him one of those looks that she gave when she didn't want to show she was excited. I am going towards Nina, Campbell told himself. He would be there at three o'clock precisely, he was pretty sure.

Here and there beside the minor road, a canal travelled parallel on an embankment. Campbell turned his head to look for a humpbacked bridge over this canal where he had noticed several times when driving south a lock-keeper's cottage for sale. This was years before people began to take an interest in canals and their restoration, but Campbell could be fairly forward-looking and had thought such a place might be worth refurbishment and modernization.

Here and there along the minor roads, vehicles were parked on the wide grass verge or not quite on the wide grass verge, and Campbell, speeding and turning his head to see if he could spot the humpbacked bridge over the canal with the lock-keeper's cottage just beside it, narrowly missed smashing into the back of a stationary tractor and a trailor full of fertilizer.

So for a time he was not going towards Nina because he slowed down and parked his car under some willows which overhung the wide grass verge, made a pillow from his jacket and thought of sleeping; but instead felt something in his eyes which he hadn't felt for years, which must be tears and seemed to do with thoughts of Margaret and the way she had covered him with kisses only yesterday and how she might be the only person ever to do that and perhaps the only person ever to love him properly.

The tractor drove into the field opposite, its engine fading as the sun came out, so that Campbell could open his car window and smell fertilizer being spread. And when the only person to love you is a person who is simple and really rather stupid and not at all the person you could look up to, what then? But what little hands she had, thought Campbell in his car parked on a grass verge in the shade of a willow tree.

That's Campbell for you. Friendly but without many friends, a man whom other men would trust in business but not meet for pleasure, a man who, wanting to be liked and loved, would have no option other than to be admired for his achievements.

* * *

We must say something about England at this time of year when both Wimbledon and the Lords Test Match are going on, not only at those places, but on radio and television, so that the whole country seems linked up. Few people don't know of these events. Few people do not feel in some sense part of them. Old ladies like Aunt Winifred may hear distant commentaries in the next room. Invalids like Nicola might lie on their sofas watching as the sun emerges in late afternoon, take their transistor radios into the garden and hear from next-door gardens other people listening as well. There is something to be said about the end of June when the flowers in the north have caught up with the flowers in the south.

Because by early afternoon they had nearly reached their destination, Charlie said, 'Let's stop, shall we?' They sat with drinks in a pub garden, near a border of bright marigolds, a stream, a little rustic bridge and slatted tables. Such lush grass! Her hand rested on the table. He covered it with his.

She will be crying for him, Helen thought, grinning at him across the table. 'It's good to see you happy,' Charlie said. 'Let's have another drink. They are about to close the bar.'

She would remember that garden as if lit by the mass of marigolds and remember the grass as emerald.

This is the sun lounger Phyllis suggested Peter buy for Nicola, so that when the sun came out she could put her legs up in the garden. This is the garden which is probably the most neglected we have seen yet, full of grass patches on the lawn where Mo dug holes for hidden treasure.

Nicola looked blooming, rested, the sun having touched and coloured her cheeks and arms. The longer the two older children were away, the more Peter felt that he and Nick were back where they started, a fine unravaged couple. But: 'No,' said Nicola. '*If* we were a fine couple, we were *meant* to be ravaged in order to produce the makings of more fine couples.'

There was so much of her mother in her that he had to go inside to pour himself a drink, but when he came back into the garden, she said, 'Why don't you go to Headingley tomorrow or to Ripon Races?' 'But I want to stay with you,' he said. 'No, you go.' Friends would call in as they had been calling in all week. 'Honestly, love, I'll be okay.' It was too much of an idyll: he might soon be bored.

The curve of her stomach under her cotton skirt only hinted at the presence which had remained so far and which would, if it survived, only further ravage them. 'Mum rang,' said Nicola. 'The rehearsal went swimmingly. Cam got there just in time.' 'How typical!'

When Mrs Arnold brought Toots home, they put her on the lawn in the playpen. What a contented child she was, compared to Mo for instance. When Mo was a baby, wherever you put her, she would twitch and scream and wave her sticklike arms, rather flail them around like windmill paddles. Toots was more like Louisa. Give her a pile of Kiddicraft plastic beakers and she would pile them carefully in correct size order to make a tower, usually waiting for someone else to knock them down.

So it was soothing with just the one baby and the sound of John Arlott's voice from Lords droning on, mentioning names like Graveney, May, Cowdrey, Bailey, Close, Evans, Wardle, Trueman, Statham; England scoring away like anything, having bowled the West Indies out for only a hundred or so. One more innings might well do it. 'I'd rather stay here with you and go on listening than anything in the world,' said Peter. At close of play he rolled up his sleeves and took Toots upstairs to give her a bath.

10

Bernard thoroughly approved of the menu at the Dolphin. At lunch today there had been a choice of several soups as well as fruit juices, then a choice of fresh salmon or roast chicken: nothing fancy. 'I thoroughly approved of the lunch,' he said to Phyllis in their bedroom. He was looking forward to the dinner. The children had been taken to the beach again. Bernard had played golf this afternoon.

The Dolphin: a Georgian construction, solid-looking from the outside, but inside a place of creaking boards and uneven corridors. 'And you?' he looked at Phyllis. 'You are beginning to enjoy yourself, aren't you? This break, this whole shiboodle?' 'Well,' said Phyllis, 'at least now I've rung Nick, I am.' 'And she's all right?' 'Well, she says so.'

Phyllis inspected the navy blue dress she was intending to put on for this evening. No one would notice what she wore, but it had to be suitable. Also Cicely approved. Bernard had read her mood correctly. She did feel suddenly relieved in general. The rehearsal had gone very well indeed. Even Mo had walked where told and stood where told. Surprisingly, the Forestiers were reasonably well organized. There'd even been afternoon tea served. And shortly, in an hour or so, a proportion of the Crosby party were to return to Glebe House for a buffet supper. Very good of Julia: such a trying time for her.

'So I'm looking forward to the dinner,' said Bernard. 'I'll pop down now and have a drink and see you in the dining room.' 'The dining room?' Phyllis spoke slowly. The tone was familiar: 'No, dear, if you remember, we are going to the Forestiers.' 'Ah yes! Of course!' Facing the mirror, she could see his eyes. The look in them was familiar. He hovered in the doorway, turned and left.

She stood beside the window for a time, breathing deeply, resolving that she must not let his absent-mindedness in regard to what must be called a domestic issue spoil her equanimity. Men didn't know. They'd never know. It was a woman's duty to inform them and then confirm that they had absorbed the information. Peaks, dear, she would say to Nina in the years to come, are invariably followed by troughs, dear, aren't they?

Charlie and Helen, having made love twice, now lay entwined. In the end it never failed them. 'It never fails us, does it?' 'Takes me back a long time, doing it at this time of day.' Their suitcases were still unpacked. The whole thing had been very spontaneous. It was tempting to think it made up for everything. 'As ever I love you.' 'And me, you,' said Helen. Once, she was thinking, could be a token of reparation, but twice did seem to speak of genuine desire rather than a guilty conscience.

At least those were her feelings until he said, 'I let you down so often.' The cathedral clock tolled six. Charlie left the bed to dress and go down and get sorted, as he put it, to make sure all his lot for the stag party were beginning to assemble. She watched him move around the room. Let her down so often? Let me down so often? But too late now to say, 'In what sense do you let me down?' Which could be as well, since he had the burden of the best man's duties ahead of him. An outward image of their closeness at this time was prime. And she herself must look her best.

Get her in a good mood and then find you've spoiled it! Bernard on his way downstairs, feeling dismissed by Phyllis, also wishing he'd had the strength of mind to ring room service and order sandwiches. Anything! He knew buffet suppers. He walked out of the hotel and along the street. I'll take a look at the cathedral, he decided, to take my mind off things. The whole kerfuffle would be over soon. He took a deep breath, looking up at the cathedral spire, sun glinting on the brass cross at its pinnacle. Sometimes he heard a question echoing inside his head: 'What has she done to me?'

* * *

Calming herself before going downstairs, Phyllis ticked off things that had gone well so far: Nick's continuing good health; hearing, also by telephone, that there was no worsening in Aunt Winifred's condition. And yesterday, Mo not being sick in the car.

Julia was changing into the pink cotton which she'd had for Vanessa's christening. Nina looked in. 'I might go back to bed actually.' 'Of course you're not going to!' So Nina spoke again in a whisper to show her mother how hard she was trying to save her voice for tomorrow. 'I feel awful, honestly.'

Then her mother burst into tears at the dressing table and Nina came a little nearer, hating the pink dress and the way she could see her mother's scalp where the hair was thinning. God, I hope I don't go bald like that. The way she put her arm around her mother's shoulders spoke of reluctance. Even worse it was when Julia said, 'It's all right, darling. I'll be all right.'

In the mirror – the pink-rimmed eyes, the red nose, the tears running down the creases in the ageing cheeks. How ghastly! 'I just don't think you can very well go back to bed.' The voice was shaky. 'Okay then.' This voice was long-suffering. 'I mean you have to be all right for tomorrow, so you might as well be all right for tonight. And think how disappointed the Crosbys would be!'

It was so many years since her mother had had the courage to be firm to her face about anything that Nina was taken aback by all this. If people were going to be weak and weepy, then they shouldn't suddenly get tough. Nina went to her own room and put on the low-waisted dress of corded silk, which was about the nicest thing in her trousseau and which she'd had made up by the dressmaker in Chichester at the last minute, having bought the material in a sale. Much more of a success really than the wedding dress, though a bit daft maybe wearing white two days running. She also had some red Italian sandals which were really super.

Laura looked in. 'That's lovely, but don't fluff your hair out. I thought the idea was to have it exactly right for tomorrow. Is Mummy all right? I thought I heard her crying.' 'Yes, she was.'

Nina could hardly bring herself to speak of this: 'But she's okay now.'

Laura stared. 'She cried before my wedding as well. It's too much for anyone, isn't it?' 'I didn't want to have a big wedding, if you remember.' 'Then you should have dug your toes in and refused it.' Laura slammed the door. What a hopeless family they were!

It was impossible to remember now the cause of it all. Easier to remember the causes of wars as learned at school. Who'd finally agreed that it would be like this? Surely not me, thought Nina, wanting to cry and only stopping herself because of the way her mother had looked just now. But wasn't it odd how you suddenly found yourself involved in something so incredibly complex and upsetting? Life held quite a few surprises. This thought could have cheered her, but she went on sniffing, partly at disappointment with her hair. They'd said the coronet wouldn't balance on straight hair and so she'd had it permed. She wouldn't really feel good until the curls had grown out; not for months, perhaps.

Charlie put three five-pound notes in his wallet, put the wallet in the breast pocket of his navy blue suit, together with the chequebook for the joint account, and went downstairs. There he kissed Phyllis, Cicely, also that bad-tempered girl who was married to Simon Crosby, and shook hands with the appropriate men. Then he said, 'Right then' and the younger men followed him to their various cars, some of them with their hands in their pockets. The only person missing was Campbell who, having only just arrived back from the church (where he'd been having an absorbing conversation with the vicar) was still changing. He'd follow them on.

Before leaving, Charlie went over to the bar where Helen, dewy, fulfilled and looking her best, leaned gracefully with drink in hand, talking to Caroline Cornelius who looked even more tasty being fifteen years Helen's junior. 'You both look beautiful. Tara!'

'Oh, I adore him,' said Helen. Caroline moved a few inches back. Helen was so obvious, so unsubtle, so nearly garish. Caroline, acknowledged to be the most poised and sophisticated of all the relations, intensely disapproved. One didn't go around saying how marvellous one's husband was in those enthusiastic tones. Caroline wasn't one to be curious or listen to family rumours. She just thought Helen rather batty.

With an hour to spare before they need leave for Glebe House, Cicely and Phyllis put on lightweight summer coats and walked through the Close, noting very little of their surroundings. What with one thing and another, it was the first time they'd had a good natter for some weeks. Anne, daughter of Joan and mother of Joanne, was supervising the children's tea and bedtime. They linked arms.

'Be at all costs calm,' said Cicely, patting her hand. 'Weddings are notoriously disruptive events.' Phyllis gave a small smile. 'Just think,' Cicely went on, 'if men were perfect where would we be?'

They walked so easily that there was never a moment when one or other of them had to suggest this pace or that path or exert pressure on the other's arm to guide. They walked as one, circling the cathedral on stone paving between mown grass, moving especially slowly through the patch of sun which lay to the west of the tall building, treading neatly on elegant low-heeled shoes. So soothing to catch up with each other's news, to discuss respective families – to say, 'How do you think Helen looks?' 'Radiant.' 'Mmmmmm.' 'How do you think Jane looks?' 'Scowly.' 'Yes.' 'Mmmmm.'

The traffic through the nearby streets of the old town had eased and the colour-washed Georgian houses across the street threw back sunlight. Cicely said, 'I have been thinking, in regard to worries, that even if one is right and things do happen in accordance with one's worst fears, having known that they would go wrong helps not one bit. They still happen.' 'Yes, dear,' Phyllis said, 'but so often we have *let* them happen.' All the same she felt a good deal calmer. It could be the presence of the cathedral, its height. It dwarfed them, yet the two of them walked tall. They had no reason to walk otherwise, although their walking tall for ever depended on their walking carefully: they must remember that they could not stay away from what they called 'the fray' for very long, since drinkers and even those not drinking would need reminding in good time that it took fifteen minutes by narrow roads to reach Glebe House.

'Yes,' said Phyllis, reporting on the afternoon's events, 'both the sister and the brother strike me as all right. She, full of common sense and he, quiet but pleasant.' 'And *she* will change,' said Cicely, reading into Phyllis's remarks some hope for Nina: 'Or *may* change. And anyway, let's face it, as they say these days, there is nothing you can do about it now.'

A single tolling of the bell above them indicated seven fifteen. There was a wooden seat in the sun. They sat, crossing their ankles. The wood was warm to their backs. They regarded a rose growing against the railings and both remembered how, when young, to sit on a bench and look at a rose tree would have been a bore, because they'd always have been afraid of missing something in those days. They both spoke of their gardens and considered how this rose, whose name escaped them, would be a pleasing addition. Being a bush rose, it would need no pruning; it grew naturally in a satisfying shape, but surely one would have to cut it back a little? Nothing in nature prospered without control.

Bernard had turned away from the cathedral. He was in a side street, looking in the window of an estate agency, the business belonging to the old friend with whom he had played golf that afternoon. As expected, prices were around thirty per cent higher down here. The place was set up rather as Campbell had set up the Wakefield office, all property particulars on view. 'Modernized,' thought Bernard. Everything must be 'modernized' these days. This afternoon the old friend who also had a son had said much the same, but added: 'Let them modernize. I'm not going to waste my remaining years sitting on the boy.'

Bernard suddenly lost interest, feeling hazy and unconnected. He'd felt that earlier in the day as well. Less hungry now. These symptoms: what were they? A lack of zest. Could it be liver? Or was this old age? Would all old age be like this? He did not consider whether the cause was the little spat he'd had with Phyllis back at the hotel. He had forgotten that as she would, more or less, forget it.

* * *

Muriel had gathered George and Joan to join herself and Richard for a quick rubber. 'You'll drink less and be able to sup more there,' she told them. 'Do we expect to get much there?' said George. 'Come on, George. Don't be such a misery. You play a weak opening club if I remember rightly?'

Joan usually tried to avoid bridge with Muriel. Luckily they did not meet very often. They were not in fact related. It was simply that Joan's sister-in-law was married to Muriel's brother-in-law.

Phyllis and Cicely passed through on their way to check on the tidiness of their persons after taking the air. Phyllis felt a little concern that her role as link between the Ramseys and the Crosbys threw people like Joan into unwelcome situations. After all, Joan had done more than her bit by conveying that Forestier cousin southwards.

Muriel was a large commanding woman. 'One last deciding hand,' she called as she saw Phyllis and Cicely returning, standing ready to go, waiting like two old crones for the guillotine to fall. 'Who says it will be deciding?' said George who hated losing, especially to Muriel. 'Well, it will have to be,' Joan said quietly but firmly, because she hated being late for things.

Richard sat back, rattled the ice in his otherwise empty glass and called to Jane who was standing near the bar. 'Jane, be a duck . . .' She was still his daughter-in-law, wasn't she? This is our first glimpse of Richard. Tall, thin, grey-haired, wearing a double-breasted grey pinstripe suit, he drank double Scotches when in company and when not in company drank hardly ever. Richard Crosby, chairman and managing director of Crosby Timber Holdings Ltd.CTH, as it was known in the family, was and is a parent company to several smaller businesses. It grew from the building firm founded more than a hundred years before, when Richard's great-great-great-grandfather, a journeyman joiner from the countryside, arrived in Leeds to work on the building of the town hall.

The only richer person in the foyer of the hotel was Harry Cornelius, also a chairman and managing director of an engineering company based in York. Harry sat on a low settee reading the *Financial Times*, but behind the newspaper he was poking a matchstick into a cavity in one of his only remaining teeth, a large molar upon which depended his entire bottom denture. A rash action, since if this tooth crumbled or gave way, he would spend the wedding of his nephew by marriage with a dangeously loose lower set. Luckily however, he was not making a speech. He waved towards Phyllis and Cicely. 'Sit down, for heaven's sake, women! Stop hovering!'

They were obedient, feeling much smaller than they had when in the shadow of the cathedral. But their presence would continue to aggravate. It was the way they sat on the edge of their chairs rather than relaxing and falling back into the Trust House upholstery. As girls they had been biddable (never as inactive or as supine as our bride) but possibly capricious, occasionally irresponsible; now they were purposeful and directed, possessors of hard-won power, iron fists holding silk gloves.

When you have dressed a little early, gone down to have a few drinks and still no one's ready to leave you feel a little out of things because no one's talking to you, you have to go back upstairs and be alone in a hotel bedroom and, as always, tidy up after Charlie. The suit he'd travelled in was thrown over a chair. Pick it up. Find a hanger. Fold the trousers over the crossbar of this. Smooth them. Then the jacket, but feel the outline of what seems to be a chequebook in his pocket. But you'd seen him take his chequebook to pay for the dinner, hadn't you?

It was known all along. It was always to be. What I have just discovered has always been known. This room, that time together in this room was too good to be true. Nothing is true. This room with its uneven floorboards, its window seat, its view over the street to other windows staring back at me, the bed we straightened together having unstraightened it together. In the inside pocket of his suit, this pocket which is divided into two and this chequebook from a bank to which we have never belonged. But to which he belongs, but has written nothing on the cheque stubs . . .

* * *

John was doing a jigsaw with Edmund who was going to be a page the next day. They sat with their backs to the other people in the room. Edmund seemed to admire his uncle. This puzzled John, although he'd noticed that small children did often take to him. Perhaps they did not sense his unease. And yet small children were said to be possessors of more sensitivity, in which case they could pierce his barriers and become aware that behind those barriers he was full of good will to all men with very few exceptions.

Nina sat down beside him. 'Changed your mind, have you?' he asked. 'About marrying Campbell? Yes, actually.' 'When are you going to tell everyone?' 'I'm not. You see, what's happened is that yesterday I decided not to marry him and today I changed my mind back again.' 'Then you won't have to send back all the presents and cheques.' 'That may have influenced my decision.' 'Mmmmm . . .' He was nearly laughing. One of the best things she could ever do was to make him laugh. 'Mmmm . . .' She picked up a piece of sky from the puzzle and put it in place, deciding that, if love existed, which it probably didn't like most people said it did, one person whom she did love was John in a very pure way. John knew what Campbell would never know in a million years.

By now they were supposed to be putting the puzzle away. Laura and their mother and Mrs Carter were preparing the buffet supper. Nanny was upstairs putting Vanessa to bed and calling her Nina by mistake and sometimes 'hasty pudding' which she used to call Laura. 'Look,' said Nanny, holding Vanessa up to the low window of the room that used to be the night nursery, but was now the spare room. 'Look, darling, a bird!' Vanessa in her cotton nightie said: 'Bird.' 'That's right, precious. And another bird. A magpie, another magpie, that's two magpies, which is good for Aunty Nina. One for sorrow, two for joy.' And Vanessa, who was at the age of repeating everything anyone said, repeated: 'One for sorry, two for joy.'

Over here, the first magpie alighted on a frond of the cedar tree, which bobbed under its weight. Then the second flew past the branch and the first left the branch still bobbing. There, under that tree, depending on the position of the sun and the direction of the wind, Nanny had first placed Laura's pram, then John's, then Nina's.

Vanessa struggled in her arms: 'You're a bundle,' said Nanny. She let her go, a fat child. Vanessa ran towards the landing, calling for her mother. Her run was that of a toddler. Far too young to be a bridesmaid, thought Nanny again. They want them to grow up too quickly these days, and her daddy a doctor who should know better.

But a wedding was a wedding and there would go on being weddings, and Nanny, for a few more weddings, for a few more families for whom she had worked, would put bridesmaids to bed on the night before and then go to the top of the stairs and call for pages.

Because the page did not come when called, Nanny went downstairs, down the curving staircase, holding on to the mahogany handrail, stepping carefully in her black lace-up shoes.

There they were, the three of them: John and Nina with Edmund between them in the corner of the drawing room, heads bent over a jigsaw puzzle, John, tongue between his teeth, trying to do the difficult sky pieces and Nina with a piece held up to her mouth. She had always done that with jigsaw pieces and often sucked them, ruining them, especially cardboard ones, making the picture loosen from the backing. 'Now you!' said Nanny to Nina. 'Sorry, Nanny.' 'I'll let you off this once.' 'Thank you, Nanny.' 'That puzzle had to be put away, I thought.'

Nina decided that, in addition to loving John, she loved Nanny. But such things were over. Such things hardly ever happened now and, even if she did marry Campbell tomorrow, she would never be with John, Edmund and Nanny like this again.

But if times like this were unimportant and passing, which they could be in the scheme of things, then which times were important? Of which moment could you say – *this* was the time, *this* occasion mattered.

'And you've got to be putting on your best bib and tucker,' said Nanny, tapping John on the shoulder. 'Haven't you, Mr Serious?' wondering how he'd ever learned to keep himself as clean as he was these days after all the trouble she had had with him. Possibly he had a young lady, but you could die if living depended on finding out John's secrets. Mr Serious!

John's best bib and tucker was a pair of cricket trousers which had once been Harold's, plus a cotton jacket, herring-bone, tailor-made for Harold in Nepal at the time he was on the way to Everest – or hoped he was – at about John's age – that long ago.

I believe there are no Nannies like her now. The world Nina came from was their place. Perhaps Nina would have felt differently about her mother had there not been Nanny and the early memory of Nanny's special contours against which you leaned and Nanny's arms into which you ran.

Polly sniffed the air and heard the bees buzzing in Julia's herbaceous border. Softness and warmth! Such essences! For a moment she felt the pull of the latitude of the place where she'd been born and bred. I must not be seduced by this, thought Polly. All the same there were no smells like this in Swaledale, no wisteria such as this which climbed into the eaves and hung over the garden door. Nor did the cuckoo ever sing in Swaledale as vigorously as she had heard it sing on her arrival.

11

Laura, always sensitive as to how any social occasion should run, realized that there was no precedent in her experience for a party like this. It was bound to be messy at the edges, with some people sitting around not getting talked to. She could only do her best. Her mother did the same in her natural but thoughtless hostess manner, pointing to the food and calling out: 'Do everybody help themselves!', expecting people to dig in, then rushing off to talk to others. Nina did very little to help in any way at all.

Nor was the food enticing. Seeing this she, Laura, had that afternoon whipped up a salmon mousse and made a quiche which was quite an innovatory dish at that time and still known most frequently as quiche lorraine. Her mother seemed to think that you could get away at buffets with serving only cold meats and undressed salads. As well as all this, the wine glasses were too small, which meant that people stood around having drained their glasses, but were too well-mannered to shoulder through the crowd for refills. Everything constrained true sociability. Her mother's way was to fling whatever was to hand at guests rather than to make them, by a display of meticulous trouble taken, feel both welcome and respected.

Jowly Harry Cornelius stood side by side with Bernard Crosby and said out of the corner of his mouth: 'How long do you think we have to stay?' And Bernard, still feeling distant, said this was up to Phyllis really.

In the kitchen Mrs Carter washed up at the sink while Nanny sat on the edge of a chair ready to run upstairs if needed by either of the children. She was hemming Vanessa's bridesmaid's dress and would follow this with intricate repairs to the heir-loom of a veil. Brides who had worn this went back along the female line via Masterson and beyond, daughters of daughters, each of whose mothers had in turn opened out their drawing rooms on eves of weddings to the families of bridegrooms – plus inviting locals to make weight.

A lot more presents were arriving. Lest the givers were concerned that their gifts were duplicates of those already received, Nina developed a new stock phrase of thanks: 'Oh, how lovely! We haven't got one of those so far.' Although she had altered it this evening to: 'Oh, how simply lovely. We haven't got one quite like that so far.' Having used one of these phrases to Polly, she felt foolish because of course no one could possibly have given her a Victorian portable medicine chest. 'Well, it's hardly lovely,' said Polly, 'but one could say quirky. I think probably a doctor would have carried it in his carriage on his rounds or some hypochondriac on an empire-building journey into some yet undiscovered hinterland.'

Nina wasn't really listening. She was thinking how towards each person that you met you offer something different of yourself. And, in regard to groups of people, it was even worse. Towards the Crosbys she was one thing and towards her family she was another. This evening was terrible. I look all right, thought Nina, which is something, but it's terrible. She said to Polly: 'I say, thanks. I'll put it in the hall for now, and make sure that it goes on show tomorrow.' 'That isn't what I bought it for,' said Polly.

'I know,' said Nina, and to demonstrate that she had taken the point, she put the present down behind the sofa where, having sharp edges, it was the cause of several barked shins during the course of the evening. It also ripped a ladder in one of Cicely Cornelius's grey nylon stockings.

'What are you going to do?' asked Polly. 'To do?' Nina looked blank. She was giving Polly every impression of what Polly had imagined she would be, a mindless girl only just out of her teens who would join the world of Joan Ramseys and try to fill her time with purposeless activities of an entirely domestic nature. 'I mean after you are married. I heard you were a journalist.'

'Well, sort of, yes.' 'Are you going on being a sort of

journalist?' 'I hope so,' said Nina, thinking, well, she might one day. 'Good,' said Polly. 'That's the ticket. Don't sink!'

I've sunk already, Nina thought. I've never surfaced anyway. She envied Polly her directness of speech, which she had always wanted for herself and always would want for herself.

She doesn't know what I'm talking about, thought Polly. It is daft of me to try and say important things at parties. But it happened that Helen was standing nearby. 'It's so easy to sink, isn't it?' said Helen. And Polly said, 'I shouldn't really pronounce on marriage. I was only married for seven years.' 'Could I ask you what happened?' Helen felt that this was the evening to be impulsive. Here might be someone who had been deserted and could speak about it.

Nina left them to it. The special relationship she felt she had with Helen didn't seem to work this evening, not in front of Polly anyway. All she knew about Polly was that she had married someone who had eventually died of something like TB and that her mother kept on saying what a pity it was that Polly hadn't married again.

Joan Ramsey had the first symptoms of migraine, which wasn't surprising. One, she'd had to do all that map reading which had strained her eyes. Two, she'd had to play bridge. Three, the strain of George not liking having Polly in the back of the car and his continual nagging about the route; but they'd got here, hadn't they?

She'd found Laura who seemed the friendliest Forestier and asked her where the toilet was. 'Oh, the loo!' said Laura. Anyway, whatever it was called, Joan went to it, locked the door and took a green pill which was her first line of defence. Or should she have taken the stronger white one, which was the second line? It might be too late for the green one to work. But the trouble about the white pill was that it made her dull and stupid, rather duller and stupider than she already felt most of the time.

Because there was no cup or glass in the downstairs loo or toilet or whatever they called it at Glebe House, she ran water into her cupped hands and lapped it like a dog to wash down the pill.

The cause of migraine in Joan's case: eye strain and social

strain or a mixture of the two. Once she asked the doctor what he thought: 'I think it's a mixture of eye strain and social strain,' said Joan. 'Then get your glasses changed and try not to meet too many new people,' said the outspoken Scottish doctor as he handed over his desk the prescription for the green pills and the white ones.

On the wall of the loo were all these Forestier family photographs, mostly summer ones of children on the beach. What a funny place to put them, but Joan couldn't look too closely, daring to strain her eyes no further. I am disabled, she thought. If I needed to be employed to earn a living, would I in fact be entitled to a disability pension?

The green pill began to lift her spirits. Sometimes it gave her flashes of inspiration, such as now, combing her hair and seeing herself in the cracked mirror and suddenly knowing that nothing was ever going to change for her ever, although since yesterday she'd been thinking about what Polly had said and thinking how much happier you could be once you realized that you didn't have to be.

'What happened?' asked Helen. 'Do you really want to know?' asked Polly. 'Yes,' 'He died,' said Polly, 'but it might not have lasted anyway. I have to prevent myself from recalling the seven years as happy since death distorts reality.' 'Why might it not have lasted? Do you mind telling me about it?'

She's younger than me, thought Polly – about five years maybe. She may be worried about the bags under her eyes or about having a less than perfect skin, but when she is my age she will see those faults as nothing compared to the diminishing areas of smoothness and the loosening of neck and jawline. 'It is debatable,' she said to Helen, 'whether it is better to be tortured and with someone or to be comfortable and lonely. As Dr Johnson once said, marriage has many pains but celibacy few pleasures.' Polly had had quite a few drinks by now and wasn't all the sure as to the accuracy of the quotation, but Helen seemed unlikely to be well read enough to contradict.

Phyllis and Cicely stood together for a few minutes observing the mixed patterned porcelain plates, the dryish salads, the crumbly merringues and over-ripe strawberries. Most of the time they had been circulating, one of them in navy blue and the other in grey. A spot of dried blood showed on Cicely's bony shin after her encounter with the medicine chest. Most people never thought of Cicely as having blood. There was a family joke: when Cicely gave birth to Tim, her one and only child, her brother George, not normally noted for his humour, said she must have laid an egg and hatched it in the airing cupboard. It is certainly hard to associate the blood and slime of parturition with someone as ethereal as Cicely Cornelius.

'I can't see Helen,' Phyllis said. 'She's gone outside with the cousin, the one from Swaledale.' 'She could be overdoing things.' 'Drink you mean?' 'Just a look in her eyes I don't like very much.'

Anne Walker, née Ramsey, stayed at the Dolphin to be with all the children there so that Jane could go to the party since everyone felt that would be best for her. Anne knitted and watched television in the residents lounge and waited for her husband Graham, who would come here if he were too late to join the stag party. Graham was an accountant. Anne was a dark girl whom everyone liked almost as much they liked Nicola. She had curly hair and had once played hockey for the north of England ladies team. As well as Joanne, now in bed and asleep, she had two sons at a prep school on the coast near Filey.

George, having established that Joan was nowhere near, looked around for Polly. You could tell about women like that. He despised and yet was fascinated. What she had said in the car about being single and the way she said it! Dualistic feelings of scorn and lust came over him. And at her age! Some twenty-five years after these events, thirteen women were killed by one man on account of feelings not dissimilar from George's at this moment. It is worth mentioning. Having failed to see Polly anywhere, he turned to talk to Richard Crosby about the day's play at both Lords and Headingley.

Nina went on thinking about sinking and how she had nothing to say and what she lacked was personality, which all these people talking nineteen to the dozen must have. She was as bad as Jane Crosby sitting there on the window seat looking discontented with her bouffant skirt arranged around her and her stiletto shoes crossed. People don't like talking to discontented people. They turn away. The only way was to look contented, so Nina forced a smile on to her own lips and went to fetch a newly filled decanter of wine, saying to herself: inside I am surly and resentful, but it gets me nowhere, I must bury surliness, bury resentment.

Laura looked around: all these older, prosperous-looking men in expensively cut suits. She'd known there was money but had not expected to be reminded of the top consultants whom she occasionally met with Jim. It all made the hospitality look meaner and the wine glasses even smaller. She managed to get Daddy in a corner and suggest he open several more bottles. Daddy said he would, but she felt sorry for him having to do it. Today he'd told her that after all this they might have to sell the house.

Across the room from Jane: a huge mirror with feathered gilt surround, although some of this decoration appeared to be missing. The only person to speak to Jane so far had been Julia: Jane admired the mirror. 'Oh I'm glad you like it,' said Julia: 'In fact I bought it at an auction for two and sixpence. People don't want huge things like that these days, but someone told me the other day it was now worth about a hundred pounds.'

Jane sat and wondered if, when she had left Simon and sorted herself out, she could open an antique shop. She'd get a pretty good income in the form of maintenance, but she could sue for a lump sum which would be enough to set herself up somewhere like Ilkley maybe where Emma would meet the right kind of children.

Harold conducted the older men to his study where they peered into the group photograph taken near Base Camp One. Some of them remembered reading of the expedition. Richard considered the floor-to-ceiling shelves of books. Very little had been said in the family, but the rumour was that Nina was becoming a Crosby with no marriage settlement. But here surely were several thousand pounds' worth of books and, if the Forestiers divided inheritance equally among male and female offspring, Nina should be entitled to a third of the capital raised by the eventual sale of the books.

On the terrace, dusk was falling and the cedar tree becoming a looming shape rather than a source of green. At the back of Helen's mind, even while talking to and listening to Polly, all the names and dates of the past few years rolled up as if on a rotating calendar. How long had he had the chequebook? How often had he used it? Was this the first he'd had, the second or the third? How many treats had he bought for others with it? Images of Charlie's hand signing cheques, tearing them out, turning his face with a smile towards another upturned smiling face?

But here was Polly – at last a sympathetic and unjudging ear. She felt confessions welling up, confidences ready to pour out, holding back so far for one reason only – that Polly was an unattached woman, thus belonging to the most dangerous class. 'You mean before he died, your husband was unfaithful to you?'

'Endlessly.' Polly was perched on the low wall which surrounded the terrace. 'And you took it? You accepted it?' Helen stayed on her feet, slightly swaying. 'I didn't lie down under it, if that's what you mean.' 'You challenged him?' 'I tried to let him know I knew.' 'Did that upset him?' 'Horribly yes, but that wasn't what he died of.' Polly started laughing. Helen couldn't help but join in. You could laugh, couldn't you, when things were over. Dare I laugh with her like this? Surely this small woman was no threat! Older probably – too old for Charlie and anyhow a Forestier, a southerner, not someone whom they'd ever meet again. So Helen went on laughing. By now she couldn't help herself, tears streaming down her face, wishing that life could always be like this, drinking and laughing at the horrors.

It isn't as funny as all that, thought Polly. Who was this half-dotty woman? Because of the sudden way they'd plunged into this conversation, they had missed out on the usual pleasantries.

As a child, John drew his first pictures, two curved lines arching away from each other to signify a bird, and Nanny had said as

127

usual: 'Oh look, a bird!' which proved to John that birds were as you saw them and not as they really were.

There was a flock of them high up in the evening sky as he was driven east by Jim towards the other party. There they were like those first ones that he'd drawn – just two curving meeting lines. 'All right if I smoke?' he asked. 'Yes of course, old chap.' The 'old chap' coming from Jim sounded false, an awkward attempt at bonhomie, but after all a stag party was intended to be warm and friendly – all boys together. 'Perhaps we should have had one or two drinks before we left,' said Jim: 'I find myself in a peculiarly unpartyish mood.' It was hard to imagine Jim could ever be in a partyish mood. 'We could always stop for the odd pint,' said John.

They drank in silence in an almost deserted pub, two men thrown together with nothing in common, except that as brothers-in-law they had often spent Easters, Christmases and the odd weekend under the same roof. 'So what do you think of this whole show?' asked Jim.

'Not a great deal.' 'So you're not thinking of getting hitched or anything?' 'It depends what you mean by anything.' This reply seemed to make Jim uncomfortable, so John added, 'No, it's not on my programme at all, I'm afraid, although I don't know why I should be afraid.'

'No, I see.' Jim's voice was wavery, his manner of speaking was always one of speculation, slow consideration and reflection. They had another pint each, bought by Jim, and watched two other men play darts.

Perhaps men could not talk to each other unless they had activities to share. But you had to try. 'I was thinking about birds,' said John when they were back in the car: 'About birds, the nature of them, you know.' And he explained about the two arched lines while regarding another flock of them in the sky above Arundel, which they were approaching. 'We shall have to watch the old liquor level I suppose,' said Jim, although this was years before the drinking and driving laws came in: 'But it's not exactly my cup of tea, this sort of caper.' 'Nor mine,' said John. Jim hadn't responded to the bird topic.

* * *

'Aye, lad,' said Charlie, meeting Mike McKorkadale at the restaurant: 'Tareet?' 'Tareet, then!' said Mike McKorkadale. This exchange is most frequently used in the Halifax area, or Calderdale as it is now known, and can be taken to mean: Hello, are you all right/Yes thank you, I'm all right and I hope you are too. So they were both all right or at any rate had said they were. 'T'old lad's not here yet then?' 'T'old lad had better be here soon.' 'T'old lad's got to put head in noose in t'morning.' This further exchange referred of course to Campbell. The fact that the wedding would not take place until two thirty in the afternoon of the next day is neither here nor there. In parts of Yorkshire 't'morning' can be read as 'tomorrow'.

This sudden use of dialect between the two men: a kind of joke – maybe to make them feel more matey. They were even less closely related than were Jim and John, Mike being a young Crosby connection, an auctioneer, but more in the business of selling contents of houses rather than property itself.

Campbell himself had only just left the Dolphin and was approaching Arundel, having passed unwittingly the pub in which John and Jim had stopped for a third and fourth pint each. A very interesting thing had happened to Campbell in church that afternoon at the rehearsal. He's seen a tomb of a crusader and, on leaving Glebe House after tea, had popped back to make a note of the long-dead warrior's name. You never knew when such titbits of information might come in useful.

'No,' said John. 'marriage is not really on these days.' Jim nodded and paused, using what must be his consulting room manner, allowing the patient to talk on while observing. 'The population explosion and all that?' he asked eventually. 'Yes, and all that – as well as the other very possible explosion.' 'Yes indeed,' said Jim, as they left the second pub.

A little further on John hit on the idea of questioning Jim about the scientific method used in diagnostic medicine. 'An immediate and successful diagnosis is, I imagine, rare,' he said. 'Oh yes, absolutely. Well . . . pretty rare.' 'So,' went on John, 'as it were, you might say – as Mrs X enters the surgery – you might say: Mrs X, you might say, it would seem that the red pills I gave you have not, apparently, improved your condition. Now we have already tried the pink pills and the green pills I prescribed for you, also a change of diet and you still have pain. So now for X-ray possibly or investigative surgery?' 'Very roughly, yes,' said Jim, and John went on. 'The approach to truth via sense experience by eliminating all other possibilities? I say, Jim, are you all right to drive?'

There was another stop during which time they discussed the mind/body problem in some depth and, consequently, psychosomatic illness. Then the car failed to start again, the trouble almost certainly being dirty plugs. John, having dealt for years with his motorbike, understood the internal combustion engine and had done so ever since the age of fourteen when Harold began not to be able to afford a dependable car any more. Outside this third pub, John took off the Nepalese cotton jacket, rolled up his shirt sleeves and threw open the bonnet of Jim's Wolsley. Jim hovered, hands in pockets, apologizing and admitting that he was unable to tell the difference between distributor and carburettor. All of which gave John confidence, because he could now walk into the restaurant where the party was to be held, having performed what could be described as a manly action – at the same time feeling rather ashamed that this should matter to him.

Twilight and beginning to rain softly. Polly, still outside with Helen, felt the first spots of it, which fell on her forearm at blood temperature. Southern summer rain was like a warm shower: it did not fall preceded by a drop in air temperature. It simply happened. Clouds arrived overhead and released it. First you heard it pattering on the leaves of the wisteria and then you felt it falling silently at your feet on the brick terrace. Then it began to add to the already highly scented night, more essences drawn from surrounding vegetation.

'I know he loves me,' Helen was saying, 'and I do forgive him in a way.' 'Why should you?' Polly was saying: 'And anyway, it's more or less impossible. Forgiveness is acceptance and acceptance is as good as giving up. Acceptance is not caring, acceptance is to shrug your shoulders, turn your back. No, someone has to do the crying.'

They moved back to stand under the overhanging creeper which kept most of the rain from them. Helen's hair had begun to shine with sprinkled droplets of it. As for Polly, she could feel the slight waves which had been put in hers the day before in Harrogate disappearing by the moment. Then Helen said, 'I couldn't be alone. I really couldn't.' 'Suppose he died?' 'I'd manage. Well, I'd have to, wouldn't I? You manage. Well, you look as if you do.'

'I manage,' Polly said. But what she didn't say was just how rotten it was always being on the lookout. Totally preoccupying it was sometimes. 'But it's not all roses.'

'Oh dear, it's not right for anyone. Shall we go in now?' Helen heard herself say this. It was one of those nights when she kept hearing herself say things without knowing she was going to say them, just as she often saw herself doing things before she'd known she was going to do them. What had she said to Polly? She crossed her fingers. Recklessness in her case nearly always spelled disaster. But disaster had already overtaken her this afternoon. 'Most people are leaving now, I think,' she said.

12

'John, this is Mike, Simon, William Ramsey and, er . . .
Gerald.' Gerald seemed to be a friend of Campbell's from his
army days. 'Mike, Simon, William, Gerald, this is John, Nina's
brother-in-law – no, sorry – I have got that wrong I think.'

Charlie was making introductions in the restaurant, a place
of varnished beams and leaded windows, hanging ships' lan-
terns and reproduction prints of galleons. The smell of food
was tempting. 'Gerald? Sorry . . . haven't you met Mike? And
this is William, William Ramsey . . . Jim . . . what are you
having?'

Jim stood next to Mike who seemed to be a cousin of
Campbell's. Around them other members of the family told
each other stories, some of them about cricket, which was only
to be expected really. Jim tried to remember what the score
had been last time he listened and which of the Test Match
team, apart from Trueman, played for Yorkshire. Most of the
early part of the evening he seemed to spend saying: 'I am not
a cricketing man myself, but I do go fishing.' He remembered
his own stag night when everyone became joky as they often
do in medical circles and wished he could remember some of
the jokes which were told on that occasion.

When Campbell at last arrived, there was much laughter and
jeering. They seemed to think he had had time on the way for
a sexual encounter. Campbell explained he had had a puncture.
This was followed by a good few 'puncture equals penetration'
jokes. 'We had trouble with the car as well,' said Jim.

Most things John did, he did with a purpose, either to
discover more about that which puzzled him or, in the case of
sex for instance, for direct enjoyment. Then there was that
other category of acts, exemplified by the mowing of the lawn

at Glebe House earlier today, which was to relieve his father of a burden. But this evening was, to all intents and purposes, purposeless. Yet here he was, and would have to hang on somehow, if only to express some kind of solidarity with Jim who seemed equally at sea. He had to see it in this way: they were here as male representatives of Nina's family. In which case, what sort of front was to be expected from them? The evening began to take on the shape of ritual or competition, but in what field? If in the field of storytelling, sporting knowledge or of monetary success, the Crosbys were going to win hands down.

John had recently begun to work on a firmer handshake. Even if he could not be expansive in conversation or compete in any of the fields mentioned above, at least he could show willing by this gesture, false as it was.

Harold dozed on the sofa of his study, his tie loosened and the remains of a bottle of Beaujolais on the floor beside him. John would wake him up when he came in to use the camp bed, then Harold would stumble upstairs to join Julia. Also in bed by now was Nina, reading yet another novel about present-day Yorkshire in which people who lived in terraced houses made love in cars parked by dry-stone walls. Polly was helping Nanny and Laura with the washing up. She hadn't forgotten Helen, but was remembering the sheer collective force of all those married women in the room tonight and speculating how, if it were not for them, there might be no more weddings. This female force assumed the dynamism of a juggernaut, the directed aim of which was to drag the bride to join them. And this regardless of their individual rewards or otherwise in marriage. As to the girl herself – she might not be that dim, but was moving in a pattern like a puppet on strings manipulated by the others and her own biology. Supine rather than insouciant perhaps.

At the Dolphin, Muriel, Richard, George Ramsey and Harry Cornelius were playing bridge again and Helen was in her room, green chequebook in her hand. What should she do with it? Replace it where she had found it? That would be in tune with policy – to lull him into non-suspicion. Or keep it hidden and let him worry? Cicely was trying to get to sleep by working out how she would deal with the drawing room at Glebe house to minimize the lowness of the ceiling. Perhaps faintly coloured paint, or wallpaper on the walls and a dead white ceiling? First of course you'd have to get rid of the picture rail.

There was a good deal of teasing of Campbell who, they all said, would have to give up having sex with someone called Margaret who, it seemed, was known carnally to several of them. Sitting next to Charlie, John was now pleasantly full of fillet steak which had been followed by ice cream and apple pie. Charlie, in charge of proceedings, wasn't such a bad bloke after all. Best man in more ways than one. And Campbell – to do him credit – seemed aloof from the general joshing and hilarity. But then, in regard to Margaret, he was hardly likely to welcome revelations of his sex life in front of members of the family of his bride-to-be. He was looking stunned, was laughing a lot as if aware that he should appear jovial, but that was all. Perhaps this was the purpose of such an occasion – to stun the bridegroom and deliver him to the church hungover. All he needed to do tomorrow was to enter, stand up, repeat his name after the officiating priest and say: 'I do,' two words which were among the simplest sounds in the English language.

On John's other side was Simon, the one who hated his wife and who seemed intent on telling Campbell how he would regret his marriage, that women were never satisfied, made insane demands of a domestic nature, went off sex and bled you to death financially.

The one called Mike was, from the far end of the table, suggesting that they should all drive to Hove where he knew a girl he'd met when attending an antique dealer's fair, who offered some unusual sex practices. Then Simon said there was a girl in Cleckheaton who permitted anal intercourse, but charged extra. 'How much?' asked Mike. 'Well, considerably more than for the average,' said Simon. John turned to Charlie to ask if in his opinion intercourse could ever be described as average. 'No,' said Charlie, lowering his voice. 'Emphatically never, but with this lot, it's all talk anyway, and it could be very very average the way they do it.' Then he added, 'I must apologize. I can't excuse them, only say they are not my blood relations.'

'Their salient feature,' John said, 'is – as far as I can see – that they don't much care for humankind – or rather for any improvement in the lot of humankind.'

'And your salient feature is that you're just a bloody optimist,' said Charlie. 'You come to Dewsbury or to Hunslet where I come from. Lot of humankind improving? That'd make you think again.'

'Oh, aren't they better off these days?' asked John, and Charlie laughed. 'Better off? Better off, my foot! The only thing to do is, if you come from there, to get the hell out of it. That's what I did. How do you think I got to look like this?' He indicated his pale suit, silk tie, polished shoes.

'But at least you care,' said John, 'or seem to care.'

Jim remembered a joke at last, more of a riddle really, about the difference between a weasel and a stoat and wondered to whom he could tell it. The soldier, Gerald, who was sitting next to him, didn't seem to be the type somehow. Unlike Campbell, Gerald had been dropped in the Canal Zone. Talk of Suez had begun. A touchy subject. At the time, Jim had a patient who, although not serving in the army, developed psoriasis, almost certainly an hysterical reaction symptomatic of the general furore which seized the nation in October 1956.

Phyllis's night was to be one of interrupted and inconclusive dreams, in which members of the family would enter and demand attention. One after another they would appear standing in her doorway, then one after another crowd into the room and all the while she would be waiting for Nicola to come and help, but know in her heart of hearts that Nicola had been delayed by the accident which was inevitable one of these days because she drove around the county so much. Phyllis would then be at the scene of the accident, running towards Nick's overturned Morris Traveller, scrabbling at the door to no avail, then bending to peer inside to see which of the children was

135

there, trying to recognize the immobile head while police bells sounded in the distance.

'I've never quite made up my mind as to the rights and wrongs of it,' Jim was saying, 'except that I do know what a sick man Eden was.' He went on to mention theories he had heard in recent months as to the precise effect of this illness on the personality. '. . . really rather intriguing!'

'If I may say so,' Gerald said, 'and with respect . . . not awfully relevant in either military or political terms.'

Across the table, John sat up. He had been leaning his head in one of his hands, finding that his elbow kept slipping off the edge of the table. 'Of course it's relevant. That's history for you, isn't it? Made by leaders who are sick. And anyway – to be a leader – to *want* to be a leader is to be a sick man, blinkered, narrow . . .'

'Hang on! Hang on,' said Gerald. John looked over, saw a pale-faced, long-nosed man. He should have recognized the type. He had been educated with such as Gerald. John faced him, elbows now square on the table. 'A leader, by his very nature, is a bastard, is he not?' 'Dear me!' – this was Gerald again – 'How fearfully naïve!' There was a cool sharp feel to him.

Jim began to wish he'd told the story about the weasel. He should have known with John around that this would happen. John, like Laura, would argue the hind leg off a donkey if the spirit moved him to. 'I say!' said Jim, 'it is fascinating, isn't it, I always think, how talk of Suez arouses such emotions. I had a patient once . . .' But it was too late. John had taken off his spectacles, wiped them with a table napkin, put them on again, was flushed and ready.

In the next dream, Phyllis witnessed the accident herself. It took place at a roundabout. The Morris Traveller was certainly Nicola's – was at any rate white. She saw it now, nosing out slowly from a minor road on to a major one, the A1 possibly.

In general Campbell did not favour arguments, at least not those which led to voices being raised. It was so unnecessary, he would always tell Nina, to raise one's voice. Life should be conducted rationally, peaceably. But in one sense this was different. High-level stuff – quite impressive. It was something to have intelligent people debating great issues at one's stag night. It did raise the tone somewhat. Perhaps he could take the role of umpire. By now, on the one hand John was attacking those who believed that Britain could still be great, and on the other hand, Gerald was attacking John, saying was he not himself descended from a family who had partaken in imperialist activities in the past? 'Gerald actually *was* at Suez,' Campbell said. '*And* he is at Staff College now. He is a Captain.'

'In that case I am entirely overawed,' said John. 'And may I take it that you're saying that, apart from those who were in action or are serving now, no one may offer an opinion? If that is so, we have become an army state. The generals are the governors.' He drained a glass of red wine, put his glass down, ran his fingers though his hair and stared at Gerald. Meanwhile others joined in, calling out such things as: 'After all, we had a legal right to the Canal,' or: 'Look what happens when you hand the empire back to blacks! They make a balls of it.'

Charlie went on filling glasses, calculating how many bottles had been drunk. The longer the argument went on, the more would be drunk and the more he'd have to worry about those too drunk to drive. (Campbell at any rate had to be kept alive for tomorrow.) He'd better keep a watching brief and stay as sober as he could.

Simon was accusing John of being the kind of person who welcomed immigrants – black workers and Asian doctors – to which Jim said that doctors, Asian or otherwise, were in almost every case both honourable and efficient. But by now he had begun to realize that his contributions were, as Gerald had suggested earlier, irrelevant. This was his last.

John said not only did he welcome coloured people to the country, but they should *all* come if they were so minded, and if they took the bread out of his mouth, they well deserved it and he owed it to them.

'Sins of the fathers, eh?' said Gerald. 'So you wish to make amends, do you? What does that solve, may one ask?' 'It solves nothing, but it salves my conscience.'

'So the nation's policies should be so directed solely for the sake of your conscience?'

John looked down at his place mat. I'm on my own, he thought. I didn't think I'd have to fight like this. He looked for Charlie who might help, but Charlie's chair was empty.

He was in the gents splashing cold water on his face. He had been joined by an unsteady Jim. 'I was beginning to enjoy myself,' said Jim, 'until that started. So I've brought a bottle in. What does one do?' 'Do about what?' asked Charlie.

'All that in there.' The two men perched on basins, arms folded, looking at the ceiling, both about ten years the senior of those left round the table. 'You mean,' said Charlie, 'about the world in general or that lot in there?' 'Well both,' said Jim. 'I'm buggered if I know,' said Charlie.

Then Jim said that he was rather squiffy, in fact almost stuporose which was a medical term for a state of insensibility. 'I can see that,' Charlie said. 'I've seen a lot of suffering, you know,' said Jim. 'No doubt,' said Charlie, thinking: poor sod – I don't suppose he gets much pleasure; doesn't look the type.

They'd reached the rights and wrongs of empire-building, the manner of its building and the use of Christianity to subdue . . . 'and to disguise our greed,' said John.

Meanwhile his mother soothed herself to sleep by reading from Revelations – how a mighty angel came down from heaven, clothed in a white cloud and a rainbow on his head. 'His face was as it were the sun and his feet were pillars of fire.' She'd almost missed her Bible reading, having felt extremely tired, but was glad now that she hadn't.

'Misguided missionaries,' said John, 'forcing a perverted message down the throats of conquered people!' Dark oak table, orange place mats, orange table napkins, waitresses hovering to clear away. Only Gerald and John involved now, apart from an occasional 'Hear! Hear!' and Campbell's conciliatory interruptions. Gerald smoked a gold-tipped cigarette, leaning back, stretching his long legs, saying: 'would you not at least concede that there was some international benefit in what occurred? Some side effect . . . at least it's now established that there is a peace-keeping force available?'

'It saved our face. That's all it did. I don't condemn it, but – to use your own word – it isn't relevant.' John took off his jacket to reveal a dark green shirt, not very crisply ironed.

'And in regard to empire – your hated empire – let me make another point . . .'

William Ramsey, by several years the youngest of those present, had been wondering whatever happened to the plan that they'd all go on to a brothel. He'd been promised this for several weeks. The argument was tedious to him. He didn't need to think about these things. His life would go on as his father's had. He had taken over Charlie's task of filling glasses and he drank and yawned and yawned and drank, eyes crossing with boredom as Gerald pointed out to John that had it not been for the riches we'd gained in our imperialist days, there might have been no welfare state. 'How was it funded? You tell me. What other country could have done it? Only one as rich as we still were in 1945.'

It serves me right, thought John, for believing that all those who oppose my views are idiots. This has shown me that I have formidable adversaries. I must try to see this as a learning process rather than a humiliating one.

'I suppose,' said Gerald, 'that you yourself have great plans with which to strike at the establishment?' 'John is in the RAF,' said Campbell, feeling that all facts should be made plain. 'Well thank you Campbell!' John said, classing Campbell for ever afterwards as a well-meaning fool.

'Ah!' said Gerald, 'so the pacifism is but skin-deep!' 'No!' Here John told Gerald that it had been easier to submit to national service – just to get it over with; and anyhow . . . But before he could explain the unmilitaristic nature of what he did, Gerald, lighting another cigarette, came in with: 'Bit of an angry young man then, is that it?' as if he had dismissed the opposition – while others murmured: 'Bit of a red!', voices reminding John that to be a red was not so clever these days what with Russia having stamped out freedom of thought and action in Hungary, killing thousands, and that communists could be as imperialist as anyone. John felt he was a lonely guard outside a camp where everyone slept in their tents.

'Yes, I've seen a lot of suffering,' said Jim. He leaned against the tiled wall in the gents. 'I'd better go and sort them out,' said Charlie, feeling for his chequebook in the inner pocket of his jacket, Jim waved the bottle. 'Have another!' Charlie found his chequebook, but went on looking through his pocket. Jim thought he'd got the joke right at last. 'The difference between a weasel and a stoat is that . . . a weasel is easily identified but a stoat is totally different. That's it, isn't it?' Charlie stared at him. 'Not funny?' 'Not particularly.' 'Oh well,' said Jim wondering when he'd get the chance to get quite so drunk again: 'What are you looking for?' 'My chequebook.' 'Well, I may be squiffy, may be almost stuporose, but I quite clearly saw you find it just now. There it is!' 'I have another,' Charlie said. 'Two chequebooks! Well I never!'

'And after national service,' Gerald was saying to John, 'you have plans – no doubt world-shatteringly reformist plans? Social work perhaps?'

Should I have shut up? John asked himself. Should I have stayed out of this? And for the next few years he would be of the mind that yes, pride had been damaged. Then later he would look back on this evening and tell himself: no, it was better to speak out . . . that those who *could* should always do so. 'I shall class myself as a thinker . . .' This sounded feeble. Gerald grinned. 'Thinkers influence,' said John. 'Socrates, Erasmus, Shakespeare, Blake, Sartre, Russell . . .'

'Ah!' Gerald held a finger up. 'A thinker! But thinkers do not always advocate the way of peace, the foolishness of war. Some thinkers have, have they not, acknowledged that the nature of the beast called man is violent. Life nasty, brutish, short, and all that. Hobbes, if I may so jog your memory.'

I need never come this way again, thought John, never listen to another Gerald, never be in the company of barbarians. I can stick to those who think like me. Along the table he could hear talk turning back to sexual jokes. Simon was telling a story

140

about a man in bed with a girl. The man wore pyjamas with a white rose on the pocket. 'My goodness, do you fuck for Yorkshire?' said the girl. The laughter drowned John's next remark. He needed to repeat it. 'I still think . . .' Charlie had returned by now. John's glass refilled . . . 'I still think . . .'

'So I should hope! You'll hardly be a thinker otherwise,' Gerald stood up, straightened his tie, his blazer buttons shining in the low light over the table. 'But let me say, as far as I'm concerned keep thinking! Things won't change much. There'll always be these here . . . this lot.' He gestured to the others slumped in chairs, careless of their good suits, stomachs bulging, men whose stomachs would bulge further in middle age: 'There'll always be these here to back me up.'

And so there would be. Such as Simon, William, Mike and others would be cheering Gerald on as at the rank of colonel he zapped terrorists in Northern Ireland, and at the rank of major general, he sailed off to the Falkland Islands in the QEII to return triumphant to retire, to sit in boardrooms and to write his memoirs. Middle-aged Gerald would nod in full approval as the nation seemed to shake itself back towards reality and at least away from the soggy idealism preached by such as John. And those who would have cheered for John tonight would shrug their shoulders, pity their children and say: we nearly did it, didn't we?

'I say! Not going, are you?' Campbell rose. 'Sorry! Needs must.' Gerald circled the table, shaking hands, ending with John, holding out his hand. John took it. The gentleman in him predominated. Why shake that hand? Why, he asked himself, and would continue to ask himself for years ahead until he saw that there was no way he could cast off what was in his blood, whether by nature, nurture or race memory. But at this moment he kept looking at that hand of his as if it were symbolic of the mess he was.

Campbell spoke of Gerald: 'Quite my best army friend, he was.'

Gerald had no idea of this. Until receiving the invitation he had almost forgotten the existence of Campbell, the young national serviceman. Now Gerald climbed into his fast, low car and drove off. The evening had been less tedious than he'd expected. After the wedding he would never see Campbell again, although he would receive Christmas cards from Campbell and Nina – later with the names of children added – and every year or so he would return the compliment. He would also be asked to act as godfather to one of these children; but would be unable (so very sorry) to attend the christening; would every few years remember his responsibility and, being by this time married himself, remind his wife to send a present to that Crosby godchild among other godchildren.

Others were leaving too, Charlie collecting cash from them, pocketing it, duties nearly over now, only problem back at the hotel. Could it be there? He remembered the pub garden in the early afternoon. He'd had it then. Mistake to bring it. He nearly always left it locked in his office filing cabinet. Must be slipping.

Outside cars revved. The gang were about to zoom at speed through Sussex lanes to Hove, heading off to fuck for Yorkshire. Campbell hesitated, stood up, held the back of his chair, seemed to feel it appropriate to make a comment. 'He is a clever man,' he said of Gerald. He loved clever men and did so wish he could be really clever also. He looked down at John, who sat there head in hands as if not seeing Campbell, whether deliberately or not there was no knowing. A tap on the shoulder could have roused him. Campbell hesitated. Charlie said, 'Come on, old lad,' and led Campbell out towards his car.

'I do have Nina,' Campbell said. 'Of course you do! And best of luck!' 'I say, thanks, Charlie' 'Lucky bastard,' said Charlie amiably. Nice chap, Charlie, conscientiously delivering bridegroom to car; one of nature's gentlemen, you could call Charlie. 'You have been excellent,' said Campbell, 'really excellent. I'd like to thank you.' 'All in the day's work,' said Charlie, closing the car door, thinking: oh yes, I can be the life and soul of anything standing on my head if necessary.

'Now, you two!' The car park was empty now, except for Charlie's Austin Princess and Jim's Wolsley. They put Jim in the passenger seat and leaned for a time against its bonnet. Clouds – a moon behind them somewhere. 'I blame my sister for all this,' said John, 'for selling out.' 'Who hasn't?' Charlie's cigarette glowed red, then redder as he drew on it. 'I just don't see how anybody . . .' John began, 'how anyone can find it that important . . . I mean can find someone so important as to . . .' 'Cause all this?' 'Exactly!' said John.

A light crossed the sky from south to north. Charlie said it was a shooting star and John said no, it was a sputnik, he remembered having read that it would be visible tonight.

Nina saw it. Getting up to open her window, she saw it above the cedar tree. You read about these things. You saw them on the TV screen, but this was real.

Part III

13

Under the dress, the boned bodice and the starched underskirt with three parallel rows of stiffening towards the hem of it. Under the bodice, Nina's breasts with pale nipples which became erect at Campbell's touch these days, but would not be used for their intended purpose for nine months, give or take a few days either way. Under the cotton starched underskirt, Nina's knickers and under these, her suspender belt holding up pale fifteen-denier nylon stockings with a tiny ladder above the knee, which didn't matter for once, but was, all the same, caught with a dab of nail varnish in order to stop it running further.

'Praise my soul the king of heaven,' sang Edmund, buttoning up his ruffled white silk shirt along the corridor.

Under the suspender belt, Nina's skin covering Nina's stomach and digestive organs and her reproductive organs including womb which would not be put to use for a week or so at which time it would ready itself to accept and hold protectively the embryo which would form as a result of the fusion of Campbell's sperm with an egg from one of Nina's ovaries.

Praise my soul, thought Campbell at the shaving mirror in his room at the Dolphin, at last we can do it without a thingy tonight because she's told me she has got the Dutch cap now as promised.

'To His feet thy tribute bring,' sang Edmund, buttoning his red silk breeches.

Below, in the sense of further down Nina, were her feet in white, silk, low-heeled court shoes which pinched and which she'd never wear again. She had wanted sandals, but everyone said it had to be court shoes. One way and another she'd taken people's advice and given in to their opinions, although she'd had an all-out argument with Laura in the shoe shop yesterday, Laura having said that no one absolutely no one ever got married in sandals. 'I expect some Spanish peasants do,' said Nina.

In the room surrounding her, Nanny, Laura and sometimes Julia. An expensive scent of a French make surrounded all of them. This had been an extra and incredibly thoughtful present from Nicola, personally to Nina as if saying: 'Welcome, sister-in-law.' Outside, sun on the lawn, and whenever Nanny looked out there she couldn't help but see Nina in the old black pram, couldn't get the picture out of her mind.

Edmund's shoes were shiny black with silver buckles. He was going to walk immediately behind Nina and was going to have to hold on to Vanessa's hand very firmly.

Still in transparent covering were the white roses, creamy arum lilies, waxy orange blossom, sprays of gypsophila and green-grey leaves, all intertwined and fastened together by the Chichester florist and constituting the bouquet. It sat there on the chest of drawers, disregarded for the moment, but at about 2.10 it would be picked up, have its transparent covering removed, be carried for a few hundred yards and be seen by two hundred and eighty-five – at the last count by Julia – pairs of eyes. The florist got up early – with the dawn chorus in fact. Nina slept through to nine A.M. until woken by Nanny who said, 'Upsy daisy.'

'Ransomed, healed, restored, forgiven, evermore His praises sing.' Edmund's clear treble echoed. Hymn 298 Ancient and Modern to which the bridal procession would enter the church via the south door, proceed between the pews for twenty feet or so, then turn right to face the altar before the longer walk. Edmund had been told to keep two paces behind Nina and his grandfather.

The sleeves were wrong, tight at the wrist and the material scratchy. Nina was always conscious of having delicate wrists and now realized that her squarish hands looked even-squarer with close-fitting cuffs. She should have chosen generous bishop sleeves to make her hands look smaller in comparison. 'Don't push your sleeves up like that. You'll break the stitching.' That was Laura.

The single strand of pearls at the neck: the idea had been simplicity, so simple as to surprise her audience, rather her congregation. Now the pearls looked insipid. The whole lacked impact. 'I look wishy-washy.' 'For heaven's sake, Nina.' 'Now you two!' Nanny's voice echoed from years back.

So much was happening outside, cars moving on the drive at the back and in front on the lawn around the cedar tree, friends and relations and people she knew or hadn't seen for years. Voices were in the passage outside the room and on the stairs. The whole place had been taken over.

On the slopes of a wooded hill eight or so miles away where the ridged expanse of the marquee gleamed in the sun, two large vans containing all that the caterers needed stood still unloading in the drive of Uncle Arthur's mansion. The first waitresses had arrived. And at the Dolphin, Anne Walker finished helping Joanne dress and came along the passage to help Phyllis with Louisa and Mo.

Nina wondered – as Nanny was looking out of the window and had suddenly gone very quiet – if Nanny knew that she was doing the most terrible thing in all her life. Then she began to wonder how Spanish peasants getting married in sandals felt about it all. Did they, having decided to do it, simply get on and do it with no particular thought for adverse results?

Charlie looking in the mirror, straightened his silver tie. 'By but we supped some.' He was talkative now, keeping things going. Perhaps he knew what evidence she held zipped into a compartment of her overnight suitcase. For the first few hours of the morning he'd been groaning with his head in his hands. She gave him aspirin, then Alka Seltzer, both out of another inner compartment in her suitcase. 'Well, we did it. We saw him off.'

She'd told him about the Glebe House do and what she thought of everyone who'd been there, including a wildly inaccurate paraphrase of her conversation with Polly about marriage generally. In the version she gave Charlie, it came out that she had told Polly how deliciously happy she was with a wonderful and attractive husband and how close they were.

The cream two-piece looked not as absolutely stunning as she had hoped. A little too like something the Queen might wear or perhaps that was the impression given by the turban. And had it not been a slight mistake to have everything so completely matching? 'What do you think?'

'Sensational!' said Charlie, which for years she'd loved him saying, but was now, she realized, a word used for no other purpose than to soothe, to calm, to anaesthetize.

His morning clothes were not hired, having been bought at huge expense for the wedding of Tim and Caroline Cornelius two years ago. Pale grey and fitting perfectly. 'You'll look the best man as well as being it.' The main thing was to keep behaving at this moment as she had twenty-four hours ago. Last night she woke when he came in and heard him moving around as if searching in jackets, trousers, suitcases.

Louisa's hair curled up around her well-shaped head, which might have been designed to support a wreath consisting of red and white daisies and pale green foliage – or any wreath come to that. Mo's had been a more difficult birth and her head had never quite developed into a truly head-shaped head because of forceps. She had a wide brow and her wreath kept slipping over her dead straight silky hair to hang lopsided over one eye.

Louisa was slim with narrow shoulders. She knew when a dress fitted and when it didn't and hers did. She could fix her own sash. The sashes were made with wide bows already stitched at the back, so all she had to do was fit the hooks into the eyes, which she did, easily and quickly. Meanwhile Phyllis was having difficulty. She had fastened Mo's sash, but there was no way it was going to stay in place other than by the use of two concealed safety pins.

There had been some discussion as to whether there should have been slots through which the sashes should have run, but it had been decided that this would spoil the line. Mo's screams echoed down the Dolphin corridors as Phyllis, for once ruffled and a little careless, dug the first pin too far in.

Nina, who'd chosen the style, had in fact here ignored advice or rather had failed to ask it. She had no idea of the waistlessness of most girls under nine or so and had assumed that if there were problems, the mother of each bridesmaid would solve them.

Anne said, 'Aunty Phyllis, do go and dress. I'll get this sorted.' What a nice girl she is, thought Phyllis, almost as kind and sensible as Nicola.

'Praise Him for His grace and favour to our fathers in distress,' sang Edmund, although he'd noticed that his father hardly ever seemed in distress, whereas Edmund often was.

Mike McKorkadale sat in Campbell's room with an early bottle of champagne and a transistor for the cricket scores. Under Campbell's white shirt was his hairless chest and pinkish body. Under his trousers, the new underpants he had managed in the end to buy on Thursday, muscular stomach, digestive and reproductive organs, pubic hair (red-gold like the hair on his head and under his arms), his penis, circumsized, which Nina still hadn't touched and probably never would, but which would be cherished yet again by little Margaret in nine months' time, give or take a few days either way, during Nina's first confinement.

Campbell knew it was on with the show now. His braces hung down over his trousers. His black socks were on, but not his black shoes. His room was at the back of the hotel, a small room, cheaper than some of the others, looking out over the courtyard where the kitchen porters scraped the remainder of the Trust House lunch into bins, clattering the lids, drowning the cricket scores from Mike's transistor.

The room was full of Mike's cigar smoke. He was making a day of it, drinking two glasses of champagne to every one of Campbell's.

Phyllis said to Bernard, 'Have you been along to Campbell's room?' 'No need,' said Bernard. 'But I still can't see why he chose Charlie as best man,' said Phyllis: 'Charlie should be looking after Helen.' Her hand shook as she fastened a pearl earring. She lifted her almost jaunty navy blue hat – with a tiny veil – out of its box labelled Marshall and Snelgrove. It was going over one eye. Cicely approved so it must be all right.

'Very nice, dear!' said Bernard. That was all it needed. If you were Phyllis, you would not have dreamed of questioning a compliment. You accepted it, knowing it meant very little and was no more than a ritual which Bernard, over the years, had learned to deliver at appropriate moments.

Cicely had helped her choose this outfit, which cost about three times as much as she would normally spend on clothing herself. It would have to last through other weddings, christenings, business receptions, important lunch engagements and exceptional functions to do with the St John's Ambulance Brigade. Also maybe the Great Yorkshire Show at a pinch if it were not too windy.

Cicely would be wearing dove grey with a touch of white and a silk scarf of grey and white with a narrow streak of pink in it. No one would have helped Cicely choose this. No one ever went shopping for clothes with Cicely. Some little person somewhere in some tiny boutique, which no one else in all the company about to assemble on either side of St Paul's church would ever have heard of, had created this. Cicely's always ideal clothes seemed to descend on her from another dimension. Only the exceptionally discerning eye for high couture would be able to analyse how she achieved her incredibly just-rightness.

This morning the sisters had another walk around the cathedral, but Cicely was careful not to talk about matters in hand, concentrating more on the contents of an interesting biography she was reading, the main intention being to take Phyllis's mind off things.

Several of the young men had not returned until well into daylight. Namely William Ramsey, Simon Crosby and Mike McKorkadale. They had all three got their legs over in Hove, about which there was still much joshing in Campbell's room. They had also made a good deal of noise in the early hours, especially William and Mike who shared a room above Bernard and Phyllis. Phyllis's troubled dreams had continued through the night.

Simon slept until eleven. When he woke, Jane had long since left the room, taking Emma for a walk around the shops. She was not going to speak to Simon today and would soon be ringing up her mother in Bingley with the news that she and Emma would like to come and stay indefinitely.

It could be said that everything that could go wrong between Jane and Simon by this time had gone wrong and that the marriage was past the point of no return. It would seem so. Question: what, if anything, could prevent them separating?

Charlie, having been in Campbell's room for a time, went back along the corridor to his own room for a clothes brush. He had to knock. Helen took a moment to open the door. She had that look. What had she been doing? Charlie stood waiting. 'Oh, God!' said Helen, 'you are getting in a state, aren't you?' 'No, *you* are getting in a state, my darling. What is it?' 'Nothing. Just the packing and repacking.' 'No, there's more to it than that.' 'There's nothing.' Which she had to say and which he knew she had to say because of the timing of the question. Having passed him the clothes brush, she went back to the dressing table, apparently checking on her mascara, but aware of him still standing by the door. He said, 'If there is something, Helen, say it now or not at all,' and left.

His eyes as he closed the door were unforgiving. He has destroyed my sense of self. Without him I have no identity. The only Helen I can be is the Helen that is loved by Charlie. The room, the suitcases now packed and strapped again, my hat beside me on the bed, the voices in the corridor, the traffic in the road outside . . . Everything that I had been looking forward to is spoiled. There is no future. But if there is no future, what about the past? What was that for? Helen sat. She would go on sitting.

'Fatherlike He tends and spares us, well our feeble frame He knows,' sang Edmund, still sitting where he had been told to sit on the bed with his feet straight out in front of him.

The original idea was that Nina's neck would rise out of the collar as a stalk from leaves and that the face, hair and the small coronet which secured the veil would be as the flower growing out of the calex. But the magazine picture which had captured her imagination had been taken at a distance and the proportions in reality dismayed. She should be half an inch

153

taller at least and the hem further off the ground in front. This was all because she had bought the shoes the day after the final fitting. She could blame the dressmaker who was old and inefficient. Or she could blame herself which made it worse, because if you couldn't get to look the way you wanted on your wedding day, whenever *would* you look the way you wanted? Too well my feeble frame I know. The veil is heavy and there's far too much of it. It swamps. I shan't see where I'm going. 'Absolutely super from the back,' said Laura. Veil on. That was better. Now she might be anyone, anonymous, a bride completely masked. Also her hair was hidden, which was something anyway.

Edmund reached: 'Angels in the heights adore Him.' He'd seen angels, wooden ones carved on the rood screen in the church at the rehearsal and one looked something like the bridesmaid called Louisa. 'Daddy, what is the difference between an angel and a fairy?'

Jim, standing at the mirror of the main guest room at Glebe House, brushing his straight, slightly greying hair with two brushes, told Edmund that both angels and fairies were figments of the imagination but nevertheless important as an idea, but that in general angels were probably more important as an idea than fairies.

'Ye behold Him face to face,' sang Edmund. His voice was really exceptional. Jim and Laura had once or twice discussed whether it would be a good idea for Edmund to try for Canterbury as a chorister when he was seven or so. Jim remembered the sunrise this morning, looking back and being blinded by this great red ball rising out of the land eastwards.

The bell-ringers left the village pub, their drinks having been paid for out of a sum supplied by Campbell, which had covered two pints each with some left over for the evening. Six ringers went up the steps through the lych gate as they had done the Saturday before for another wedding. They also practiced every Thursday.

Out of her cottage near the pub stepped Flossy Booth, a spinster of the parish, who was, years back, left at the altar waiting for the bridegroom and for ever after did her best to be included in wedding photographs. It was to be expected of any bride here that she would be handed a bunch of flowers by Flossy to be included in her bouquet. It was said to be unlucky not to accept this contribution.

Harold left his study. Polly was in the garden sitting in an old canvas deck chair under the cedar tree. 'Enter the father of the bride,' she said, 'and very distinguished too.' She also made a joke about this being his finest hour, but he seemed too lost in thought to notice.

On the whole by this time everyone who had time to talk was talking about anything except weddings, the purpose of them or their personal feelings about the wisdom or otherwise of matrimony. It was all too near for that. Polly had dressed early, knowing that the bathroom would be much in use for the rest of the family, and was concentrating on keeping cool so that such make-up as she had on did not run. She'd had a nice day up till now, what with the sun shining since early morning, and had walked down to the sea with Nanny and the children. She wondered once again about the south and what would lure her back to live in it. Old age and infirmity perhaps. A less gloomy but more immediate worry was the mistaken choice of black shoes. Why ever did I come, thought Polly. Like it or lump it. The expatriate belongs nowhere.

Harold sat in another canvas chair, but restlessly, looking into the distance as if he knew he should be making conversation to her and the various other relations who had begun to mill around. Eventually he got to his feet in a jerky fashion and went back into the house, busily.

Then John came out. This pleased her, since not only was she his godmother, but she saw him as more representative of the rising generation than any other member of the family. She wanted to discover how he saw life.

Nina looked out, guessing they were not speaking of present events, but of something from a world into which she might never penetrate because of today. This morning she asked John how it had gone last night and he had shrugged his shoulders, saying: 'How do you imagine that it went?' and nothing more. She would always remember this minute – looking out of the window, and the bells opening suddenly in rapid downward succession, all six of them, instead of beginning as they did on Sundays with a one-note toll. Bells celebrating. It was going to happen as you'd always realized it would happen in the end. Only you hadn't realized it would happen in exactly this way.

Under the bells Polly had to raise her voice. She found herself saying things she would not otherwise have said. 'The only reason I want to go on living, John, is to see what happens.' 'That seems a good enough reason.' He wrinkled his nose.

'You were always a kind little boy. Just an impression I got maybe, although you never spoke very much.' 'I *might* have been *very* unkind. You had no evidence to the contrary.'

She saw that he had begun to look more like his father and pictured how he would look at his father's age when inches would have gone from his height. He was the sort of young man whom years before she would have passed by as undistinguished, since in her youth she always went for the more obvious attractions of dash, good looks, achievements. But now she appreciated his smooth skin, firm chin and clear eyes, all attributes of which he was no doubt totally unaware. 'So why do *you* want to go on living, John? Silly question, but I'm curious.'

He looked up into the branches of the cedar tree. 'I suppose,' he said, 'because to stop breathing intentionally is, I'm told, as good as impossible and I wouldn't have the guts to stop it any other way.' Then he began to tell her what he had learned the night before – that those who had the money were unthinking and that those who had the power were all for war and therefore what hope was there?

'Perhaps I'm jaundiced,' Polly said, 'but I never thought there *was* much hope. So every tiny but hopeful thing that happens is a plus for me.' She wanted to encourage him. She might be getting soppy in her old age, but all she wanted for him was that he should be loved, that someone should see through his rigorous idealism to the softness underneath and cherish all of him – his thick hair, his straight forehead. Those horn-rimmed spectacles! She wanted to lean forward, remove them from his nose and say, as people did to plain girls in films:

'But John, you're beautiful!' And yet he was, no doubt, as obdurately selfish as the next man, as psychologically incompetent and inept, as unintentionally cruel and clumsy in his dealings with whatever girls he'd known. 'I don't remember what I wished you at your christening,' she said, 'but now I wish that there were more like you.' There is a piece of me in him, she thought, a scrap of gene or chromosome we hold in common. 'It *is* worth continuing.' Through the bunched branches of the cedar tree, a patch of sunlight found its way. It fell on Polly's hand as it rested on the wooden arm of the chair. The bones of the hand were clearly delineated, representing the underlying truth of structure.

'I wish that I could tell you,' she was saying, 'just how good it can be.' She inclined her head in the direction of the church. 'Not *that*,' she said, 'but this!' she raised her hands, elbows at right angles as if indicating the air around. 'So much I wouldn't have you miss. It's hardly ever what you hope will happen, but sometimes something happens which is better and surprises you.'

He kicked at a chunk of mown grass which he had left unraked when he mowed the lawn for his father yesterday. The overnight rain had moistened the piece, stuck it together. The blades of grass were already less separate. It was almost gunge and soon would be more liquid than solid.

The trumpeter: a schoolboy Julia had heard at a local school's concert and who happened to live along the village street. He was to 'take up' music, as Julia termed it, and was today to play the descant in the last verse of 'Praise My Soul'. He walked towards the church and was feeling pretty nervous (carrying his second-hand trumpet in its battered case). He was passed by cars carrying bridesmaids turning into Glebe House drive, bridesmaids being hustled out of cars, hovered over by mothers, grandmothers, photographed individually and together by grandfathers and fathers and then taken inside for last-minute visits to the loo, careful lifting of white silk skirts, last-minute refixing with kirby grips of wreaths and especial attention to Mo's sash.

Muriel wanted a photograph of Simon, Jane and Emma

together – perhaps the last one taken. So they stood, Jane with her chin up, small face, small eyes, pointed chin. No one would believe his cruelty. She gripped Emma's hand until the child twisted her wrist in pain, feeling her mother's engagement ring through white lace glove digging into her hand. Simon took his daughter's other hand and held it lightly in his own. He was, thought his mother, fearfully good-looking. Everyone would think so. No one is as hateful as Jane, thought Simon. Other women would crawl over broken glass for me – I'll show everyone.

All this took place in the drive of the house where the sun was beating down, while at the back Polly talked in the shade to the other relatives, John having left for the church where he was chief usher.

14

It is what people do, isn't it, through a glass darkly perhaps or, in Nina's case, through the dark glassily because she couldn't see where she was going and neither, presumably, had any of her female ancestors wearing this veil. Coming downstairs she gripped the banister, thinking suddenly out of the blue that she was taking a woman's first steps towards self-slaughter, then telling herself that she had taken these months before and these last steps were simply the result of earlier actions and therefore part of the same process.

As she came to the garden door, the bells stopped ringing for a moment. They were supposed to stop ringing as the bridal procession entered the church. I'm late, thought Nina, then as the bells started up again, she realized that she *was* the bridal procession.

The scene from above or as laid out on a map: the church down there with its spire pointing up towards us, to be reached by the procession by way of the kitchen garden, but to be reached by guests along the road, having parked their cars wherever possible. Many kind friends had offered driveways, although whoever offered a driveway automatically had to receive an invitation, which partly explains why the numbers waiting in church (or approaching it at this moment) so far well exceeded Harold's estimate of two hundred and fifty.

Shiny cars, people getting out of them, men in black and grey carrying top hats or in some cases wearing them, women in violet, pink, red, yellow, orange, mostly with wide skirts and stiletto heels. Picture hats, off-the-face hats, sailor hats, filling the lane and spilling on towards the church. A place *en fête*, the gentry celebrating.

Flossy Booth watched them, having known it would be a big

do. Also she recognized the photographer from the local press who would be looking out for her.

Opposite the church, the farm, a solid mellow-brick house but with its appearance somewhat spoiled by the recent addition of a Dutch barn made of corrugated iron and painted battleship grey. Any cowpats left by the herd of cows which went along this road four times a day had now dried out, making it easier for guests to pick their way. The lane ended here at the church, there being no way ahead except into the cemetery.

A breeze arose, causing ribbons on women's hats to flutter, likewise the heads of wild roses which grew along the cemetery railings. Some of these Flossy went to cut, having nail scissors in her pocket. In this respect she was well organized, although she lived in a great muddle not to say a revolting mess: twice in recent years she'd had her house cleaned out by the council, whose workmen found layers of gungey organic material not dissimilar to the overnight grass mowings of Glebe House lawn under the cedar tree. In Flossy's case, the gunge was a result of rotting potato peelings and cabbage leaves. Not that she went in for eating much in the way of fresh vegetables, her diet consisting mostly of baked beans and sliced bread upon which she survived but could hardly be said to flourish. Every wrinkle on her face was ingrained with dirt. Her hat – well, you would not have wished to pick it up or hold it close. Her hair – only strands of this showed under her felt hat and those thin wisps are best left undescribed. Her cottage had no piped water, only a tap outside; nor any heating apart from a smelly old oil stove which she only used when the temperature outside fell below freezing. In the south that is, admittedly, less frequent than the north and maybe in Yorkshire Flossy would only have survived until sixty or so, whereas now she was seventy. To the wild roses cut from the cemetery railings she added a few stalks of campion, buttercup and bugloss from among the grass growing at the foot of the churchyard wall.

She was first remarked upon by a female Forestier cousin who remembered her from Laura's wedding, and said to her husband as she linked her arm in his and as he bent his head to step up through the lych gate: 'Oh look! There's that funny old woman!'

Inside the church, ushers looking upright, military and purposive, nodding and gesturing to incoming guests. Women stepped elegantly sideways into pews to sit, then kneel with handbags placed on the oak pew seats, their husbands also bending the knee, but not necessarily kneeling, perhaps propping their elbows on hymn book shelves, lowering their heads on to folded hands. More people than you would expect nowadays were versed in how to behave in church.

A very few members, before entering their pews, paused while facing the altar in order to genuflect: the Roman Catholics, of which there were a few more on the bridegroom's side than on that of the bride. There are in general more Roman Catholics in Yorkshire than in Sussex, although since it is a larger county this is not surprising. Most of the male Catholics from Yorkshire would have gone to Ampleforth which, being famous anyway, needs no introduction here. Ampleforth at this time had just become even more famous, having produced the best A-Level results in all the country of any public school.

The only Roman Catholic with whom we need concern ourselves was Mike McKorkadale, who had no particular conviction in his faith but had, in spite of being a brusque, jolly and not especially reflective bloke, genuflected from long habit, perhaps remembering his late mother – Sheila McKorkadale, sister to Richard, Bernard and Helen.

The pews were filling and the whole church now transformed from yesterday by the addition of flowers on windowsills, on wooden stands placed in front of pillars and by the lectern and on the altar, all arranged by Celia, a childhood friend of Julia's who had studied under Constance Spry, then the most famous name in flower arranging. Celia's ambitions flower-wise were rather higher than Dorothy's would have been – thus more expensive, and Julia had to use up a tiny legacy received within the last year from the estate of her late Aunt Minnie Masterson. This just about covered the cost of the flowers, although Julia had rather hoped that she'd have a bit left over for a better dress than the one she would be seen wearing on her entry into church shortly.

The organist was Mrs Jenkins, the mother of the trumpeter. She opened with a quiet rendition (later to crescendo) of 'Sheep May Safely Graze'. She was a graduate of the Royal College of Music, teaching music at the local secondary modern school, which would in a few years time join with the local grammar school to become the local comprehensive school. Most people would think this was a god idea to start with, although very few among those present would have dreamed of sending their children to it. In fact the only person, other than the trumpeter, in state education was the oldest bridesmaid, Hermione Forestier, who was now back at Glebe House waiting by the garden door to set off with the other bridesmaids and with Nina and with Harold and with Nanny.

Coming into church now, to sit a few pews back on the bride's side: Hermione's grandfather, Colonel Lawrence Forestier, the uncle of the bride who would propose the bride's health later. In his pocket, notes on his speech. Every now and then during the service he would take out a stubby pencil and scribble an additional refinement to his speech. He was practised at this kind of thing and spoke in public frequently – at regimental dinners, annual dinners of local Rotarians and so on. He had done well at Laura's wedding, so both Harold and Julia said why not ask Lawrence again. He had the right touch and made people laugh which was the main thing really, wasn't it?

Much nodding, whispering as white service sheets were picked up in gloved hands, turned over, read, put down again, hymns noted, other names of bride and bridegroom noted – Campbell James and Nina Rose Anne.

On the bridegroom's side a few pews back, a gap, the cause of some concern and whispering of: 'Who was bringing her?' Yes who *was* supposed to have brought Helen to the church? Phyllis looked up at the angels on the rood screen and hoped that all this whispering had not been over-obvious.

The rood screen: the carved heads of angels, five of them, the central one looking out along and over the chancel as if in flight, as if, had she had a body, she could have taken off and headed, wings held back, towards the belfry end where she might have folded her wings and settled. I say 'she' but the angels were essentially androgynous. Four others flanked this central one. Two had straight hair and two had curly hair. They represented to most people, either consciously or unconsciously, both human innocence and heavenly responsibility. Their surfaces were smooth, rubbed with the carver's finest grade of sandpaper, then polished – perhaps a hundred years before this wedding, when the rood screen was introduced into what had been a plainer building.

Polly also looked up at the angels, but she thought: I see! I see! They are there to make me look heavenwards and by so doing, were I an ordinary and unthinking worshipper, I might feel more reverent. What a clever old established church it is!

Whispers, nods and sheep safely grazing all around until the tune changed to 'Jesu Joy of Man's Desiring'. What about woman's desiring – oh for heaven's sake, thought Polly: I am full of it. Her desire was directed, passingly, at almost every man who entered and sat down. In between thoughts about the nature of church worship, she was playing in her head the game of asking herself which of these godlike creatures in morning dress she would kick out of bed.

Helen sat there. Since no one had come for her, perhaps she was not there at all. I do not exist. It is better that way. I would rather not exist. Then, in her mind's eye, Helen saw the church now full, Charlie about to enter, all the women looking at him, thinking maybe he was on his own . . . She jammed her hat on, unlocked the door and ran downstairs.

By the drawing room – by the open garden door – the younger bridesmaids hopped up and down while Emma, Joanne and Hermione, the outsider, were telling each other what they were best at at school. Joanne was rather hoping she would be able to make a best friend of Hermione and mentioned that she'd been a bridesmaid twice before whereas Emma hadn't. 'How many times have you been a bridesmaid, Hermione? I say, Hermione, how many times have you been a bridesmaid did you say?' 'I can't remember,' said cool Hermione, head and shoulders taller than the rest, swinging her tightly packed posy. 'If you're head bridesmaid, you'll get the bride's bouquet thrown at you when she goes on her honeymoon. You'll get Nina's bouquet thrown at you, you will,' Joanne went on.

On the lawn, slightly raised above them, stood Nina, a shrouded awesome figure, Nanny beside her arranging the veil. Edmund gripped Vanessa's hand. He'd been gripping it ever since his mother had left them to go clacking away along the terrace and the brick path on her red high heels, clutching her huge red straw hat, dashing ahead to take her place in church.

Mo stood facing Edmund, staring at him, Edmund staring back at Mo. Mo bent down towards Vanessa and, putting down her posy, played peep-bo with her, poking her face very close into Vanessa's, which was not something Vanessa liked strange children doing to her. Edmund looked away. He knew Vanessa's face was about to crumple and that she was about to scream blue murder. 'I wish you wouldn't do that,' he said to Mo. But too late. Vanessa started screaming as expected and Nanny had to leave Nina and hurry on down the steps to the terrace and remove the child, the one with the wreath flopping over one eye who kept losing her posy, the one Nanny suspected all along might cause trouble. 'Now you!'

Louisa leaned down to make a fuss of Vanessa, so that everone would see what a capable and grown-up person she was and that she knew how to talk to little ones better than Mo did. Harold had stepped into his study for a moment. Now he came out again, went up the steps to offer Nina his arm. Nina had some difficulty finding her own arm and producing it out from under the veil, which Nanny had to straighten once again.

Vanessa was going to be a problem. She had stopped crying more or less and was holding Edmund's hand, but there was no way she could hold her posy in two hands in front of her as ordained. No, Vanessa's posy would just have to hang down in her left hand. Several people had warned Nina that little baskets would have been more practical.

Mo was fed up after being told off by Nanny, Louisa and more or less everyone present. She stuffed her nose into the red and white daisies of her posy. Emma hopped on one foot along the bricks, fed up that Joanne was talking to Hermione and being more bossy than usual. She hopped along on one red silk dancing pump which was held firm to her white socked foot with red elastic. Edmund let go of Vanessa's hand, put both hands into the pockets of his red silk breeches to hitch them up. Then wiped his nose on his white silk sleeve. 'How disgusting can you get?' said Mo. 'Quite a lot more disgusting than that as it happens,' said Edmund. 'I hate hymns and flowers,' said Mo, 'don't you?' 'Not particularly,' said Edmund, whose father had told him hate was a word only to be used after much consideration.

'Fall in, everyone!' called Harold, and the whole procession, Nanny alongside as marshal, took its first steps along the lawn, on to the path which ran between herbaceous borders, passing between delphiniums, aquilegia, banks of white daisies edged with yellow pansies. They came towards the archway which led into the old vegetable garden. Over and around this arch there curved a rambling rose. Nina should have practised yesterday in the veil, since the Brussels lace was now threatened. No one had considered the extra height of the coronet and veil might be snared on a trailing thorny strand of Dorothy Perkins. Had they foreseen this, someone could have fetched Julia's secateurs and snipped it away. But it was now too late for that. Pause at this point while Nanny disentangled, standing on tiptoe, Nina having to stand very still meanwhile.

Pause and pray for those about to enter holy matrimony, although why should you, since the state is voluntary and undertaken by all parties willingly? In church, a few seconds break in music, hush and rustle, some people no doubt praying, some remembering perhaps that they once prayed, some thinking – and Joan Ramsey was a case in point – that it was rather warm and could she slip her shoes off for a while until she had to stand and sing or would her feet swell, making it impossible to get her shoes on again?

They went into the kitchen garden on the cinder path, holly hedge to the right and to the left the brushing of asparagus fronds. These swept along the bridal skirt: bridesmaids reached out hands, ever so soft to the hands they were. It wasn't much, the Forestier asparagus patch, but Julia said it was the one vegetable she simply had to grow: but probably wouldn't any more now Carter had gone.

Not that she was thinking about Carter in connection with

asparagus as she knelt, though she may have given a passing thought to Dorothy. The bride's mother wore soft sky-blue cottonish silk – actually rayon – a never very satisfactory material, cheap but easily creased. Her hat was magnolia pink, a small round straw which Laura had helped her choose and was quite successful. She felt at home kneeling and undramatic, only relieved that everything had gone so well so far. So far so good, so thank we all our God, which hymn was not included in the service sheet, the second hymn being 'Love Divine All Loves Excelling'. Hymn one you know about. No, Julia's dress was not sky blue – it was softer than that – air blue would be closer: and with large white blobs like clouds.

Phyllis looked across and gave a little smile on catching Julia's eye. Although Julia was not looking directly at Phyllis. In fact, being fairly short-sighted, she was just looking around generally. And Phyllis's smile was rather more absent-minded than usual since her thoughts were focused on Helen's absence. How inconsiderate were those who were obsessed, how self-indulgent.

At some stage Nanny saw that Edmund needed help. She moved up to walk beside him and to encourage Vanessa. This meant that Nanny had to stick close to the holly hedge, leaving the path, making her best shoes dusty, risking her best and only good pair of nylons. Pray for Nanny with her one good pair of nylons and one good suit and a hat borrowed from her sister – a round white felt hat with navy blue hatband. Also pray that when this is all over and Nanny, as planned, goes to stay with that same sister up in Wolverhampton, Julia would remember that she'd promised Nanny she would pay her train fare, because Laura would have left by then and Laura was becoming the one who remembered such things.

A penny for your thoughts, Nanny? *My* thoughts, darling? What do my thoughts count? Well I never, fancy asking! Well, I never, did you ever see a monkey dressed in leather! Nanny, Nanny it was you who kept us well wrapped up in winter and who noticed when we first showed signs of illness and said to Mummy, get the doctor. Nina once nearly died of whooping cough. Nanny saved her by sitting up night after night with her. Precious darling, treasure, live, said Nanny, keeping the steam kettle going, and Nina lived and here we go again towards the second arch – the rose that used to ramble over this one died – and into the alleyway, nearing the source of the sound of bells. Children hardly ever die of whooping cough. At least they didn't for a while and it was during that while that Nina bore her children. What a lucky girl she was. While Mummy had Nanny, Nina had the National Health Service in its heyday at her beck and call.

Bells right across the sky above me, stretching from east to west and north to south. The less you see, the more you hear. Surely the veil had slipped somehow. The coronet had shifted – it felt further back on her head than it should have. 'All right, sweetheart?' Daddy said, and she said, 'Yes, okay I think,' and he gripped her arm, pressing it against his side. She hadn't felt that close to him since years and years ago just after Nanny left, when he used to come into the bathroom and wrap her in a bath towel, which was something she couldn't imagine him doing at all, but which he must have done or she wouldn't have remembered it. He sang – what was it – Rule Britannia, Britannia rule the waves, Britains never never never shall be marr-i-ed to a merm-a-id at the bottom of the deep blue sea.

What was it I used to sing to her? What a business it all is, this big show, this great disaster towards which I bear her, never knowing, never having had the remotest idea of what goes on in her head if anything. She'd never have made a journalist. Lazy girl, not having her mother's energy, but she seemed to have brains once. More hard-headed than her mother. Less – what is it – swampy? But underneath that veil are eyes that remind me of her grandmother, *grande dame* beldame Masterson who went under the name of Rose but was surely called that for the thorns and not the blooms.

Nearer the second arch and a breeze fluttered the veil, lifted the front of Nina's organza skirt, blew some holly leaves to cling to it. After the rehearsal it had been noted that dead leaves from the holly hedge were scattered and bunched on the cinder path. John had raked them back under the hedge but now they threatened the thin silk of the bridesmaids pumps. Holly leaves crackle as you walk on them. Holly leaves always here, thought Harold, never get rid of them properly: the next procession this way will, I dare say, be the one which carries me horizontally in oak with brass handles and no epitaph to speak of.

My white shoes crunching holly leaves. Shoes that pinch and that I'll never wear again. Who cares what happens to them? Tread firmly. Hard-going on the holly leaves and cinders: like walking up a hill. It all reminds me of . . . I don't know what. Even though Daddy holds my arm I feel I'm helping him somehow. I'm choosing, I have chosen.

Into the alleyway between the flint walls, where the older girls and Edmund looked not up ahead of them but at the ground in front of them, solemnly. It was rather like marching into school assembly when you had to be quiet and orderly. People standing in the churchyard could see the top of the veil bobbing along. At the point where the alleyway met the lane there was an iron bollard to prevent cyclists whizzing in and out, and here Nina and her father would have to separate to go either side, likewise Edmund and Vanessa, likewise Louisa and Mo, Joanne and Emma, but not Hermione who walked alone at the back.

In regard to money, everyone on the right-hand side of the church – the bridegroom's side – with a few exceptions who were children or young people who had not yet come into their own or reached their full earning power – had money or, having close relations who were rich, at any rate had access to it. The two richest people: Harry Cornelius and Richard Crosby. The difference in wealth between those two is not easy to assess since their capital was not necessarily concentrated in their respective businesses, but spread over other investments, the value of which would fluctuate and anyway, it being a Saturday, the stock market was closed. It would also depend on the strength of sterling against the dollar.

None of which is to say, however, that there was no one on the Crosby side who did not feel the pinch from time to time or that on the Forestier side there was no one who did not from time to time have a flat wallet. Lawrence, the proposer of the health, for instance, was not doing badly on a colonel's pension and a few investments.

The person with the most money on the bride's side was absent. But no one had expected Uncle Arthur to come to the church. He was at the moment being dressed by his personal servant and helped into his motorized wheelchair in preparation for his brief appearance at the reception – and complaining rather. Not that Uncle Arthur was now as rich as he once was. The sale of his mansion would cover his gigantic overdraft, but the old people's home in Bournemouth into which he was about to move was the most expensive in the area. Plus he would be paying for an extra room for his personal servant. All that he would leave, finally, to his daughter in Australia would be in the region of five thousand pounds after death duties, Uncle Arthur never having taken the prudent measure of 'making over' any part of his fortune during his lifetime in order to avoid them.

From a side aisle appeared the bridegroom. He sat in the very front pew of all, the pew with no pew in front of it, the pew almost immediately below the angels. The bridegroom: pray for him. You know that no one is unflawed and a great many people end up thinking they are married to just about the worst person in the world. A very few end up believing they are married to just about the best. It is possible in fact for one person to believe both, depending whether it is, let's say, Wednesday or Friday. So, in regard to Campbell's many flaws, let us pray that Nina will learn to live with them as long as need be for her sake. And pray that, for the same number of years, he will abide with her flaws, which should be pretty obvious by now. Your prayers depend on your belief in marriage, whether you believe it is for keeps, a useful social edifice or at its best the most successful way yet devised in which to raise a family.

Also in the front pew on the right, our very lovely best man. Dearly beloved, let us pray for him as well, whether he be lost sheep, nice guy or errant bastard, at whom a woman three pews back across the aisle stared wide-eyed and awarded him first prize for desirability, thinking, my God that is *Him*, giving Him the capital H of the deity, whom (atheist though she was) she thanked for the sight of the back of His neck where His hair curled to a well-barbered point, to the fall of His shoulders in the perfectly tailored morning coat, the stomach-churning profile as He turned as if aware of someone looking at Him. His mouth suggested – be it or be it not a cliché – humour, warmth and a soul-stirring hint of toughness, all of which, with something of a dull thud, hit Polly well below the belt.

In fact he was turning to look for Helen, but on the way he paused, stopped mid-turn, caught her eye – not Helen's eye since she was still three miles away, leaning forward anxiously in a taxi, dabbing at her mascara – but Polly's eye, Polly's two eyes, two grey Masterson eyes with straight eyebrows. I cannot help but gaze and gaze at him, though Polly. Dearly beloved, we are gathered here; and there is mystery; here is the glance that beckons and entices. Let us pursue it, let us relinquish all for it, let us crush man's innocence and at the same time worship him.

15

The bride's brother, ushering duty completed, slid into the pew already containing the bride's mother, the bride's sister, the bride's sister's husband. He faced forwards, studying the east window, which told the story of St Paul's conversion. A mustard-yellow beam of shocking intensity poured down on to a road of Prussian blue where Paul knelt stricken, hands to eyes. Atrocious, and an insult to St Paul moreover. After all, no fool, St Paul, who had worked out how to make the Christian message marketable. And, thinking of the masses being conned, what about this lot here, sitting in conspiratorial silence, contributing passively to the perpetration of an act as false as any that there ever was, a masquerade as empty as the silly simple songs which would be sung.

Don't pray for John. He would reject your prayers while at the same time allowing you freedom to pray. You might say to John: 'I prayed that you would recover from illness. Let us call it illness X and let us say that you recovered.' But John would say there was no proof that he would not have recovered anyway. He would add that it could equally well be said that because he had eaten, for example, lettuce, he'd been cured by that.

John, it should be mentioned, was about the poorest in terms of immediate cash flow availability of all present. Moreover he remembered as he knelt briefly (having decided that since it was all a façade anyway, there was no point in making the gesture of not kneeling and that most people wouldn't even notice how he comported himself) that he had borrowed two pounds off Jim the night before to pay for a last round and had no cash with which to pay him back.

More music for expectant congregations: having given them

'Jesu Joy of Man's Desiring' as well as 'Sheep May Safely', Mrs Jenkins now extemporized, intertwining snatches of both tunes. Above the organ, at eye level, a mirror, through which she could see to the far end – to the door of entry, the south door. The signal would be the appearance of the verger and the lifting of the cross. At this point Mrs Jenkins was to play the first phrase of the hymn.

The wind rose countrywide at that point of the afternoon – at Lords, Headingley and Wimbledon, where, in the shelter of the centre court, it caused no problems. But Nina's homeland was on the coastal plain and her procession met the wind face on. The veil blew back to cling against her face, sticking to her pancake make-up.

Waiting for her just inside the lych gate, the press cameraman. He'd worked with her for the few months she had been on the paper. Useless she'd been and when he'd spotted her the other day in a street in Chichester she had passed him nose in air, stuck-up bitch deserving to be shown at her worst, but he had his professional pride, which was more than she did. Girls who couldn't make it in a career copped out and married rich blokes. He'd grabbed her once on a reporting job, couldn't even force her lips apart to kiss her properly, she'd given him some story of wanting to get to know him better first.

Flossy's bunch of flowers: to the wild roses, campions, buttercups and bugloss, she had added cow parsley which gave off powdery pollen. This blew in the wind which was shaking the elms between the churchyard and the cemetery. The rooks were restless, circling above. Nina would remember those familiar cawings and the sound of the wind rustling the leaves and how she couldn't look up as she usually did to the tree tops. Once in a high wind a branch had been blown down and carried on to the road outside the church, landing just here where she was now treading.

Around the lych gate, scattered small groups of villagers, mothers and children, providing a chorus of: 'Ah, look! They're coming!', the little girls in white with red silk sashes and a little boy leading them, clutching his tiny sister's hand. 'What a duck! What an angel!' although on the whole I think they were only curious and somewhat critical, these women watching, checking on general effect of colour scheme and texture of material.

Flossy positioned herself inside the lych gate near a tombstone. The bunch of flowers was wrapped in newspaper, that same newspaper for which Nina had worked and for which the photographer still worked.

The procession reached the lych gate. Two stone steps up here, so a general pause while the bride lifted the full skirt and placed one white shoe on the first step, then the second, bending her head under the heavy veil. Nearer the church somewhere was the girl who had taken over from the girl who had taken over from Nina. She would report that it was one of the prettiest weddings in the locality so far this year. This girl would persist in the work which Nina had found tedious, unrewarding and badly paid, and go on to be a feature columnist on the woman's page of a national newspaper, specializing in tips on housekeeping, some of which Nina would find useful.

'Take them, Nina.' Nina, having negotiated both steps, now stood upright. Out popped Flossy from behind the nearest tombstone. Let fall the dress, Nina, and stretch your hand out from under your veil and take this bunch wrapped in the newspaper which should remind you of what you once wanted to be. 'Don't drop them, Nina!' said Flossy. Which was strange because she seldom spoke and Nina had never heard her voice before. 'Don't drop them, Nina,' Flossy said again as the camera clicked and clicked again. 'Hey, Nina!' called the photographer as Nina went on facing Flossy and not the boy who had once taken her aback by kissing her suddenly and without any preliminary conversation. And actually he was good-looking and wasn't to know that, had he taken things more gradually, he would have got much further with her. Who knows, he could have had his way with her and where would we be now? Not, it is arguable, where we are now, in church waiting to hear the change of tune – some of us determined to resist the urge to turn our heads towards the door of entry.

As she took the flowers, the heavy gold hand of the clock on the church tower jerked from 2.30 to 2.31 and the bells still poured into the heights. What is bad luck in marriage anyway?

Does it mean that the marriage will not last beyond the first, second, the tenth or even the twentieth year? Or is it that it will be unfruitful, or is it that it will be over-fruitful?

It could be that she took the flowers because any movement to thrust them away might further have dislodged the veil. She would say one day that she took the flowers because she took the flowers because she took the flowers. And add, 'This photograph: that's me there and that's Flossy. That is Daddy. He is dead now. Mummy's still alive and awfully well, amazing really for her age. I have forgiven her, I think.'

Or perhaps she took the flowers because, although arguably one of the most egocentric people in the world, she did care about not offending people. Because offended people, like the cameraman for instance, keep turning up and staring at you in an offended fashion. Crying: 'Stand for a tick, Nina,' in a taunting tone. Who wants to make more enemies in life than absolutely necessary?

Nina took the bunch of flowers, removing them from the newspaper and shoving them into the expensive sheathed bouquet made early that morning at the expensive florist's shop in Chichester. Then, putting her right arm back within her father's arm, she moved on, she and Harold, followed by the train of children, Flossy flanking one side of them now, Nanny still the other, young photographer in front of them, walking backwards, clicking the camera all the way.

Outside the porch: 'Hey, Nina!' he called again. She turned and a gust of wind blew the veil. Here's the picture: the veil, in spite of its weight lifted by the upward gust, a blur like a sheet flapping on a washing line, bellying up.

They must be coming any minute now, thought everyone inside the church where a bird was swooping in among the rafters. It excreted in the centre aisle, splat on the floor a few inches from the third pew back on the bridegroom's side, at the edge of which stood Richard Crosby, who was pondering a conversation he had had with Harry Cornelius that very morning concerning the possibility of an imminent general election. Always a possibility of Labour getting in – always a dodgy time in high finance – could presage a rise in income tax: Richard planned an appointment with his chief accountant.

Not that Richard Crosby need concern us much. He would die soon. Simon would take over as chairman of Timber Holdings and steer the company into and through the 1960s, through the years of Labour government which, in spite of Richard's prognostications, would be prosperous years for those who build. Simon would need to earn an especially large income – partly to pass on to his divorced wife, Jane. Also Simon himself would remarry an even more ambitious and demanding girl than Jane, a girl who would expect a high-flying life style, would have several children, want to buy them show jumping ponies and take for granted holidays in places like Sardinia and Mustique.

Come to think of it there were at least four people in the congregation who would be dead within a year: Richard of a heart attack at his home in Northallerton; Lawrence Forestier the health proposer, of the same cause at a cricket match in Hampshire; Julia's friend Celia, who did the flowers instead of Dorothy, of cancer in a London hospital. Also Flossy, now outside in the churchyard with her hands in her pockets (having got rid of her flowers), in a geriatric ward in hospital in Chichester, where she would be taken, having been found huddled and more or less unconscious in what passed for her bed. And here she is in the album of wedding photographs, snapped from the back as she moved quickly between the photographer and Nina, Nanny fiddling to secure the veil, about to add a kirby grip, holding the grip to her mouth to open it before inserting.

In the hospital Flossy would only survive a few days. The official cause of death: pneumonia; but since she would have been given a bath for the first time in God knows how many years, a much more likely explanation for her death is shock. Her house, having been cleaned out for the enth time by the council, would then be sold for a few hundred pounds to a small local builder who would modernize it and resell it for more than double the purchase price. From such small enterprise evolved Crosby Timber Holdings.

The bird again. Phyllis noticed it. Birds in buildings signified for Phyllis, death. One came into the room at Pound Close on the day her mother died. A starling. Phyllis, a bird lover but

175

one who only loved them in the open air. Phyllis, always having Nicola in mind and Nicola's embryo, couldn't help but hope that if this bird presaged the death of someone close to her it would be that of Aunt Winifred.

It was: a few minutes previously in her sleep in Harrogate, aged ninety-one. Funeral private, no flowers, donations to the Distressed Gentlefolks Association, please. The news would come through when they got back to the hotel that evening. Phyllis would have to begin planning the best day for the funeral. She would always remember how Aunt Winifred died on the day that Campbell married.

The bells stopped ringing. The wind dropped. So did Nina's veil. She took her Daddy's arm again to prepare for entry. No one lives for ever, she remembers thinking. In there she could hear the organ stop playing, then hear it start up again. The cue. Right now, Nina, ready? Okay? That's right. Step inside. Once only. Good performance, eh? You know what you have to do. The lines are written. Easy peasy. Not a crime you are committing, God rest your soul.

You married him because he stood there waiting at the altar. You married him because you had arrived here through the garden on your father's arm. You married him because there were so many people waiting. You married him because you wore the dress and veil and carried flowers. You married him because last night you saw a sputnik and decided this was real, because of all the presents and the house you had, the honeymoon you were about to have; because you'd asked for wedding presents and because he'd come into the office, taken you to dinnner, slept with you and sex was okay really and a lot of fun sometimes. You came into the church.

But you would tell your daughters: THINK before you do this thing. Choose – don't be chosen; and they would look at you and wander off into the world and come back saying: where did thinking get us, Mother? But surely thinking's better than not thinking, you would say, and anyway life's far from perfect, dears, the passing on of wisdom being something people do as they get older.

* * *

First through the arched door came the polished silver-plated cross lifted to the perpendicular by the verger. Second passing through the porch and under the arched door, the choirboys who did this every Sunday in their surplices worn over robes, some of these on the short side revealing dark grey worsted school trousers and thick woollen socks and black shoes.

Military service had given the verger a straight back. He held the cross as he held his rifle in the army when given the order to present arms. His favourite processional hymn was not 'Praise My Soul the King of Heaven' but 'Onward Christian Soldiers'. The use of martial music for religious purposes worried him not at all. And maybe within limits he was justified. For if there is to be a high degree of panoply, a ring of grandeur in proceedings, then let's have it good and loud so that it sticks, the meaning of it all, goes deep.

Rustles as two hundred and eighty people rose. A few missing from the last time we counted heads. A few hadn't made it. The Humphrey Mastersons' car broke down on the coast road from Portsmouth and they spent Saturday afternoon waiting for the AA man who had been called to numerous breakdowns, this being the finest Saturday of the summer so far.

One chord, then a few notes to remind them of the tune and then they sang, pretty well all two hundred and eighty of them, some full of confidence, some careful, doubtful of their skill to keep in tune. But those who knew the hymn let rip and here she came, the bride, this person coming veiled to join this other person, and within not many minutes they would be, the two of them, required and charged at the dreadful Day of Judgement when the secrets of all hearts shall be disclosed, etc . . .

Yesterday at the rehearsal all these pews of varnished oak were empty. The ecclesiastical space was grey, hollow. Yesterday the footsteps of the bridal party echoed to the rafters, but today! The smaller children looked around in wonder at the difference. Was this the same place? The colours, multitudes of them, the smell of flowers and scent which had been dabbed on wrists, hollows of necks, behind ears, sprinkled on lace handkerchiefs, now vaporizing in the warmth engendered by these rows and rows and rows of . . . Goodness – it was awesome! Edmund missed singing the first half of the first verse with the shock of it. But Louisa loved every minute of it, singing every word and note, wishing she could be always and for ever walking into church singing and with people watching her.

The bridegroom and the best man, having stood, now moved towards the chancel steps – slightly right of centre in order to leave room for the bride when she arrived. Another angle on the best man's profile was revealed. Beams from the clerestory fell upon one ear, highlit the bone behind it, the soft skin on the neck, the white shirt collar – no more than a centimetre of it – above the morning jacket. His cheek: in spite of being blonde, there was a shadow here. She thought of him shaving in the morning, towel around bare shoulders. Praise Him praise Him, first verse ending.

She is coming, Campbell thought. This is it.

Praise Him praise Him, here we go, thought Charlie, looking down the aisle for Helen. Still no sign of her. That woman gazing at him still. What eyes! Who was she?

Move slowly, take it slowly. On the bride's skirt, buttercup petals slipping down, also pollen from the cow parsley, a trail of these confetti-like on the stone flags. Mo, head down, also noticed as they neared the chancel steps a splodge of bird poo if she was not mistaken. Praise Him Praise Him, the vicar waited on the chancel steps, which the verger was the first to reach, moving right to place the cross in the waiting slot. Choirboys filed through to the choir stalls right and left. The vicar centred himself and the bird shat at his feet then flew up to the rood screen and settled on the middle angel's head.

Procession halted, remaining standing in order. Praise Him praise Him. Loudest singer (woman), Julia. Loudest singer (man), George Ramsey. Praise Him praise Him. That up there is called a rood screen, Edmund thought, or is it called a rude screen? He was otherwise amazingly good at spelling for his age. Mo standing behind him wished she was a boy with a nice round head and thick smooth dark hair. If they had let me be a page, she was thinking, I could have worn red breeches and black shoes with a silver buckle. The bird flew off again and settled on the crusader in which Campbell had been so interested the day before.

'Well our feeble frame He knows,' sang Polly. Oh that He should know my frame which yearns but is not feeble. No, it's man who is so feeble, surely. Man is such a nervous fawn inside. He is a bambi to be coaxed. I'll have to hold my hand out gently, draw him, tempt him softly.

The most nervous person: the boy about to lift his trumpet and join in with the obligato where it says that angels in the heights adore Him and we all behold Him face to face. The sound of brass sent shivers down the spine of nearly everyone. Surely no one is immune to that. The sun fell on the gold wristwatch of the best man and the hairs on the backs of his fingers. Bow before Him? I would crawl over red-hot coals towards him.

Arguably the most miserable person in church cheered up: Jane Crosby who, even though brimful of hatred for the man she had married nine years ago, did consider for a moment that her wedding dress had been far prettier and a much better fit than Nina's. And that veil was a disaster.

I don't want this to end, thought Mrs Jenkins. My boy my boy plays like an angel. This is life and breath to me. Thank God for music in my life. The oldest person present was Mrs Jenkins's mother who happened to be staying the weekend and who was asked along – a last-minute thought of Julia's at ten o'clock that morning, message delivered by Nanny when she took the children for their walk. Add one to the congregation.

Nanny, squeezing in next to John, looked up and saw the bird and thought: look, a bird. Likewise, John for the first time noticed the bird and thought of Nanny saying, 'Look, a bird.' He was singing, knowing the hymn only too well, having been in the choir at school where chapel attendance was compulsory. All against the grain it was, but he could sing pretty well. You should be able to guess what he was thinking, but he sang.

If music be the food of love, thought Polly, give me excess of it but let me keep my appetite. The most committed person, in the sense of true unquestioning belief: the bride's mother. The fattest person: Harry Cornelius. Edmund looked up at the middle angel and the bird. A place resounding with raised voices and a trumpet soaring over them: can the fabric of a building be untouched by what goes on in it? Can't these stones retain some trace? In the silence at the end of this, is nothing left?

Door closed. Nothing to be heard from outside. Helen came up the churchyard, panting. She leaned against a flat box-shaped tombstone. The young photographer knelt on the grass and took a picture, Helen fanning herself with her cream silk turban and looking down at her shoes. The young photographer was to go on to make quite a name for himself, working for a London press agency, having exhibitions and eventually publishing a book of photographs. 'Wedding Guest' was the title picture.

Harold, having told the vicar that he gave this woman to be married to this man, went to sit down. Julia moved up to make room for him, Laura shifted to make room for Julia. By which time both Campbell and Nina had agreed to keep each other in sickness and in health, etc. Rather had responded with 'I will' when asked if they would do these things. Shortly after this, Charlie passed the ring to Campbell and Campbell put it on Nina's finger. A wide gold ring and well designed, inscribed with date and both sets of initials. Nina felt she should say thank you somehow. If it was a gift, that is. Well was it? Should she think of it as a gift or not?

My son, thought Phyllis, remembering the feeling of sickness when she came round from the chloroform and was handed this red-faced, red-haired, squawking bundle of sensations which they said was her son. 'Your son,' said the midwife. 'This is your son.' It took Phyllis days to be pleased with him.

Bride and bridegroom kneeling, the vicar putting his hands over their two hands and praying that those whom God had joined, man should never put asunder. Here several couples who were particularly in tune or getting on pretty well these days, give or take, clasped hands. Among these were Jim and Laura. Here the bird flew out of the south door and was seen by Helen, about to move towards the church. Here Mo began to want to wee. Here Nina realized that she hadn't spread the dress out in front of her but had been kneeling on it so it would be creased when she stood up again. That bird was a sparrow,

Phyllis decided, having seen its flight. Here Joan Ramsey wondered if she could extract a green pill from her bag and get it into her mouth without George noticing because he always said if an occasion made her ill she should stay away from it.

Outside the wind gusted and died down again. Further away people went on doing what they usually did on Saturdays. In the marquee rows of glasses were being laid out. At Headingley, Illingworth was bowled for 29 and at Lords Trueman bowled Walcott for 14 – caught by Bailey. At Wimbledon Cooper beat Fraser in the men's singles and in Harrogate, Nicola sat on the chaise longue in the garden, hearing about these events on the transistor. Toots was in the playpen piling beakers in a tower and Peter was cutting the privet hedge, clip clip.

Bride and bridegroom still kneeling, their heads, shoulders, backs at the same angle, parallel, matching, both pairs of hands folded. Inasmuch as people can be seen in pairs, they were one at this moment, whether suited or unsuited. Man and woman, Polly thought, in essence, into Eden out of Eden. There is no life without duality. Two cells make one. This new cell sets out from the beginning always in search of another. What is missing throughout is the opposite. The heavy door creaked open, closed again. Someone on tiptoe entering. Helen – to sit in a pew far back.

'Love Divine All Love Excelling' sang the congregation. Helen always moved by music. Joy of Heaven to earth come down. Ancient and Modern 520. Have I lost him? Trust is all he wants. I shall resolve to music and with trust I'll keep him. Helen actually the best singer with a fine and rich soprano. Jesu, thou art all compassion, pure unbounded love . . . yes yes. Please visit me with thy salvation and I promise I will trust, believe in him.

In the *Penguin Book of Law* (chapter on divorce) it says that on the break-up of the marriage the wife can claim a share of all the family assets (house included) even if they are in the husband's sole name. Nina signed the register and emerged. And after all that had been sung already, there was 'Oh Jesus I Have Promised'. And here she was with veil thrown back, ready to look down over all the congregation, a married woman, legally because our church is the established church. Nina, ready for the best bit which was walking down the aisle to Mendelssohn, and would now walk entitled to a great deal when you come to think about it. She would not starve, she would not freeze. She might not have exactly what she wanted, but she would have the power to ask for it. She would be Mrs Campbell Crosby and her credit would be good. Whatever she had done up to this point mattered not at all. The words she had spoken earlier, those concerning love, obeying and the rest of it, mattered only in a moral sense and, unless she became insane, became excessively promiscuous or walked out she would be immovable from 33 Firs Avenue.

Towards the door, his arm in mine, door open, people smiling, waiting, photographs – we'll frame them – they will fade a little but we'll still be there, Campbell laughing, throwing back his head, showing his uneven teeth, shiny face, all energy and vigour, young and with broad shoulders that will stoop in time.

Yes, Nina, now you can be as you will. You can be lazy, nagging, sluttish. Legally you are not bound to cook, clean, wash his socks or entertain his friends. Of course he might make claims against you, but success of claims depends on precedents and if you can afford a clever lawyer . . .

Your mother, head on one side, holding hat. Phyllis now to be known by you as Mum, her hat more firmly fixed. Father, sagging trousers, coat too long for him, such a little man he was, however did he get even halfway up Everest? Bernard, stout and solid just before retirement and decline. But there they are, the four of them, whatever did they let it happen for? It happens, Nina, these things happen. You'll stop asking in good time and learn. Oh Jesus, you had promised, hadn't you?

You will also learn to take the blame for lost socks, lights left on, unironed shirts, less than pristine sheets, bills unpaid, children crying in the night or during dinner parties, broken windows, large electricity bills, telephone bills, for having friends he doesn't like, for taking him to films he doesn't like, for spending too much time with the neighbours at Firs Avenue, for going off sex during post-natal periods. For the much blame, you will not forgive him.

Bells ringing, guests crowding round, organ playing back in the church, bridesmaids bounding, cars waiting, last dry petals dropping from the buttercups, last drop of pollen from the cow parsley, one pink campion petal, one blue bugloss petal.

What did you want? I wanted not to be what I had been. I wanted change. I wanted time. I wanted what I seemed to need until I found it wasn't necessary.

Dark days to come, despondency. Your job will be down there in the messy ends of life, without which there is nothing learned. Therefore grow through adversity. You did this willingly. Okay, I did this willingly. Throw back the veil. Walk down the aisle for the grand finale. This is your beginning. We shall not pray for you.

A holly leaf stuck in my shoe. Must have been there all the time. I was coming through the garden on my father's arm. No, that was earlier.

Now I go down the path between the tombstones, people's voices, car door open, skirt lifted, someone helps me and I lean forward like the Queen to wave, lean back, probably looked happy and excited, probably was, just another day it was like all days are, car moving, who was driving it? No matter, all was done for me and me done for.

A hand in mind. Whose hand? So familiar, so strange. I saw him the other day. He does look old, I thought. No doubt he thought the same of me. He does look bent, I thought. Did I do that to him?

16

At the far end of the marquee, part of the canvas wall had been unhooked and removed to make a wider exit and let in more air. Beyond this opening was the edge of the top lawn. Below the top lawn came a slope down to a lower lawn. On this slope the bridesmaids took to rolling, one after the other, except for Louisa and Emma who did not wish to get grass stains on their dresses.

The bride's uncle, Col. Lawrence Forestier MC, said he remembered the bride in shorts and wellingtons with her front teeth missing. He mentioned that he had noticed that she had much improved since then. Scattered laughter. Moreover he understood that she could spell, which very few people could these days. Murmurs of approval. Hear! Hear! And so on. Once a thing has happened it always seems as if it never could have been otherwise.

The colonel stood in front of the white-clothed table which stretched along one side of the marquee. The wind blew against this side, so that the slope whereon the bridesmaids rolled was on the sheltered side. To the right of the colonel, the recently married couple, both leaning slightly against the edge of the table, on which their hands also rested, hands nearly touching, Campbell with one finger stroking the top of Nina's hand. Each in their spare hand held a glass of champagne.

The bride's uncle told the assembled company of this vivid memory he had of the bride in wellingtons and yes of course she had improved considerably since then, although he would not say the same for the world around him. Light laughter, mostly from those of his own generation because nearly all of them thought the world a worse place than it was when they were young. How inane can you get, thought the bride's brother.

Between the bride's uncle and the couple, the wedding cake, three-tiered, and beside it a long-handled knife supplied by the caterers. The bride would hold the knife, the bridegroom would place his hand over hers and . . . She was going to the beach, her uncle said, and was warned by her parents that a storm was rising. 'Oh is it?' said young Nina. 'Yes, be careful,' said her parents and young Nina said, 'Well, I am going anyway.' More light laughter here, though no one quite knew why they laughed.

Further to the couple's right, the best man. Once a thing has happened, once a glance has been exchanged . . . No! You can stop there. You can, if you choose, go no further. The bride's first-cousin-once-removed had by now realized who he was. She had seen him kiss Helen outside the church. So it was him was it? It would be, wouldn't it. Just my luck. My feelings about the whole thing have become a little mixed. I suspect however that there is no stopping me. There are advantages. With a man already straying, less guilt on my part as well as less on his, I hope. Where is Helen?

By the time the bridal couple would be ready to cut the cake, the major domo would have whipped away the top two tiers. The top tier of all would be handed to the second-in-command of the catering team who would wrap it in greaseproof paper, seal it in a tin (extra charge for tin) and place it in a cardboard box in which it would be transported (along with the southern batch of wedding presents) for use at the christening of the first child. That was the plan.

Not far away near the front of the crowd which faced the table stood the wife of the best man. Rather on her own she stood, with her chin up and her glass held delicately by the stem, just as she'd imagined when trying on her outfit: Helen looking into the distance as if full of important thoughts and as if she did not mind standing on her own. I must not change my mind, she was thinking. I must not lose the inspiration that I had in church. I know this to be the only way to keep him loving me, if it is not too late. Outside the church I went to kiss him and he said, 'Are you all right?' and I said, 'Yes I'm absolutely fine. I love you.' Upon which he kissed me and said, 'Good.'

The bride's uncle said a few words about the bride having joined the press corps and how impressive that was, the woman being the weaker vessel and so on . . . 'Ahem ahem.' Some laughter here. Bride's brother crossed his eyes and looked at roof of tent.

The bridegroom was tapping his foot. What an irritating habit this was! His mother raised her eyes to the canvas roof. Nearly all his life she'd tried to break him of this habit. All part of his suppressed energy but inexcusable and very very irritating, always doing it he was, even when sitting down and watching television, moving one foot up and down. 'Cam, please don't do that,' she'd told him endlessly. It was now up to Nina.

'Now yet again – today our bride,' her uncle went on, raising his voice over the buffeting of wind on canvas, 'might say, I'm going anyway.' For she was off now, heading out like any young and brave explorer to a strange and foreign hinterland. Pause for laughter. Someone cleared their throat. One person laughed and the colonel added that this place was one which many present would consider to be home and beautiful.

And it is and it can be especially so on a spring day as the light is growing and you can drive or ride or walk along a ridge, birds circling, and it can be on a summer evening in a suburb as the pubs close and the day's still with you, and it can be on an autumn morning as you drive in sharp air on an open road to Beverley. Climb down from Heptonstall and find the stream beneath the woods. Approach York via the surrounding plain and see the sun catching the towers of the Minster from miles away.

'Hear hear,' said nearly half the audience. The best man stood to the right between the table and the crowd. He had made his own speech proposing the health of the bridesmaids, managing to remember all their names. Now his eyes rested as often as he dare let them on the bride's cousin once removed, who was standing well back in the crowd but isolated somewhat and clearly visible. The more he looked at her the more she crossed her fingers that he would go on looking. Once you know a thing might happen and you want that thing to happen you will go all out to make it happen.

'And so my niece is about to venture forth into this strange and foreign land and on the evidence of recent proceedings, we can take it that one of the natives in particular has behaved, let us say, in a warm fashion towards her.' Titters, ripples of them. Wind in the marquee, creeping through the open side, making the edge of the tablecloth flutter. The cake was as high as Nina's head, including the veil and coronet.

During recent hostilities – by which, for the information of younger readers, Uncle Lawrence meant the Second World War – our speaker spent some time in Yorkshire. It was summer, not that one could call it summer . . . Loud cries of 'Shame!' And, as was inevitable, he was called upon to become involved in that sporting preoccupation at which people up there seemed to feel that they had some God-given excellence. Which of course was not the case. More cries of 'Shame!' Helen noticed Charlie looking in her direction, but not at her, rather he was looking at the space above her head or possibly behind her. She began to turn, but checked herself. I have resolved, she told herself. Phyllis could see Helen and noticed that Helen's recently filled glass of champagne was tipped sideways. champagne was dripping on the coconut matting which was the floor of the marquee. She also noticed that Campbell's foot-tapping had become leg-twitching and that this was rocking the table.

Uncle Lawrence thought the place at which he was stationed was called either Cleckheaton or Heckmondwike or could it have been Osmondthorpe? And while he was quite sure that many of the assembled company were well able to tell the difference . . .

Jane Crosby wasn't listening. She was possibly the only person present to whom these feeble jokes meant nothing whatsoever. She was one of those many Yorkshire people who don't even know or care much whether or not the north is looked down on by southern people. For people like Jane, where they live is the whole world to them, in which the pain or otherwise of living looms larger at all times than where this painful or otherwise life takes place. And some of it is beautiful and where it is not beautiful, it is as often as not on account of history and the ancestors of the Crosbys who built and spoiled. Yes, certainly for greed, but also to the cost of others, among these the ancestors of Jane. The Bosomworths came from an area much less beautiful than most and from a line who had survived with difficulty. So we should not blame the Mrs Bosomworths of this world for encouraging their daughters to pursue the rich young Simon Crosbys of this world and screw them for every last pound they can get out of them. They have good reason and should go on doing so. There remain new generations of Bosomworths living at survival level under leaky roofs in houses and in tower blocks built by Simon in the booming sixties.

Joanne Walker, having had enough of rolling down the slope, came quietly into the marquee, skipped over to her grand-mother and took her hand. We don't know much about Joanne, but it would seem she was a nice, kind child. Joan felt comforted. Everything today had been such a haze. The pill she had taken after coming out of church should have been taken earlier. All she could do now was try deep breathing.

The place where Uncle Lawrence had been stationed – whatever its name – it was here that he was called upon to form, from among those under his command, a team to play the home side. While the story went on, Polly imagined herself at home, seeing the river below and the road beside it, watching for the car which would be silvery-grey. She'd seen him getting into it outside the church. She'd see it coming. It would go behind the clump of ashes. How soon would he come to Swaledale?

The bowler on the opposing side to Uncle Lawrence may well have been related to one F. S. Trueman. Cheers, applause. Not a fine day. The match began and to the west clouds thickened.

The car would reappear from behind the ash trees. I am seeing it, thought Polly. She would be waiting in that way one waits for lovers, hoping; also dreading that there will be in his eyes a lesser passion than expected. I must stop dreaming, but it's such a little thing to ask of anyone, as well as all the world to ask.

George Ramsey, before the speeches started, had been having an absorbing conversation with John about Yorkshire dialect or rather dialects, for as he had pointed out, they are multifarious. The study of dialect was his hobby. He stood, legs slightly apart, as firmly as if planted in a corner of the marquee.

Mo had also had enough of rolling down the slope and thought she saw a birds' nest deep inside the evergreen hedge which formed the boundary of the lower lawn. Trying to climb inside, she lost her wreath. By now her sash was slung from her shoulders across her chest like a soldier's sword belt, which was how she had wished it could have been all afternoon.

Campbell's leg twitching became hip-rocking. Nina hardly noticed it. She looked out across the crowd, still making the most of being the centre of attention because it wouldn't last much longer. Already her smile felt somewhat forced. All these people who had come to see her married – could she *really* be the centre of their attention? The centre of attention for each person is themselves. Therefore, she decided, I am not the focus, in which case what's the point of standing here dressed up and feeling so important?

Was it the wind which caused the canvas roof up there to ripple and the ribbons on hats to dance and the air itself to become as if full of darting black flies? Focus on something, Joan told herself. Focus on an object which is static. If that moves, then all is lost.

Who was he looking at? Helen again resisted the urge to turn around. To trust must be to ignore all evidence. I swore in church that I would take all knowledge as it came my way and hold it close, drink it in as if it were champagne. She raised her glass and found it empty.

Charlie was feeling vulnerable. We have seen him feeling vulnerable before. But those who claim vulnerability also have unreflective moments when they behave with amazing confidence, moments which are completely forgotten when they are comtemplating once again their vulnerability.

But she was Helen and he loved her and he always needed her approval. He moved towards the table, put his weight against it, reaching for a bottle from which to fill Helen's glass. Charlie's weight against the table kept it, for a time, from rocking. He wanted to help Helen. Did he, we must ask ourselves, want to help Helen so that she would pat him on the head and wave him off, even if the journey were towards another woman?

In regard to other women, there were plenty of better-looking younger women of the type he fancied present. From what you know of Charlie in regard to Polly so far, would you say that he was interested, curious, planning how to approach her, trying to get a look at her legs, speculating about the body under the clothes, still wondering who she was? Don't forget that Helen hadn't told him what Polly looked like when describing (inaccurately) their conversation at Glebe House the night before.

Uncle Lawrence's speech continued. We'll miss the bits about a partial umpire who refused the visitors a claim against the failing light. He now referred back to the story with which he had started, the one about Nina setting off in wellingtons with shrimping net and saying she was going anyway.

Charlie watching Helen, seeing her mascara running, hat askew, eyes full of that reproachful look, Charlie lifting bottle, outside grass slope empty now, all bridesmaids having had enough of rolling, Hermione and Louisa swinging Vanessa between them, holding one arm and one leg each, Emma saying that Vanessa would be sick and that would serve them right. Mo and Edmund by the hedge, Mo telling Edmund that while looking for the birds' next she'd seen through the hedge into another garden which was absolutely gynormous and like the jungle in Tarzan films on TV. There was this gate she'd seen as well which could lead into it. Would he like to go exploring? Edmund, imitating Jim's voice, saying, 'Rather!'

Joan Ramsey focused on the cake, a distant white tower with crenellated walls. Uncle Lawrence wished Nina on her journey power, health, hapiness, prosperity. Very nearly finished now. We shan't hear any more of Uncle Lawrence. Sighs of relief all round no doubt. As mentioned earlier, he would soon die, living only long enough to make one more speech, the next one being on his war experience, to the Chamber of Commerce in Winchester where he lived.

'She is going anyway. Good luck to her!' So was the cake,

the top tier designated for the first christening. 'Ladies and gentlemen, the bride!' said Uncle Lawrence. The major demo echoed: 'Ladies and gentlemen, please raise your glasses to the bride.' 'The bride!' said everyone.

The person with the quickest reactions on this occasion: Jim who leaped forward, caught half the middle tier as if diving for a close-to-wicket catch, having played no cricket since the summer before he caught poliomyelitis at the age of sixteen. The rest of this tier fell at his feet, broken lumps of rich dark impacted fruit, icing and marzipan on the matting.

The most looked-at person: Helen, pushing through the crowd, dashing to the spot, kneeling down and beginning to shovel the smashed top tier into a pile, not even taking off her gloves to do this. Her turban fell to the ground and was retrieved by the major domo who helped her to her feet, handed her the hat, then reached for a tray and a pair of silver scoops.

Joan wasn't sure if it had happened or not. Black flecks enveloped her, hurtling, diving, obscuring more than half her vision. She clutched Joanne's hand and groped her way towards the opening and would have fallen and rolled like any bridesmaid down to the lower lawn, had it not been for Joanne who led her grandmother carefully, steering clear of guy ropes until she found an ornamental tree below the terrace of the mansion, under which Joan collapsed, leaning against the narrow trunk, legs curled under her, holding her hat in front of her eyes; but even under this, the furious shapes dodged and lunged in all directions. Later Joan was to move upstairs, assisted by her daughter Anne, and left in a darkened bedroom for the rest of the afternoon, vomiting into a bowl provided by Uncle Arthur's housekeeper. Then later still driven by a silent and disapproving George back to the Dolphin, put to bed again, missing the evening dinner the Crosbys gave for close family on both sides after the bridal couple had departed.

Polly would be remembered as the voice who broke the silence which followed the sliding forward of the cake. 'Christ Almighty!' she called out and slapped her hand across her face, since in those days violent blasphemous expletives were less to be expected on social occasions. Campbell would be remembered as laughing uproariously, more so than anyone else, as if he had been waiting all day or for all his life to release this gust of laughter, which was not that of someone amused, but of someone who, not getting sufficient laughs out of life, had a suppressed volcano of them. He always and forever laughed like that at incidents of this kind, but could never make other people laugh however much he wanted to.

'Well held!' said George Ramsey to Jim, who thereafter became included in the continuing conversation about Yorkshire dialects.

In regard to the toppling of the cake, stories varied. In some, Campbell was held responsible, some Charlie, and some Helen. Some people tried to make a moral of it, eg that at a wedding something awful had to happen, always does, isn't it amazing eh?

'Cake hit ground. Could have been worse. Could have been the tent,' wrote Harold in his diary that night. Phyllis's attitude was not dissimilar. Rather as in Japan they welcome small earthquakes, believing these release underground pressure which might build up to a single cataclysmic one, so did Phyllis welcome what was after all no great disaster.

Charlie had his arm round Helen. Polly, seeing how he cared for Helen, decided this made very little difference to the way she felt. He would be chary, wary and require complete discretion, at which she was a dab hand.

Helen felt guilty as if it was her presence that had caused the accident. Nina's attitude is interesting: she kept thinking: well it's not *my* fault, now is it? I was only standing here. (Only married for an hour or so, mind you.) Nanny thought: what a shame when someone put so much work into it; and Louisa was thinking: now I can say I have been a bridesmaid twice and at one of the weddings the cake fell over and I saw currants and icing sugar, curly swirls of it all smashed.

Mo didn't see it. She was by that time pushing forward through the forest of undergrowth beyond the hedge, followed by Edmund.

Charlie, bending over Helen, passed her a handkerchief, whispering that her mascara was running. She didn't dare ask him for how long it had been running. What does anyone do without someone to tell them their mascara is running? 'Listen, darling,' he said, 'why not sit? Hey, Nanny! This is Helen, Nanny. Helen, this is Nanny. She and I met outside the church. She'll look after you. I'd better go and check up on proceedings. I'll be back.'

In the days when Uncle Arthur kept a team of gardeners, the ground had been richly fertilized. Here now grew cooch grass, docks, enormous leeks with round seed heads from a crop planted years back. These had seeded and reseeded themselves and rustled above Mo's head as she pushed them aside. She kept Edmund's red trousers in view and followed him as best she could. White butterflies flapped around her. She shot out a hand to try and catch one. 'Edmund,' she shouted, 'when is a butterfly not a butterfly?' 'When it's a caterpillar. Easy peasy.' So she'd have to think of something else with which to impress him.

He'd helped her climb the gate, saying: 'I say, can you cope?' Then she'd got her sash hooked over one of the upright pointed wooden stakes. They'd tried unlashing the wire to open the gate, but couldn't, so they'd climbed. In the end she wriggled out of her sash and left it there as a valuable red silk clue to her whereabouts for those who were eventually to come in search. The search party would be led by Nanny. Caring and being watchful was her livelihood. Behind Nanny would come Phyllis who of course . . . well you know Phyllis, say no more. Although, since neither of these women were of an age to move at speed, they would be preceded by a runner, fleet-of-foot Hermione who would be the first to reach Edmund and Mo.

Since the wind had now dropped, Uncle Arthur had been wheeled out to sit on a space of the upper lawn below the dining room window, but since the sun was strong, his manservant had placed him under a laburnum tree. Uncle Arthur, although by far the oldest person present, was not to die just yet. A thin old man with the outline of sharp knees showing through the ancient black-gone-green morning suit.

Bernard leaned over, one hand on the back of the wheelchair, and raised his voice. 'Lovely place you have here!' It had seemed to Bernard that it was behoven on him as one of the leaders, as it were, of the visiting team, to communicate with this old man, the doyen of the Forestier side of things. He offered condolences on the passing of the mansion into other hands and expressed to Uncle Arthur regrets that the days had gone when such magnificent surroundings could be privately maintained.

Not of course that Uncle Arthur comprehended more than one word in ten, although he gave the impression of trying to hear – by cupping a hand behind one ear and crooking his head to one side. Eventually Bernard changed the subject and, speaking louder than before, said: 'Lovely wedding!'

Uncle Arthur's voice was thin. 'At my age, one is nothing.' The hanging laburnum seed heads shifted slightly in the breeze. One seed pod fell on to the shoulder of his morning coat. These days he was dressed and undressed by his manservant who was the person of greatest importance to him. Now he turned his head towards the marquee, hoping to see the manservant returning with a glass of champagne. Not that Uncle Arthur, who in his time had consumed vast quantities of it, could now drink much champagne or any other alcohol. It only caused even more restless nights and affected a recurrent bladder problem. 'At my age, one is nothing,' he repeated.

'Not at all,' said Bernard, 'I won't hear of it!' The conversation was forcing out of him a degree of joviality he did not feel. He observed the paper-thin skin on Uncle Arthur's face and hands. How terrifying was old age!

'Now, if I were an animal,' said Uncle Arthur, and Bernard waited, noticing how people were now moving up towards the house. 'Ah! So you envy animals?' he said.

'No, no, no, no!' Uncle Arthur looked out over the grounds which had been his or were still his but only just. He sounded fretful. Poor old man, thought Bernard. 'No, no, I do *not* envy animals. Most animals have been put down by the time they are as old as I am. That's the point. Supposing every time you visited the doctor you thought: are they going to have to put me to sleep today?' He chuckled, went on chuckling, his whole frame shaking, so frail and brittle he was that he might well crack a bone. Bernard made to move away, but Uncle Arthur's mouth was opening again. A clawlike hand came up to clutch at Bernard's jacket. He felt obliged to lean down towards that pale clean face again. Such blue eyes the old man had! Having drawn him down, Uncle Arthur let go, making a gesture with a long bony finger towards the tent. 'They had to marry.'

'Oh I don't think so.' Bernard stood up. Uncle Arthur clawed the air. 'For the survival of the species, you see.' By this time the manservant had arrived and stood there, a glass of champagne held on a tray, waiting for the old man to stop shaking with laughter.

Back in the marquee, George Ramsey was explaining to John and Jim the variations between vowel sounds which could be heard within the whole of Yorkshire. The differences were, he emphasized, as wide as those existing between John O'Groats and Lands End. 'I had a patient once,' said Jim. 'He was from Yorkshire. He asked me once if he was *forced* to take the medicine I'd prescribed for him . . .' 'Ah! Now . . . forced to!' George paused, having been diverted from the previous course of his peroration. 'To be *forced* to . . . Yes, indeed . . . that's very common. It speaks, we could say, of more necessity. A southern native would say, "I have to" or perhaps, "Must I?", both of which carry far less weight, in my opinion.'

'Are you saying,' John asked, 'are you saying that this is significant? Does it, would you say, reveal a trend in character?' George paused again. A lengthy pause, during which Jim considered slipping away to find Laura and to ask her where Edmund was. Vanessa was beside him, clinging to his leg, rubbing her mouth, which was covered with ice cream, against his hired trousers. He picked her up and wiped her mouth with his handkerchief.

George Ramsey: confident, sure of himself – well, we must assume so – evidence from that characteristic Yorkshire habit of taking his time as if what he was considering was of such moment that it deserved each second's pondering. All this regardless of those who waited for an answer. Insensitive to others possibly, but particularly insensitive in George's case, it must be argued, was his neglect of Joan, whom he had seen leaving the tent in some distress. No doubt he had seen Joanne accompany her – no doubt expected Anne, his daughter, to be in attendance. On a scale of one to ten, who would get the lower mark for husbandly concern, George Ramsey or Charlie Garside?

Meanwhile his daughter Anne, having settled her mother in bed upstairs, was relaxing in a corner of the marquee, part of an animated foursome, chatting: she, Caroline Cornelius and both their husbands, these two young men having arrived late last night, stag party absentees.

I introduce you here to Tim Cornelius. He had been entertaining prospective customers from Australia, and where better to have taken them these last two days than Lords? Tim: attractive, charming, highly esteemed by all who met him (son of Cicely – had she done a good job here?). At any rate, he and Caroline made an enviable pair. They were top young Yorkshire at its prosperous best. Admittedly their interests lay almost entirely outside the county, much of their fortune being spent at jet-setting spots such as Glyndebourne, Ascot, the Alps in winter and Cowes in August.

Tim was not without generosity. In a moment he was to approach Campbell, shake his hand for the second time that day and congratulate him. Campbell was delighted at such reinforcement from a contemporary whose opinion he enormously respected. Then Tim took Nina's hand, less firmly so it seemed to her. She froze. He sees there is nothing to me. I have realized suddenly that, whereas I've always thought I was okay inside, that's not enough. What you are has to show on the surface or it might well not be there. What a rotten thing to discover on your wedding day. She shook her head to forget.

George Ramsey, back into his stride by now, though whether he had answered John's question neither of his listeners could be sure. Both had been diverted, Jim by the struggling Vanessa and John by the sight of a girl who stood alone in the opening of the tent.

In the dining room people circled the laden table, admired the casseroles, arrays of wine glasses, tumblers and other gifts, the total value of which could have been anything between five hundred and a thousand pounds, this leaving aside cheques and oddments already in the marital home or waiting to be unwrapped at Pound Close when the couple returned from their honeymoon. This was to be spent in the south of France, but on the coast almost into Spain and therefore cheaper.

By the time she reached the ovenware end for the second time, Polly was beginning to think this was not the best place for him to find her. She would be lost in the crowd. People pushed past her, leaned across her to peer at labels, saying 'Yes, those are tremendously useful,' or: 'Yes, I had one of those, but hardly ever use it,' or: 'Look what so and so gave them!' with the implication that so and so had spent either more or less than one might have expected. Polly found her way to the bay window and saw Charlie coming up the covered walkway, looking in her direction. So she turned to face back into the room, experiencing one of those moments when you feel, if not like drawing back, at least not blatantly appearing to entice.

Edmund, being that inch or so taller than Mo, saw before she did the sun reflecting on the glass roof. He also saw pale green leaves sticking out of broken panes. Now he knew what he was aiming for. 'Would you have come here on your own?' Mo called. 'Yes, probably.' Then he added for honesty: 'I would have *wanted* to.' 'But wasn't brave enough?' ''Course I was brave enough.' She couldn't see his eyes when he said this, being several yards behind, so she'd never know if he would have been brave enough or not. Fronds of vegetation kept bouncing back at her, scratching her arms, thistles pulling at threads from the white silk of her dress.

If Joan lay completely still with her eyes closed, breathed slowly and lightly, she might avoid further vomiting.

'We have another expression which may be relevant here,' said George Ramsey, 'which is: "I'm not bothered."'

* * *

'I'm not bothered,' said Mo, when Edmund asked her if she minded having torn her dress and got it dirty. 'Then that's okay,' said Edmund. They were resting by a gooseberry bush, the stalks of which had grown a long way out from the centre. It was disappointing that the fruit was hard and very green and sour. Mo knelt on the hard dry weedy earth, tucking her dress under her knees.

'Let me elaborate,' said George, shifting on to his other foot and looking up at the canvas roof. Jim looked around for Laura, and out of one corner of his eye saw Nanny sitting on a chair next to Helen, Helen with a glass in her hand and a bottle on the floor beside her.

John saw the girl who was watching from the edge of the marquee and remembered that she was a school friend of Nina's who'd come to stay at Glebe House several years ago.

There he was at the far end of the table, having just entered, hands in pockets, strolling casually, appearing like everyone else to be reading labels, craning head slightly, moving some-times sideways, nodding at someone he knew, but not being delayed and definitely on his way towards her, stopping only to rest his hand on the shoulder of a small relation who turned up her face to smile at him, then raised her shoulders, giggling. I must consider the pleasures to come, decided Polly, and forget the unforeseen complexities we shall discover in each other as we each learn that no one is as we first see them.

'You said there would be fruit,' said Mo. 'Sorry about that. There will be more where we are going, I expect.' They sat down for another rest. Mo licked her forearm which was bleeding. 'What sort of fruit?' 'Grapes I shouldn't wonder.' He pushed his fringe back from his forehead.

George was enjoying himself more and more. These two apparently intelligent young men went on paying him attention. 'Your Yorkshireman will, for instance, say, "I fully intend" rather than "I mean to."' John asked, 'Are you saying that you are in general more purposeful?'

* * *

'What was the bravest thing you ever did?' said Mo. She still had the taste of unripe gooseberry in her mouth. 'Jump off a fairly high wall,' said Edmund: 'What was the bravest thing *you* ever did?' 'Drink washing-up liquid,' said Mo: 'Quite a lot of it.' 'My grandfather climbed Everest,' said Edmund, 'but not all the way to the top.'

Louisa would be able to wear her dress again for parties. Mo's would be stained and torn, but she would grow into Louisa's and wear that for parties later. She would remember wearing it party after party.

Phyllis was on her way to see Joan, up the enormously wide, curving staircase with its massive oak banister. Below her women were queuing for the lavatory, the one which had 'Ladies' pinned to the door that afternoon. Muriel was down there too, her voice booming as she said goodbye to Julia. The Richard Crosbys were about to leave. There was nothing especially Yorkshire about Muriel. She was part of a network of upper-class women who exist all over England, sharing accent and preoccupations. Muriel, a no-nonsense sort of person, saying to Julia: 'What a splendid do! Do come and see us when you're visiting the young.' 'I'd simply love to!' Then Muriel added: 'He's a good sort.' 'Who?' asked Julia. 'Campbell!' Muriel laughed loudly.

Edmund kicked at the bottom of the door to force it open. The greenhouse stretched away from them, seeming endless. The smell was one of dead, dried-up geraniums which lay along shelves in cracked earthenware pots. Stuffiness: the only air coming in from broken panes. The windows could only be opened by the operation of rusty metal winches. Mo reached up to a shelf and lifted one of the pots, pulled at a dead stalk. Pale, dry, hard-packed earth fell to the ground. 'Fancy not watering them!'

He was beside her. 'Bride or bridegroom?' 'Bride,' said Polly. In front of her, silver, cutlery, canteens of knives and forks, serving spoons, all to be polished and replaced after being used by bride and bridegroom or people calling on them or having been invited by them once they had become a household. 'What did you give them? Show me.' So she led him past the dusters Nina would or would not use to dust her furniture and windowsills, past a pack of dishcloths with a label saying: 'lots and lots of love and kisses from Edmund and Vanessa', with a chalked picture of a bride and bridegroom with a yellow sun in the sky above them.

Saying nothing, he came behind her, touching her elbow, sometimes as if to guide her. 'It's at the far end,' she said. It is up to me now, Polly thought. He has made the first move. I am about to make the second by accompanying him through the crowd, passing the dishes in which Nina would bake rice puddings, semolina puddings (Campbell being a great one for puddings), bread and butter puddings, tarts, pies, flans, although she'd never be that good at pastry.

I have felt his clean breath on my face, seen his smooth cheeks at close quarters, looked into his pale eyes, imagined running my fingers along his eyebrows, touching his ear, pictured world-spinning moments. Man and woman made He them with such desires, but man set up a system which, accompanied by household wares, ensures that once desire has faded, goods remain. Responsibility of ownership maintains stability.

Saucepans, three sets of them, including a prestigious Prestige copper-bottomed set from Peter and Nick with tons of love. Someone pushes us together. Only our wedding clothes between us. Our love will not be bound with sets of saucepans. We may hardly ever even eat together. Our love will have to be entirely self-sufficient.

Electrical goods: two toasters of identical design, from which would pop two slices of toast into the hands of Nina to be put into that toast rack over there and passed to Campbell.

Love on its own until the loved one feels its weakness, love unfettered or love uncopper-bottomed? Love called cheating. Is it cheating? Oh please don't say it's cheating.

A plug-in warming plate for use at dinner parties. Entertaining friends makes for solidarity. Love in isolation has no solidarity. An electric blanket wraps love round and cossets it.

'Are we getting warm?' asked Charlie. 'Not far now. Head for the linen.'

'There you are, grapes!' 'They're tiny. More like pips.' 'They're grapes all the same. At least they *will* be grapes.' 'It's much too hot in here.' So they sat outside on upturned wooden boxes. Mo tucked her skirt decently around her knickers and pulled at the elastic of her red shoes. 'Look! A frog!' 'Where?' 'Under that clump of rhubarb. It means there's water somewhere.' 'What, the rhubarb?' 'No, the frog.' 'It doesn't have to.' 'If there wasn't water, then the frog wouldn't be here. Anyway my grandma has a greenhouse, so does my Aunty Helen, so does my Aunty Muriel. Everyone I know has a greenhouse and there's always a tap or a hose.' 'Or,' said Edmund, 'at any rate a well I suppose?' 'At least a well,' said Mo. 'Let's look for one.'

'So you gave them sheets?' 'No, look under the table.' He bent down, reaching for the tie-on label, on which her name and address was written, then stood up again. 'Have you a good memory?' she asked. 'When I need one.'

Phyllis stood in the darkened room. Here, an overpowering smell of vomit. 'A little fresh air perhaps?' The heavy curtains and behind them a closed window and with such warmth outside, unbearable, unhealthy. 'Yes, thank you,' said Joan, not because she wanted fresh air, but because it was easier to say yes to it than explain how she wanted nothing other than complete and utter silence and complete and utter darkness.

'There *was* a frog.' 'I didn't see it.' 'I saw it and I heard it.' 'Heard it?' 'It croaked. Listen!' Nothing. No sound, only the distant babble from the marquee and a tractor somewhere. Not even a bird singing at this quietest, deadest, warmest time of afternoon. Flies buzzing though. Mo put her ear to the ground because if the frog was moving somewhere near, she might hear it as you heard a train coming on a railway line. She listened to the earth. Down under this there would be worms sliding, beetles and woodlice pushing their way through, moles making tunnels. Edmund lay his head close to hers on the ground. They stared into each other's eyes, listening, forcing each other into more and more silence with their fingers against their lips, lips pursed.

'I'm about to go on holiday. Do you like picture postcards?' 'As long as they're not of hot sandy beaches, palm trees and blue sea to make me envious.' 'Don't be envious.' An inclination in Polly to gulp here. Oh, he is unhappy! From whatever part of her had been most affected up to now, the focus of emotion moved. Love deepens. Somewhere – was it in her stomach – something lurched. Not the heart, although that may have missed a beat.

The frog leaped, making them both widen their eyes as it flashed in an arc across their vision. There it was – over by the door. 'Look, its neck is moving in and out and its eyes are bulging. We have frightened it.' 'No, it isn't frightened. That is how frogs' eyes are, bulging.' 'You could catch it.' 'No, follow it. It will lead us to water.' Mo got to her feet.

I can still turn back. I can do that right up to the moment he first rings. I can even fail to answer the door when he knocks. The choice is mine. I can survive without him. I can look out of the window, consider the clouds, listen to the skylarks, make plans for my old age.

'My holiday lasts a fortnight.' So it would be July, perhaps the best time of all, since warmth, if warmth does come to Swaledale, is established by then and days still long. Some hot summers when the river is low, white stones show in the river-bed. In the silences after sex we shall hear sheep. I shall lie with my head between the angle of his head and shoulders. I shall turn my mouth towards his neck.

'It's there, Edmund. No, it's gone again. I heard it plop into some water.' 'By those boards.' 'Let's move them. You take one end.' 'Okay.' 'Heave ho!' 'I say! Look!' 'Strewth!' 'Deep!' 'Mind out!' 'Hundreds and hundreds of feet down!' 'No, thousands.' 'No, not thousands.' 'Let's try echoing.'

* * *

It was time for Nanny to leave this lady who kept telling her how fond she was of Campbell and how he was always coming to see her and telling her how much he loved Nina. This lady said she loved Nina too. None of this was the sort of thing people tell Nannies, but this lady kept helping herself to more from the bottle she had beside her. She had had quite sufficient in Nanny's opinion, although it wasn't for Nanny to say so. She even asked Nanny if Nanny had ever been interested in gentlemen herself. Poor thing – having no children was probably the trouble.

Laura, having told Nina it was time to go and change, saw Nanny as she crossed the marquee and stopped to say, 'Oh, Nanny, have you seen the children?' Nanny pointed to Vanessa who was in Jim's arms, leaning her head against his shoulder, sucking her thumb. 'What about Edmund?' Laura asked. 'We've been having such a lovely chat,' said Helen to Laura, who had never seen a woman of Helen's kind – or any woman come to that – quite so drunk before. Perhaps Nina was right: this might be one of those real-life tragedies you sometimes read about. Helen waved her glass in the air. She promised to let Nanny go in just a minute, but asked if it wasn't a holiday for Nanny the same as everyone? She evidently didn't understand that Nanny didn't work for Laura.

A glimpse of water far below. Their voices came back: 'Mo . . . Mo . . . Mo.' 'Hello . . . hello . . . hello.' 'Let's drop a stone and see how long it takes to splash.'

'Shall we go and sit somewhere?' The only person to notice Charlie and Polly leave to go along the corridor was Cicely.

The stone took ages and ages before they heard it splash, and as Mo dropped it, something else also fell from her hand. All the bridesmaids had one of these, a gold charm bracelet – a present from the bridegroom. Grandma had said hers was too big for her. She would lose it almost certainly. 'Oh dear, my bracelet's gone as well,' said Mo.

* * *

Phyllis drew back the curtains, loosened the window catch. The windows overlooked the lawn. She had long sight, only needing glasses for reading and close work. She saw Nanny by the gate, holding up Mo's red sash. Surrounding Nanny, other brides-maids, including Louisa, Joanne and Hermione. This is it, thought Phyllis.

'I say!' said Edmund. 'What a bit of luck! Your bracelet hasn't gone all the way down. I can see it stuck there on a piece of moss or something. See a stick round here anywhere? I might be able to reach it.'

The saloon of Uncle Arthur's mansion at the far end of the corridor: a whitish light in here on account of the marquee outside. A semi-circular bay window with cushioned seats. Otherwise all saloon furniture had been sold: only remaining item of value, a hanging chandelier – heavy, ornamental, fashioned from hundreds of crafted drops of milky glass, known to be of Italian origin and especially made for Uncle Arthur's grandfather, Julia's great-grandfather, Nina's great-great-grandfather. On the cushioned seats looking up at this, were Charlie and Polly. It was about the only thing to look at other than into each other's eyes. 'What do you think?' A relief to sit down, especially when he crossed one leg over the other, revealing slim ankles. A man's ankles can be disappointing.

'Here,' said Mo. 'A bamboo. Will that do?' 'I say, thanks! I think so. Here goes!' To reach the bracelet, Edmund had to lean from the opposite side of the well and stretch. At least half his body was unsupported. 'Sit on my legs, will you.' So she did, looking up at the trees and sky and tall brick wall while he smelled the dampness beneath him, sensing the coldness of that place down there which had not seen the sun for so long. Like another world it was and only the frog alive or maybe dead down there. Only drips to be heard. Like a dungeon.

The human frame can only stand so much, thought Phyllis. Old women shouldn't have to run like this, but it is my fault for not being firm to start with, for letting her come with us, for giving in to Nick or rather Peter. She, Nick, has always been my feet of clay. That's loving people for you. Firmness is all.

For Mo, after a time it became quite boring because she couldn't see what was happening inside the well. Whenever she leaned towards the opening, he said, 'Don't move!' So she talked to him, telling him all about herself and her life so far. 'My real name's Melanie. If I had been a boy, I would have been called Jonathan. I wish I had been. I put the kitten in the spin-dryer once. It didn't die. Have you got a spin-dryer?'

Tongue between his teeth, end of stick in touch with bracelet. Just there! Got it! Could he lift it? Raise stick, but all the time keep point of stick against slippery wall opposite or bracelet would slip off again. 'Hang on, Mo, don't move for heaven's sake!' He was being as brave as Grandpa was on Everest. This well could be as deep as Everest was high.

'The chandelier? What do I think of it? Not interested.' He took her hand, spread the fingers. 'Of this I am in awe however.' 'Don't be.' I wish I hadn't said that, Polly thought. Awe helps. Awe speaks of mystery, keeps things going, holds him so that you can at some stage enfold him and encourage him.

Nina was ready. Out of the window, beyond the marquee and the hedge, she saw people moving downhill, running. Nina had long sight. The going-away dress was grey with white collar and cuffs. She wore it with a candy-pink sailor hat and white accessories. More her style than the wedding dress perhaps – a stab at the demure. Fashionwise, she'd have a stab at anything.

Polly's hand felt bony. His felt large and warm. To *be* enfolded – there lay danger.

George Ramsey stood centre marquee holding Vanessa, looking after Jim who was running, having thrust Vanessa into George's arms. Her mouth was open and he guessed she was about to scream. He looked around for someone who would take this child from him.

Who can say how long Mo's weight would have held him?

Voices were calling both their names, voices coming nearer. 'Want any help?' This was Hermione, who knelt down grabbing his legs, pulling them, dragging him along the ground and away from the rim, which meant the bracelet fell off the end of the stick. And after all that trouble!

Because of all the people coming, Mo didn't hear the bracelet plop to the bottom. Which was more disappointing than losing it. She didn't like it that much anyway. Her hand was being gripped by Grandma. She'd never forget, looking up at Grandma's face, the most frightening sight of her life so far. Grandma had changed colour. Mo thought her arm was going to be broken.

At about this time Vanessa was sick down George's morning suit.

Laura was still running, stumbling. She had already fallen twice, broken one high heel, thrown both shoes away. Jim had overtaken her. Now he was there at the well holding Edmund. Hermione was saying: 'That was a narrow squeak,' and Mo was asking Grandma what a narrow squeak was, but Grandma was telling people to fetch that big stone and put it on top of the boards to make quite sure.

'Goodbye for now,' said Charlie, squeezing her hand before letting it go, 'and I mean for now.'

People gathered by the front door of the mansion waiting for the bride and groom to leave. They were discussing this and that. Serious topics included the Organization for European Economic Co-operation, which was beginning to be planned at this time and which most people thought would be an extremely good idea. Another thing discussed was the end of national service, which would mean that every young man here under the age of twenty or so would not do as Campbell, John and others had done. Many people had mixed feelings about this, believing young men needed discipline. A very few, like John himself, had, arguably, a more optimistic view of human nature.

John watched the car disappear down the curving drive with streamers and JUST MARRIED signs tied there by Mike McKorkadale and others. John looked at the girl beside him. Lust, yes, but there had to be more than that.

Something missing. Julia put her hand across her mouth. Good heavens, she'd forgotten the confetti!

The saloon now empty, except for Jane who had wandered in there, standing, an isolated figure looking up at the chandelier. Cicely saw her through the open door, went in, said hello, started talking about chandeliers in general and particularly those made in Italy. She'd seen some very fine examples on her trips with a group of rich people like herself to centres of European culture, which were conducted by a professor of fine art at the university every spring. 'You ought to come with us,' said Cicely. This was the nicest thing anyone had said to Jane all day. She really looks quite pretty when she smiles, thought Cicely.

17

It was the speed that did it, gigantic, lurching speed. Get anything to move as fast as this and force it upwards by the manoeuvring of the wingshape and it would fly, zoom, whoosh and there below was the airport, then the fields nearby and tiny cars moving along narrow roads at the pace of snails. Nina clutched Campbell's hand. If only life were all new clothes and arriving at an airport on a sunny evening, feeling like a film star walking up the gangway then turning as if to wave.

An adventure with nothing to worry about until they returned and the sea down there like rippling silk while up here you were asked what you wanted to drink, given food completely free, a tray with different compartments with miniature packets of pepper, salt, sugar and mayonnaise. Such riches when you had just left what was too complex to be judged as yet. In a few months ahead she would have to think of it as successful. Then in a year or so she would look at photos and think: God how awful I looked and why didn't I take more trouble with the shoes and width of hem or refuse the veil?

In the huge hotel room overlooking the Mediterranean they romped and wrestled, calling each other nicknames which Nina would look back on years later with embarrassment as being very childish. There was sex and more sex which came at the end of each rough and tumble. They had to share a table in the hotel with a couple of Americans. 'Actually we're on our honeymoon,' Campbell told these two, which was quite unnecessary and probably only too obvious in any case and meant that the Americans called them 'You two lovebirds'. The man was an accountant. Campbell managed to impress him with his business know-how, but Nina kept on having to get away from the wife who wanted to give her housekeeping tips and tell her about her daughter who was also just married. And when the two of them were out each day and bumped into this couple anywhere, they'd say things like: 'Stay happy now,' or: 'Be nice to each other!'

None of it was exact or right or true or really Nina, but who was she to know what was exact or right or true or really her any more? What was true was hidden under the events of each day, under new clothes, burned shoulders.

Further along the coast in a more upmarket part of the south of France was a hotel with a court surrounding a swimming pool where Helen and Charlie spent every morning, sitting, reading. Then in the afternoon, after a short siesta, they would take the cliff walk down towards the beach which spread out, acre upon acre of it, at low tide. And nothing was said except: 'I love you' several times a day, and all those things that people who have been married for ten years or so say to each other out of habit and out of the good and busy parts of sharing a life. To all the other guests they looked to be very close indeed, often holding hands as they set off to the beach, often laughing, Helen particularly, by the swimming pool; and they attracted other people, drank with other couples in the evening.So much to think about on holiday: getting a good tan, deciding what to eat and when to eat and whether the chair you want by the pool will be available.

So far so good and nothing said and maybe nothing *to* be said. Truce time, Helen told herself, but a truce with the end of lulling him into non-suspicion as the days went by with mornings by the pool and afternoons on the enormous beach and dancing in the evenings, which she did so well. An unexpected bonus too, when Helen discovered that she could put up with Charlie chatting to other women here. After what she'd been through, all this seemed quite trivial.She'd sit back watching him, relaxed, oozing blatant confidence as if to say: this is my man; you just try prising him away from me.

One man in the hotel took a fancy to her or seemed to do so. She caught him looking at her long legs, now a perfect gold. He sought her out for dancing in the evening. Was this a solution, to attract other men? Possibly. Worth considering, at any rate for a time to test it out. And it worked, for a time, made Charlie during the first week even more loving. He could hardly wait to get her upstairs and make love to her. It was an absorbing new aspect of his sexuality.

She'd destroyed the chequebook, torn it up and thrown the pieces into the English Channel on the crossing from Newhaven to Dieppe, but realized this prevented nothing since on his return he could always get another.

Julia got simply masses of letters saying what an especially lovely wedding it had been, so the time of the wedding stretched on. Then she went to stay with Jim and Laura in a rented cottage in north Cornwall. Here Edmund learned to swim. One night Julia heard Jim and Laura quarrelling in their bedroom, which was a pity and she had to stuff her ears when Bible reading.

Phyllis was planning to take Nicola to Sandsend for a real rest, but first there was the business of Aunt Winifred's funeral to be got over. Nanny was back in Wolverhampton doing lots of knitting and making smocks or romper suits for little girls or boys she had looked after – and sometimes for little boys and little girls of children she'd looked after in her long career, also wondering if she could not live off sewing plus her old age pension – plus the small amount still paid to her by the family in Halifax for whom she'd worked all those years back after leaving the Forestiers.

Polly waited in Swaledale, but made an effort to see friends because she mustn't count on anything. The view became drier and paler and it looked as though it was going to be an amazing summer, getting hotter and hotter and less and less green, the river drying up to become several shallow streams winding between white boulders. In regard to the wedding she remembered she had said some pretty silly things to people. She often frightened people by being too sharp and clever. If she were to be a successful, social person, she needed her whole personality stripped down and made good again, oiled and reassembled, but it was too late for that. The spare parts which could have rendered Polly into a more approachable person were now obsolete.

They were running out of cash. Campbell had taken all he could afford to take out of the bank without exceeding the limit of his overdraft. 'Did you bring any travellers cheques?' he asked Nina. 'No, of course not.' 'Thought you might have.' 'How could I?' She had spent her last wage cheque the week before the wedding.

First she wanted a straw hat to keep the sun off, then her sandals were too thick and heavy, although he seemed to remember that she'd shown them to him soon after buying them and said they were just the thing for the honeymoon. Now she wanted espadrilles. She hadn't been anywhere as hot as this before. Then the bikinis in the windows of the fashion shops along the front were that much more eye-catching than her own. She had wanted these things and he'd bought them for her. 'What about the wedding present cheques?' he asked. 'Oh well . . . they are for household goods,' said Nina. 'Oh I've put them in a special account.' He would never ever know for sure when she was lying.

They always had an ice cream each on the beach. The ice creams were a lot tastier than English ice creams but much more expensive. One day at the end of the first week he said he didn't want one thanks, and she said, 'Well I do,' and he said, 'All right then,' but she enjoyed hers less with him sitting looking out to sea and banging his foot on the sand. 'Why don't you want one?' 'Because if you must know we are running short of cash.' 'Oh, so that's why you asked me if I had any.' Some days it almost seemed as if he were missing work and not enjoying this.

'I'd rather have an ice cream every day than wine at dinner,' Nina said. They were having wine mostly because the Americans had wine. Campbell didn't like to seem poor in front of other people.

Then, in spite of the new hat, she got so sunburnt that she couldn't face the beach, so one morning they caught a bus into the old city where they walked on the shady side of narrow streets. Many old and interesting shops, especially book shops.

Campbell found this huge old tome about battles between the English and the French on French soil. He could just read French so he bought the book, paying by cheque, leaving the book behind until the cheque was cleared from England, which meant that they had to go back a few days later to collect the book, on which occasion he found another book, almost as expensive. 'I thought you were at the limit of your overdraft,' she said. 'Perhaps I miscalculated.' The two books together cost more than twice as much as everything he'd bought her so far, but she reckoned now he wouldn't grumble about her wanting ice creams and maybe another suntop she had seen in a boutique a few doors down the street from the bookshop.

He spent a long time talking to the bookshop owner, who spoke quite good English. All the same Campbell raised his voice as if this helped understanding. Nina became bored, so went and sat in a café having a *citron pressé* and an ice cream, then another *citron pressé* and another ice cream, which took all the francs she had in her pocket. Campbell came to find her but wouldn't sit down and eat or drink with her because he wanted to get back to the hotel and read the books.

'Isn't it odd,' said Nina as they left the café, 'how if you're really interested in something you don't get so hungry?' 'I don't think so,' Campbell said. Anyway they walked to catch the bus and passed the shop where she'd seen the suntop, Nina slowing down here. 'I'm sure I'll never see one that I like more,' she said. He shoved a pile of francs into her hand. 'Don't you want to come and see me try it on?' 'No thanks.' He waited outside and when she came out, not having bought the suntop on account of feeling flustered, he walked on fast, making it difficult for her to keep up with him in the heat. He often said she had no stamina, which was a very sweeping statement and was proved in time to be inaccurate.

Back in the foyer of the hotel they met the Americans who said: 'Hi, you two lovebirds!' and Campbell smiled rather icily, but Nina stood close to him, realizing that, although they had quarrelled, she didn't want other people to know. 'See you later!' said the Americans and: 'Stay happy now!' By dinner time they'd had sex again and it was all made up. As long as there is sex around, you can usually make things up.

Next day he said, 'Go back and buy the suntop,' but while she was buying it, he went back into the bookshop to talk endlessly to the man again, so Nina, wearing the suntop, which made her shoulders feel somehow elegant, went on and up to the top of the narrow street where they'd never been before and where there was a cathedral, right on the edge of the high, walled part of the old city. She felt the height and coolness of it. An old man offered a candle for a few centimes, so she took it. There was a tray where people placed candles, lit them, then bowed their heads or knelt facing the altar, probably in rememberance of someone dead whom they had loved.

She placed the candle in a slot, trying to think of people she had known and loved who were dead, but couldn't honestly think of anyone except her mother's sister who had died in India but whom she had never really known. Loving people – what was it? Was it, as she had decided months back, needing them? Whom do I love? Those whom I need. In which case love was the wrong word. But she placed the candle, feeling as if she were crossing her fingers against fate. God and cathedrals were to do with wrong-doing. Sin might not exist as such, but there was the verb 'to sin' and she had sinned and knew that she would go on sinning. If she were a Roman Catholic she would have confessed perhaps, but to confess righted no wrongs. And you only confessed if you were disturbed by having sinned and she was not disturbed or didn't seem to be. She placed the candle in the hole in the copper tray alongside other candles, then lit it and felt good doing this. Her hair had become straightened by the salt in the sea and bleached on top after ten days in the sun and would catch the light.

And she would place her memories of having sinned down there alongside the truth and keep on looking at the world as if nothing had disturbed her. Because nothing had. But she felt the lighting of the candle was a good thing to have done in the dark cathedral. She came out into the blazing heat of the narrow street, thinking suddenly: one day I'll be disturbed, but shan't know what it will be like until it happens. In the silence of siesta time, the slap of her espadrilles echoed down the centre of the empty street which led straight downhill.

* * *

Time to buy postcards. Helen bought these and sat by the pool writing them. 'Any to spare?' Charlie asked. He never wrote postcards. She always wrote postcards for the two of them. 'I've done one for your mother,' she said. He nodded. There were three left over, but when she went up to the room during the next day, she found only two. 'So did you send a postcard?' she asked casually as she could while they were walking on the beach down by the tideline hand in hand. He let her hand go.

When could he have taken it? When could he have written it? And posted it? They'd been together all the time. Surely if he needed to send a postcard to an unknown person, he'd have gone and bought one, rather than rousing her suspicions by taking one of hers? They walked on side by side instead of hand in hand. The sand dipped. Here lay a stretch of water trapped on the beach, still water reflecting the sun like a gigantic mirror. Helen had a choice: she could follow up her question which he had not answered or she could say nothing.

How can I love her when she is so hard to love? How can I love her without the strength I get from loving someone else? Their feet splashed through the stretch of water. Don't do it, Helen. Please don't ask. Or this beach won't be wide enough for both of us and I shall have to turn on my heel and walk away from you, not having the strength for this.

At least there would be relief this evening when they'd dance again, Helen with the man who seemed to fancy her and Charlie with the man's wife. The other couple would see them through until the next day and the next day until the day they left. Then Helen remembered yesterday siesta time. He left the room. I remember now: I woke and he was not in the bed beside me, but came back later, kissed me, said he'd been down to the pool to fetch his cigarettes. But I had cigarettes by the bed. We always share our cigarettes. We always share . . . I know! He gave it to the receptionist to post. Lunch time today I saw him wink at her.

'Min. 60. Max. 80. Hottest for ten years. Going like iron at Newbury. Letter from woman, says left white gloves in church. P.C. from Julia saying similar weather prevails in Cornwall.'

Harold stayed at home, with Mrs Carter comng in to cook

his evening meal for him. After he had eaten, he left the dishes in the sink and Mrs Carter came in to wash up in the morning. At first he slept well without Julia, but woke up one warm night and realized he would never finish what he had begun, but all the same would go on doing it as if to finish it; simply because he'd started it. 'To seek what is impossible is madness,' said Marcus Aurelius.

Joan had a card from Helen. 'Hot sun, blue skies, bliss.' Polly had a card which said, 'Sorry about the hot sun and blue skies, but no alternative. Hoping this finds you as it leaves me, in anticipation.'

Towards the end of Julia's second week away from home Harold, hoping for more air in the bedroom one night, opened the window to its widest and it fell off its hinges, crashing on to the brick terrace. 'Window fell off hinges. Have rung builders. Depressed.' In the middle of the night he remembered that he hadn't read the thermometer that day. 'Imminent fall of House of Forestier,' he wrote next day.

John came home, national service over. He had forgotten his mother would be away. He mowed the lawn. He tried to fix the window back on but the woodwork was the problem, not just the rusty hinges. The builder came and fixed it but said it wouldn't hold for long. Nearly all the window frames needed replacing. He would send an estimate. 'Shouldn't you get estimates from several builders?' John said to his father. His father said the best thing would be to sell Glebe House. 'Surely not!' said John, horrified, but even as he said it he realized he was being selfish, wanting his home to stay as he'd always known it. 'Perhaps you do need to move,' he said. 'Where to?' said the old man. His father asking him, John, where they should move to! How the hell should he know? Was the old man beginning to depend on him? I think I'll go abroad until my money runs out, John decided.

Nicola said no thanks not Sandsend just now, partly because Louisa hadn't broken up from school yet. 'Couldn't Peter manage her and you just bring the little ones?' suggested Phyllis. 'No, honestly, Mum. Actually we've booked a place in Brittany in August, just the five of us.' 'Do you think you ought to travel that far?' Phyllis was having to stifle something which felt very like pain of rejection.

Aunt Winifred's funeral was over. Her will: in addition to the main bequest to the Distressed Gentlefolk's Association, there was an annuity to her companion, Rose. To the young doctor, she bequeathed some valuable books. One way and another this young doctor was collecting some very fine pieces, often benefiting from the wills of old ladies in Harrogate and leaning more and more to private practice as the years went on.

After speaking to Nicola, Phyllis rang Cicely, only to discover that Cicely had gone away for a few days. It was most unlike Cicely not to have told her of this plan. 'I'd thought she might like a few days at Sandsend,' said Phyllis to Bernard. 'Why not go on your own?' said Bernard, who was busy at the office until Campbell's return. 'It seems such a pity in this weather not to go,' said Phyllis.

Before dinner, after showering the salt away, Charlie lying on the bed, wearing blue cotton shorts, one leg across the other at the ankle, reading, smoking, while Helen stood by the window feeling his presence behind her, forcing her to move further from him towards the balcony. 'What's the matter, Helen?'

'Nothing.' Trying to make the nothing sound like nothing, but an unsuccessful attempt. He threw the book across the room and turned his face into the pillow. 'Get me out of this,' he muttered to no one in particular, or perhaps to his mother who had often neglected him in favour of going out to work to buy him his grammar school uniform.

Helen clutched the balcony railings. If she stayed with him, she would be forever afraid of losing him. But had never lost him yet. Was it her fear that kept him? Was it like the nuclear deterrent, which would go on being a deterrent until it failed?

Jane was advised to stay in the marital home. Her uncle, being one of the sharpest solicitors in Bradford, fully intended to get the best deal possible for her. Maintenance and a large lump sum. This would enable her to set up her antiques business in

Ilkley. She would start by attending auctions in less advantaged areas, buying from those poor streets from which the Bosomworths arose small items of Victoriana, for which people who shopped in Ilkley were beginning to clamour.

What would have kept Jane and Simon together? I suggest the following: extreme poverty, disablement of either party or some kind of national crisis, one from which there would be no escape, not even for the extrememly rich, nuclear war maybe.

Mo only remembered the well, the frog and Grandma's face afterwards and not much else about the wedding, except that there was always this photo of her with her wreath slipping sideways, a group photo taken outside the church. She would remember in more detail an event a few weeks later when Mummy was crying in the middle of the night and Grandma coming the next day saying she would take Mo to Sandsend and Mummy saying no, this time they were all going to stay together, Mo lying on Mummy's bed and hanging on like grim death.

The doctor said to Nicola that the embryo would not have been viable, but he would say that, wouldn't he? She should have asked him exactly what was wrong with it, but couldn't bring herself to.

Helen was on the dance floor with the other man, then being led by him towards the terrace by the pool where he began to kiss her, to which she could not respond whole-heartedly. Physically she felt like doing so, but knew she must remain above suspicion. Whereupon he accused her of being cold. 'Let me explain,' said Helen, and began to talk about her problem. As she talked she saw, by the light of the Mediterranean moon, that he was bored, excruciatingly bored, utterly uninterested in her life and tragedy.

Charlie came out to find them both, the other woman on his arm. Later he said that this other woman had burst into tears and tried to tell him how unhappy she was. This was more or less the end of their relationship with the other couple. It had solved nothing in the end.

* * *

217

Nanny began to realize that it might not do to stay in Wolverhampton. Her sister's husband would yawn or leave the room whenever Nanny started telling stories about the children she had looked after and what she was making them in the way of smocks or romper suits. She helped in the shop from time to time, but sometimes made mistakes with change. She went out once a week to buy *The Lady* which advertised both permanent and temporary jobs. She also bought the newspapers which advertised cottages to rent and wondered if she could afford one of these and pay the rent by sewing for as long as her eyesight was strong enough.

'Max. 83. Min. 63. Also Merry Widow has returned. Seems Carter has had his fill. Relief all round. Could be good moment to broach subject of house sale to Jo.'

John motorcycled south and south nearly into Spain. Sitting on a peak in the Pyrenees, it occurred to him that no one had asked him for a very long time what he planned to do with the rest of his life. It was as if his parents, having got Nina off their hands, had finished with family. He would probably go on the dole. After the wedding he had wanted the girl who followed him around, but hadn't had her, wondering if by holding up on lust, something else might come of it. How stupid could he get, he asked himself now.

Another beach: this time north Cornwall, after Julia had gone home: Jim making a sandcastle for Vanessa, Edmund off with shrimping net among the rock pools, Laura sitting with her hands around her knees, watching Edmund and knowing she would never get Jim to change his mind. We have nice children: let's have more of them. To wish to have a child by someone is to wish to have some part of that person duplicated or reproduced. But Laura had to reassess her life. Perhaps she would make a better job of just the two. She began by planning new curtains for the dining room to make it a pleasanter place for entertaining. She shivered, remembering the scene at Uncle Arthur's well, and wondered if Jim would have agreed to another child if Edmund had fallen down it.

* * *

For Nina and Campbell sex became even more rewarding with all this practice. The only difference for Nina was the insertion of the Dutch cap, but she reckoned she could leave this out without Campbell knowing, especially since Dutch caps were known not to be one hundred per cent effective. She could always say, 'Yes, what bad luck . . .' For those who are less emphatically enchanted with a partner, there are other reasons for giving birth. Perhaps they are looking for solutions. Or did she remember the fleeting sense of emptiness she had felt at the reception on taking the hand of Tim Cornelius? Oh, Mother, is that why you brought me into the world?

In northern Spain, the Basque country, John met up with an English girl, wanted her, had her. Afterwards he found he was remembering what Polly had said to him under the cedar tree about life being worth continuing, remembered her sitting there with her arms held up at right angles. They made love, he and this girl, in his small ridge tent, shadows of trees blowing, shapes seen through the canvas. But not love, he thought.

There might not be another summer like this in my life, thought Phyllis, standing in the garden at Sandsend and pointing her binoculars at the sky over the North Sea: Phyllis up the chine pointing her binoculars between the stubby trees, Phyllis on the cliff looking out for puffins. I am too dependent on people needing me. I thought love was being needed, but it is in the end only needing to know that those you love are all right, with you or without you.

Crossing the Channel, Helen's long white scarf blew out behind her as she leaned against the ship's rail. Somewhere Charlie paced the deck as if he knew what was in store for him. It would be now or never. She would insist on driving. The coast of Sussex. Perhaps in view – St Paul's church, but she couldn't keep on looking. She must get down to the car before he did, her set of keys in hand.

Bernard arrived at Sandsend. 'All this travelling abroad,' he said. 'Can't see the point of it.' The only time he had crossed the Channel was with the golf club for a week in Portugal a few years back. The foreign food had not agreed with him.

'Campbell and Nina will be flying back this afternoon,' said Phyllis.

Campbell was effusive when saying goodbye to the Americans, talking so much she thought they would miss their plane. In the foyer of the hotel Nina waited. Well, so be it, if they missed their plane he would have to think of some solution.

'Charlie and Helen will be driving home today,' said Phyllis.

The M1 would be open in a few months' time, the first fifty-five miles of it from the north end of St Albans' bypass near Luton to connections with the route to Birmingham near Dunchurch. So the A1 at this time was still taking the traffic north. But midweek, mid-afternoon was not too busy. She would wait until they had negotiated the North Circular. Sometime after that, she would accelerate.

No one can say I'm mad, thought Helen. Mad people would not plan like this. I will start by saying that I understand, that I understand completely. I have accepted it. Moreover, I have not only accepted, but have accepted that he cannot talk about it and that it is a necessary part of his relationship with me. I love him nonetheless, I'll say. I will tell him that I know that it will go on happening, but that I will forgive him always.

Last day of summer term and a young woman picked up her children from their private school in Biggleswade to drive them home. These days children sit in the back of cars strapped in with safety belts. Not so then. Three little girls, one in front, two in back, bouncing around talking of their school reports and coming summer holiday. Their mother slowed the Morris Traveller before nosing out across the A1. She saw nothing coming.

Charlie's reactions had always been quicker than Helen's. The life of that family is a hundred times more important than ours, he thought, as he grabbed the steering wheel. The Austin Princess passed to the rear of the white Morris Traveller. The mother saw nothing, but the oldest of the little girls looked out of the back window and saw the silver car swerve left then right, then left again until it headed back on to the straight road leading north,where it swerved again and pulled over on to the grass verge. 'Mummy, Mummy, Mummy we nearly had an accident.' The mother braked carefully on the far side of the A1, halted, told the children to sit still, got out, looked back. A few hundred yards to the north, she saw a man get out of the passenger seat and go round to open the driver's door. He helped a woman out. They seemed unharmed.

High summer in the south: hot, dry and golden. High summer in the north: hot, dry and golden. Nina went on sunbathing in the front of her garden in the morning and at the back in the afternoon, dragging the car rug – a present from the Lawrence Forestiers – also cushions, book and transistor radio. Sometimes she wore the bikini she had bought for her trousseau and sometimes the one she bought on honeymoon. Here is Nina and Campbell's house facing on to Firs Avenue. At the back was a golf course, but not the one to which Bernard belonged. On this side of Leeds, there are at least four golf courses. You could, theoretically, tee off on one of these and play eighteen holes four times over, give or take the crossing of some gardens, a few minor roads, one major road, also a good few new housing estates which have spread out since then as Leeds has grown, reaching out towards villages such as the one in which the Crosbys lived. Golfers looked over the beech hedge at Nina, or sometimes leaned down to peer between the leaves at the suntanned back and the spotted pink or the blue and white striped bikini. Sometimes she would still be there when Campbell came home. 'Hello, darling, had a good day?' 'Hello, darling, yes thank you.'

Polly waited. Surely they must be back by now. There was nothing she could do but wait, which would always be the case. The river was low. There was no weather to arrive or leave because blue sky remained.

* * *

He looks at me with caution, more so than before. But I know he wants to be here. He is always asking me how I am. We are thinking of getting a puppy. Lena is getting old. She can't jump like she used to, doesn't run for sticks so fast. I sat there, head on steering wheel. There was silence. I remember hearing birds twittering somewhere. I felt sick. Death might not have been instantaneous. Neither for us nor for that family. We might have been in wheelchairs, all of us. Worse still, I might have been in hospital and he unscathed. I saw his hand on the handle of the passenger door. He was going to jump, then changed his mind. His reactions have always been quicker than mine. I might have been left in hospital in Biggleswade and he . . . The other day he said, let's buy a snooker table. We plan to extend his study to make room for it. Whatever happens outside the home, there will be more and more here to draw him back. Perhaps I have nothing to fear.

Because of the lovely weather and being outside so much, the house didn't seem to get very dirty at all. They were also out on many evenings because newly marrieds get asked out to meals. And when they were at home it was too hot to bother about more than salads, so there was very little at the beginning to test her and her wedding presents, although Joan Ramsey's old fridge came in very useful. But the sun goes in and when it does, Nina will go indoors.

'Max./Min. Thermometer kaput. J says if we must sell, we must. Handkerchief in evidence, went to prune rambler roses. Later perked up, says cottage for sale in village.'

He comes out of the house, stands there, home from work, hands in pockets, bit of a nip in the air, he says, smoothing his hair. The house will grow, extend itself to bear the burden of our mutual struggle. I am unable to discern if within him there is resignation. His look – less guarded than it was. Something about him standing there against the door of the conservatory reminds me . . . But it was his idea to get the puppy and the snooker table. And I thought, what a loving gesture . . . Hold hard! Gulp! Stand stock-still, trowel in hand under the laburnum tree.

Weather on the move again, coming from the west, clouds building, but bright sun here, river filling and gleaming, stones covered, birds caught in westerly airstream, hovering. Knowing who was on the phone at once, so planning not to look out of the window, so going upstairs and looking up at the sky from there, a rectangle of scintillating light, a piece of sky framed, swallows in their last dance criss-crossing the blue rectangle. Look, Polly, birds leaving Swaledale as the silver car slips into the flat-bottomed valley.

In Yorkshire the word for autumn is back end. It comes sooner. That's the difference. Nina lay on the floor in front of the gas fire, reading. Then she put down the book and picked up her shopping list. She chewed the end of her biro and thought about the thing that preoccupied her and was part of her. For what she was about to feel for this, the word love would be inadequate.